M. J. FARRELL

is the pseudonym for Molly Keane. She was born in Co. Kildare, Ireland, in 1904 into "a rather serious Hunting and Fishing and Church-going family" who gave her little education at the hands of governesses. Her father originally came from a Somerset family and her mother, a poetess, was the author of "The Songs of the Glens of Antrim". Molly Keane's interests when young were "hunting and horses and having a good time": she began writing only as a means of supplementing her dress allowance, and chose the pseudonym M. J. Farrell "to hide my literary side from my sporting friends". She wrote her first novel, *The Knight of the Cheerful Countenance*, at the age of seventeen.

Molly Keane published ten novels between 1928 and 1952: *Young Entry* (1928), *Taking Chances* (1929), *Mad Puppetstown* (1931), *Conversation Piece* (1932), *Devoted Ladies* (1934), *Full House* (1935), *The Rising Tide* (1937), *Two Days in Aragon* (1941), *Loving Without Tears* (1951) and *Treasure Hunt* (1952). She was also a successful playwright, of whom James Agate said "I would back this impish writer to hold her own against Noel Coward himself." Her plays, with John Perry, always directed by John Gielgud, include *Spring Meeting* (1938), *Ducks and Drakes* (1942), *Treasure Hunt* (1949) and *Dazzling Prospect* (1961).

The tragic death of her husband at the age of thirty-six stopped her writing for many years. It was not until 1981 that another novel—*Good Behaviour*—was published, this time under her real name. Molly Keane has two daughters and lives in Co. Waterford. Her latest novel, *Time After Time*, was published in 1983 and her cookery book, *Nursery Cooking*, was published in 1985.

M. J. FARRELL

LOVING
WITHOUT TEARS

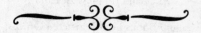

WITH A NEW INTRODUCTION BY
RUSSELL HARTY

PENGUIN BOOKS – VIRAGO PRESS

PENGUIN BOOKS
Published by the Penguin Group
Viking Penguin, a division of Penguin Books USA Inc.,
375 Hudson Street, New York, New York 10014, U.S.A.
Penguin Books Ltd, 27 Wrights Lane,
London W8 5TZ, England
Penguin Books Australia Ltd, Ringwood,
Victoria, Australia
Penguin Books Canada Ltd, 2801 John Street,
Markham, Ontario, Canada L3R 1B4
Penguin Books (N.Z.) Ltd, 182–190 Wairau Road,
Auckland 10, New Zealand

Penguin Books Ltd, Registered Offices:
Harmondsworth, Middlesex, England

First published in Great Britain by
Wm. Collins 1951
This edition published in Great Britain by
Virago Press Limited 1988
Published in Penguin Books 1991

1 3 5 7 9 10 8 6 4 2

LIBRARY OF CONGRESS CATALOGING IN PUBLICATION DATA
Farrell, M. J., 1904–
Loving without tears/M. J. Farrell; with a new introduction by
Russell Harty.
p.   cm. — (Virago modern classics)
ISBN 0 14 016.218 6
I. Title.   II. Series.
PR6021.E33L69   1991
823'.914—dc20   90–45027

Printed in the United States of America

INTRODUCTION

I am reasonably convinced that I must be almost the last person in the world to be asked to introduce you to another of the novels of M. J. Farrell—otherwise the now better known Molly Keane. Honesty forces me to admit that this will be a thoroughly biased and prejudiced account. How could it be other?

She is my friend, my confidante, my partner in two or eleven little personal deceits, my model, my teacher, my critic, my correspondent, my main source of Irish gossip, my social guide and my heroine. Do you wonder, then, that I feel a little nervous about this task?

If you have researched such a catalogue of the ties that bind you, it is quite possible that you may have debased some of the currency of introduction. I don't think I have, or will.

I wouldn't say that it was love at first sight. I can't speak for Mrs Keane (I can, actually, but I am in sufficient awe to pretend that I can't!), but when I read her novel called *Good Behaviour* and then the bald circumstances of her past private and mainly silent thirty odd years, I made a solemn little vow to myself that I would undertake an investigative pilgrimage. I travelled to her home in Ardmore, near to the complicated city of Cork, hanging on to the estuary of the beautiful Blackwater River, in Southern Ireland, with all the nervousness that I could summon. And that is a quality not lightly to be sneezed at.

In the remotest hope that you are not yet acquainted with the details of Mrs Keane's life, allow me a minute or two to take you there. When I thought (oh, the foolishness of the innocent) that I had discovered her, she had already been short listed for the Booker Prize. She had already organised her dress, her hotel, even the private celebratory dinner consequent upon what she thought would be a winning night. It didn't happen. Sometimes, in novels, and even more horrible, sometimes in real life, things don't work out exactly as you had planned them, in a delirious or an intoxicated moment.

"Prizes are all right if you win them, and hell if you're short-listed and don't," she said.

She had recovered from this slap around the literary teeth when we met. If the truth were to be told and, in truth, who needs the truth, she was riding what our American cousins would call "a high". The high, in Mrs Keane's case, was that the sales of the book had permitted her to buy two new tyres for her car. And when you're thinking of all those people, in their high expectation, sitting in a guild hall in London, smiling at cameras, convinced that literature is important, scornful of television cameras but careful to present their better side to the camera, you can imagine the curling lip of disdain consequent upon the purchase of two tyres.

I have frequently maintained that there are, basically, only two categories of individuals ... only two separate lists into which you can place all your friends and enemies. That is, precisely, drains and radiators. The drains we need spend little time on. You turn on your tap, and the fount of your good humour, wisdom and experience, is emptied, like some dull opiate, into these drains. The radiators speak for themselves. You are unhappy when they are not at full regulo, and throbbing in your life.

It was precisely in front of this radiator that I learned the shamelessly dramatic details of Molly Keane's life. M. J. Farrell, wouldn't you know, was a name over a pub. She was riding out, elegantly, in the crisp December air, well placed in her saddle, admiring glances cast in her direction, when she spotted this useful pseudonym. She was writing novels by this time, but she daren't admit it. The county would have been shocked. The invitations would have ceased. A silent, deadly and enervating revenge would have been taken against a woman who had used (as in *Loving Without Tears*) her recognisable landscape as a backdrop to her fiction. Better a fine seat, at this time, than a sharp quill.

And make no mistake. That same quill was, in those days as in these, dipped into an essence, like ink, that could paralyse, if not poison. Hear her talk of a ball at such a house as we find here. One proud mother took her plain daughter to the ball and vowed to herself that, tonight, the girl would sparkle and that, this same night, she would drive back to the big house with every prospect of a future son-in-law. She would not admit to herself, and could not admit to others, that she had mothered an exceedingly plain daughter. She took it upon herself to practise a little harmless social engineering. She ordered an enormous cellophane box to be delivered to the house just before they left for the ball. When they arrived, the butler was instructed to place the girl in the box, to stand her, like a gigantic doll, inside the entrance, and to wait for a passing beau to lose his mind, but exercise his privilege, and tear the protective wrapping from the now-sweating doll. You, of course, already know what happened ... nothing. The cataclysmic end to this plain girl's big night out was the tearing sound of a ripping knife, from her own mother's wrathful rescue; humiliation, confusion, tears from the victim, and sniggers from those who bore a discreetly distant witness.

Molly Keane's own life is the stuff of prickling fiction too. There was, initially, the pamper and privilege of a "big house" and all the seemingly attractive impedimenta of a settled wealth. There are odd glimpses of a past where, maybe, things were not working exactly to an ordained social order. Like the night that the Sinn Fein came to burn down her family home. There were due warnings. Her father sat on a haystack to watch his property burn, mouthing one singular oath; "I'd rather die in Ireland than live in England!" Beat that, if you can, for a set piece of fiction.

It can be beaten, but only by a further domestic incursion into Molly's private life. She was a fashionable dramatist of the late fifties, in London. It was a time, after the war, after that peculiar period of release called "The Festival of Britain", when we pretended that life was going to go on as we had known it, except for plastic, something called "contemporary furniture", the fading of the "New Look", and the glimmering introduction of a limited television service. All these separate manifestations of a stirring up of the old order should have served as a warning to M. J. Farrell that "things" (whatever "things" may have been) were not going to be the same again. She persisted with Shaftesbury Avenue, where she was a licensed darling.

Then, just before her opening night, her handsome husband became ill. He was taken into hospital. She was busy supervising the final touches to her latest West End play. She had a call from the hospital asking her to come round. The nurse, who believed in the expediency of swift surgery, took her into a private room, where there were pictures of generals and admirals on the brown walls.

The nurse said, "Mrs Keane, take a seat. Your husband is dead."

You pause.

"I must say, I was rather taken aback."

Oh, the gentility of it all. And, oh, the horror. And, oh, the power and the command and the style and the guts of someone able to take hold of that wretched moment, and force it into the pattern of what you want your life to be. Which she did.

Since history was being dramatically rewritten, with the arrival of a certain John Osborne at the Royal Court, the pragmatic Mrs Keane decided that a natural end had come to the dramatic life of M. J. Farrell. Her obsequies were unobserved. Quiet. Dignified. Silent. She went back to Ireland, to raise two girls in reduced circumstance. There was no noise. No fuss. Those friends she had made were already grappled by hoops of steel. The others were, perhaps, drains. As far as she was concerned, and she was concerned, make no mistake, the ink was a dessicated deposit in the bottom of the well. The curtain was down.

The same curtain could not have risen more dramatically. As literary history now has it, Dame Peggy Ashcroft, snuffing her way through an attack of mild influenza, staying in Molly's house, demanded fresh reading. There was a copy of "something really rather ordinary and insubstantial". A draft of *Good Behaviour*. Ashcroft read it and recognised it. The machines started up again. Agents, publishers, juries, panels, critics, the lot, jumped upon the new-rolling, fresh-painted, other-named Molly Keane.

This is where I came in. I think it impertinent, if not actually impudent, to forewarn the reader of the subsequent novel exactly what to expect, what to look for, relish or reject. That would be like watching a video of the holiday you are about to take. And unbecoming. It would, in Mrs Keane's terms, be a matter of delicate bad taste.

Signposts I may legitimately indicate. A certain bitterness. Indeed, a certain cynicism. Her pathological interest in the disadvantaged. Her unaccountable marriage to the sea. Her interest in bodies, and beautiful ones at that. Her obsession with that part of a woman's life where apple-cheeked innocence gradually gives way to the lay-lines of experience. Ireland. Roots. A certain domestic grandeur. Deception. Gardens. Silver. The table as a bed or a market place. Animals. Sick bulls. Dogs. Croquet. The Army and Navy Stores. The richnesses of a privileged life and the long littleness of it, too.

I need not continue, since the form and order of a well organised radiator follows this current outpouring of an overflowing drain.

Russell Harty, Yorkshire, 1987

LOVING
WITHOUT TEARS

* 1 *

IN THE light of an early afternoon in June, in the flat hour succeeding lunch-time, a man and a woman sat in a room overlooking the sea.

The woman was writing with a tremendous show of intensity. The man was playing the piano. He strummed a little tune with the definite persistence of a woman knitting. As with a knitter his busy hands stole attention from his face. In his hands and through his playing came the impression of gentleness, of emotion controlled. But a disappointed mouth denied the gentleness in hands and music. So did the lines beaten into a long face by some struggle that may have been won or lost; only the marks of its endurance remained. Whatever suffering had been, an absolute sanity looked out from the heavy-lidded hazel eyes when the man raised his head and listened, not displeased, to his own playing. The bones of his flat thin shoulders moved under a tough, rust-coloured jersey; he sang, and sang vilely.

The woman put down her pen with an exaggerated rattle of annoyance and slewed round towards the man, the piano, the sea.

" Oliver, must you sing? Your singing does destroy me."

He looked across the room. His eyes laughed at her and at himself.

" A tiny drawing-room voice perhaps, but rather sweet I always think."

She got up and went towards him. Bosom and backside as round as four thrushes' nests of the current year; long, steely flanks and ribs sprung as neatly as a bird's cage. She held her chin so high against the flying years that it gave her a silly look, sometimes, as if sheer poise must fling her on her back. Her hair had been white since she was twenty-nine—a dramatic bleaching for her husband's death. At forty-seven it was vital, plastic and elastic to a frightening degree.

"Forgive me, dear"—the ice melted in that complicated instrument and weapon, her voice—"I'm like some ghastly penguin flapping about. What's the time?"

He gave her a look, indulgent, reproving, hopeless, and looked down at his watch.

"You've been asking that at ten-minute intervals since lunch-time."

"What a bore I am. Tell me again." She was rearranging a pile of illustrated papers with vigour and decision.

"It's three o'clock and your son will be home in one hour from now."

"It's the longest hour in the two years he's been away. Two years! But he won't have changed." She sighed, contentedly, and as though to reassure herself of the past, so dear, so unalterable; her eyes fed on the room that was hers as much as the children were hers—only hers.

Oliver knew that possessive contented look of Angel's. A tiny graveyard chill ran down his bones, the absolute opposite of the greedy life in her. He loved the room, too, as he loved every flying bastion of this absurd Victorian gothic castle. This tiny castle, perched hysterically on the edge of a cliff, like a castle on the Rhine. But instead of a river's majestic passage at its feet, there was the sea, an inlet of the Atlantic on the south coast of Ireland. Gentle on this summer day, the sunlight and the sea-light flooded in through the preposterously mullioned windows. There were three windows in the room, all looking on the sea, and the centre window was built out in a great bow. To stand in its curve and look down into the clear water and swinging weed was an experience which Oliver never tired of contrasting with the rich vulgarity of the room behind.

Oliver adored Angel's unaffected pleasure in Buhl cabinets, in richly-carved marbles, in pseudo-Italian painted furniture, in gilt sconces from Austrian churches, in elaborate white wall vases from Mrs. Spry, in flower paintings, in photographs of her children by Marcus Adams, of herself by Lenare, and of her late husband by Keturah Collins. These things were hers and part of her, and so, of course, were the children. She was asking:

" Will he have changed, Oliver? Of course not."

There was no genuine anxiety in her question, and complacency irritated Oliver unreasonably.

" He'll be unrecognisable," he answered sourly. " Face it, dear, this reunion with your young fighter pilot is bound to be a fearful frost."

" Well, you forget, my own baby after all."

So he hadn't got through. She had not a glimmer of doubt about the changes he foresaw in this returning child. She went on, conning it all up:

" Nineteen when he left me, twenty-one now. What's the difference? "

" Just that you'll meet a young stranger. A superb young stranger, bronzed by two years of Italian sun, staggering home under a load of medals and embarrassment."

How would she take that? As he expected she looked out to sea and murmured:

" Home to his mother."

" Oh, come off it——" At the piano Oliver cracked out a couple of beastly chords, " Home to life, and life starts when mother stops."

She said, a little reprovingly:

" Julian knows I understand about absolutely everything."

" Perhaps I'm just a battered old cynic with one lung, but if I was Julian I think I'd prefer a little whoopee with someone who understood about absolutely nothing. Anyway, for a start."

She countered that easily. " Of course I'll provide the right young girls for him to play with. That's what you mean, isn't it?"

She would, too.

" Right, darling, I give it up. You will provide, you will give, you will take—you won't just pray heaven fasting to teach you how to leave your son alone?"

Angel was used to this form of affectionate abuse—she much preferred it to any lack of interest, so now she said gently:

" Don't, please, be such a posing old cynic—you're just as excited as any of us to welcome Julian home."

One of the three doors opened and a very small person in a pink dress staggered through it, carrying a glass accumulator vase as big as a church and as full of lilies as St. Margaret's, Westminster, decked out for a rich June bride.

" Even Tiddley," said Angel, indicating the little creature, almost invisible behind its burden, " isn't more thrilled to welcome her cousin home. Aren't you, *petite*?"

Tiddley heaved the lilies on to a French piece with a white and brown marble top and a good many brass frills, before she gasped: " Just all the Tiddley can do. *C'est tout ma possible*, Aunt Angel."

" Far too much on a hot day, too," Oliver answered.

" And *Possi-BLE* as in *Les Misérables*, if you must speak French."

" Oh, yes," she was standing on a chair, savaging the lilies into position and balance in the violent way that good flower decorators use, " *Ma possible*." There was never a change in inflection. " Thank you, Oliver."

" Don't you mind him, darling," Angel comforted. " We've spoken French for years to help the children's accents. It's second nature now. And your heavenly lilies—but is that just quite the best place for them?"

" Don't they look lovely?" Tiddley got down off her chair. She breathed hard with rapture and exhaustion as she gazed up at her beautiful decoration. " I couldn't cut my lilies for anyone but Julian." She was small and dark and strong. She looked like a plump little choir-boy whose voice might be just going to break.

" Only fifty minutes till I see him." Angel skipped any more admiration of the lilies. Tiddley was a bit too pleased with them.

" After two years." It sounded more like Tiddley's two years than Angel's.

" Nearly three," Angel corrected, taking back her years, " I can't count seeing him in hospital before he went abroad."

Oliver thought it was time this competition in sentimental memories stopped.

" Not quite the same thing, is it?" he offered, smoothly. " All those brutal nurses bundling about."

" The nurses were always lovely to me," Angel reproved him quietly. " Of course, I have a little way with people. Tiddley, just an idea, shall we move the flowers over here?"

" Where?" Despair.

" Against the sea—White Flowers against the Sea—oo, careful, darling."

9

"I believe you about the nurses," Oliver said as he took the vase from Tiddley and put it in its new position. "You certainly get the best from us all." Then he picked Tiddley up to fix her flowers. Everyone liked picking Tiddley up, but she was always put down unmolested.

"Perfect," Angel breathed, "I knew I was right. Now, pet, have you got the vegetables for dinner—the new peas, the mushrooms, the tomatoes?"

Tiddley looked guilty. "I'll never manage it in time, darling. Julian comes at four."

"Well, need you see him till tea-time?" There was a briskness here. "And, my sweet, why that silly pink dress? You can't do any real work in it."

Confused, Tiddley spoke the truth. "I just thought I'd like to be *un petit peu gai peutêtre* Julian's first day." She started parcelling up a book, meticulous as a saleswoman in Bumpus.

"Oh, Tiddley, he won't mind what you wear, darling." Angel's laugh was the most caressing gurgle. "And he's used to your old corduroys. What are you parcelling up now, dear? Do get on."

Tiddley's fingers flew. "It's just a little present for Julian," but she couldn't resist a boast. "A book he's always wanted about repairing small marine engines, out of print for years. I wrote to seven different shops and I got it."

Angel gave her a sweet, unthinking smile, but Oliver said warmly:

"How clever of you, Tiddley. Now he'll be happy for days performing unmentionable operations on his poor boat."

"Wait till he sees his *Julietta*"—Angel had the genuine thrill of giving—"a whole lovely new engine I've put in her—such a surprise!"

"Such a mistake." Oliver's disapproval was whole-hearted.

Tiddley's reaction was slower. It was a moment before her hands doing up the book lost their quick intention and she accepted disappointment, seeing her silly little gift in its new proportion. She finished knotting the string only because it was begun and put the parcel down on the piano.

"Not much use now," she said bleakly. She walked into the big bow window—they called it the lighthouse when they were children—and looked out beyond the garden and down into the sea. It was like being alone in a lantern. A refuge for sulky children and disappointed ones.

Angel prided herself on her quickness to see trouble. "After all, darling," she comforted, "it's the lovely thought that counts, and Julian will be so touched. You always spoil him, Tiddley, just like you spoil me."

Tiddley could never resist even the shadow of gratitude. It warmed and restored her. "You're unspoilable, Aunt Angel." She turned willingly from the lone sea. "It's one of the nice things *Le bon Dieu* gave you."

"How French all your friends are, Tiddley," Oliver yawned his reproof; and added, "Run off to your garden, bless you."

"And dear, put on your corduroys." Angel never allowed her advice to slip.

Tiddley paused. Her hand was on the door-knob of the lighthouse window that opened on to the flagged terrace, below which well-contrived steps led down through a steep garden towards the sea. Something still troubled her.

"Aunt Angel, I believe that man rang up again," she said, with the complicated evasion that prefaces an unpopular request.

"What man? What about?" Angel was rearranging

Tiddley's lilies, and at each change Tiddley drew in a sharp breath, but she did not protest.

"The schoolmaster," she said, "about my little piano. You won't sell it to him, will you?"

"The little schoolroom piano," Angel corrected gently. "Well, if he makes a decent bid for it, I must. After all, Funny One, you can play your three tunes on this piano— or on your old mouth-organ."

"Oh, I'd hate to go back to my mouth-organ." Tiddley spoke contemptuously, as one does of an out-moded delight. But her voice just shook when she added: "I'm so fond of the schoolroom piano."

"It's rattling with photographs and quite out of tune." Oliver could not resist seeing what might come of this probe. It was unkind, it was faintly surgical, and Tiddley reacted like a frog in a forceps.

"Who asked you to stick your oar in?"

Were there tears? Oh, these poor girls. These poor girls of twenty-three with kind aunts. He played a faint, falling phrase on the piano, a little garland for the pain. Then he teased in contradiction: "*Mille pardons, Mademoiselle.*"

"You are not to tease my Tiddley." Angel made admirable use of the diversion. "I want her to have the best piano in the house"—with affectionate raillery—"don't I, darling? I understand her. You can trust me, can't you, Toosie? Now off you pop—corduroys, French beans, tomatoes, mushrooms —and, *concentrate*!"

Tiddley hesitated. Then she went.

Oliver sat on playing his phrase over again. He looked up as the door shut.

"And don't you dare sell her little piano," he said, as though in conclusion of an argument.

"Not for anything." Angel was big with agreement. She

hesitated and amended, "Well, certainly not for less than ten pounds."

"Poor little Tiddley," he sighed, and crossed over to the fireplace to take a cigarette from an awful jade box.

"None of your own?" Angel suggested.

"None I like."

"These were meant for Julian."

Without comment he gave her one and lit them both.

"So monumentally insignificant," he went on about Tiddley. "So desperately vulnerable, so Tweedie, so tweedissima. So born with a cairn terrier in its lap."

"Now, no picking on the perfect orphan niece." Angel's delicious white head went back against an olive satin cushion. The chin went upwards till it attained the perfect angle. An artist in attitude, her eyes demanded approval. But Oliver was leaning with his arms crossed on the marble chimney-piece and his head laid gently against his arms.

"Weeds the garden, washes the dogs, mows the grass, grows wonderful flowers and tomatoes and mushrooms." He was thinking of Tiddley still. If he had sketched the least gesture of admiration towards Angel he might quite possibly have won back for her the piano. Ignored, she said sharply:

"And don't forget she does owe me a little bit of love and service. Haven't I given her everything since my poor silly sister died. Everything, literally, since she was six years old—but I've looked after her, I've made her happy and I adore her."

It was all so true. And Tiddley, in her limited way, so happy. Why did he care? He thought: I've twisted myself too close in all their lives. I, that have no other life. I, that Angel delivered surely from sickness and despair and death. Angel, my smug saviour, my loving tyrannous creature, my heavenly example of all silliness, whom I find so touching and so tough. What he said was:

"We all value a really good slave, but if I were you I would not sell her little piano." He wanted to scold Angel, and he wanted to put into some form of words the grave-wreath for girls' hopes he had made for the piano.

"And please, why not?" Angel reacted sharply to criticism. "She wastes an hour every day practising, and one hour a day, Oliver, is three hundred and sixty-five hours in a year."

That gave him a genuine spasm of indignation. "Where would she be if she couldn't play 'The Isle of Capri,' and 'Vienna, City of my Dreams,' and that awful new one, in the schoolroom after dinner? Angel, think—when there's a mist on the sea and her lilies are smelling their heads off out there."

"Nonsense. It's too windy for lilies out there. She grows them in the kitchen garden as you very well know."

"All right, all right, something more homely. Clove carnations, if you like. Quite intoxicating enough, too. Poor little Tiddley—'Let me not be mad, not mad, Sweet Heaven,' that's what she means when she lets herself go on the schoolroom piano."

"What a curiously unpleasant and unkind light you put poor Tiddley in." A genuine escapist. Angel spoke from her heart in refutation of Oliver's outcry. Then she flapped out of touch, like a bird feigning a broken wing: "Any helpful suggestions about my daughter? Just to close the lecture." She paused, and as he did not speak, went on: "Slaney may be only eighteen but you probably think she's full of unhealthy yearnings, too."

"Well, dear"—he threw his cigarette away and decided to forget Tiddley's cause for the moment, and enjoy himself— "in my opinion it will take more than a schoolroom piano to satisfy Slaney's yearnings, and I don't look on them as so unhealthy either."

"Really, Oliver—the child tells me everything—everything."

Her Slaney, her beautiful, guarded, wholesome child, so happily too young still for the world and war work. Yesterday only, the curled beauty of children's parties, to Angel her dresses were still as much a mother's affair as in those days, so close, so far. Her food was a mother's occupation, too. As a gardener tends nectarines, so did Angel minister anxiously to skin and hair and health of body. As well, she disciplined the beautiful body towards an excellence in the sports best calculated for its exhibition—a garlanded, shampooed young heifer, her looks a miracle, her thoughts unknown, Angel led her daughter by a ribbon towards the supreme sacrifice and glory of the right marriage.

"So really, Oliver," she said, "what can you mean? The child does tell me everything. There's not an idea in her lovely head beyond her sailing, her pedigree Minorcas, her fishing, her swimming; or is she," the mother pondered, "a little worried about her high dive?"

"You haven't noticed how involved Colonel Christopher Hawke has become in the pursuit of these outdoor sports?"

"Chris?" The tinge of anxiety in her voice turned into a lovely singing note of relief. "Oh, dear old Chris, the darn decent fellow, the jolly pukka chap"—no words could have conveyed a poor sap more strongly. "Really, Oliver, you're pathological, dear, if you think Slaney is interested in Chris."

"Why not? A hearty and brilliant young soldier by profession and an attractive young animal by God's grace."

It was more of an attack on Angel's complacency than a defence of the decent chap.

" I'd have noticed "—she was unperturbed—" Slaney would have told me."

" She would, would she? I do envy your self-confidence, my dear."

Angel looked over Oliver's head and out to the blue June sea. " It's simply," she said, " I just happen to trust both my children. I trust and confide in them as utterly as they do in me."

<h1 style="text-align:center">* 2 *</h1>

FAR BENEATH the silly castle Slaney and her Colonel lay in the sun. They lay on a cliff ledge close grown with heather, as flat as a table and as hot as a shelf in a moderate oven. No wind blew here. The cliff leaned above them. The sea breathed below. Sea pinks and bell heather flamed pink and purple against the unrelenting blue of sky and water. Everything was wonderfully bare, clean and salty.

The Colonel sat up and looked round the corner of the rocks towards the boat quay. It was empty except for boats. The *Julietta*, the *Silver Gull*, and his own *Curlew* slurred their shadows in the water and moved regretfully over them. The Colonel looked farther round to see again some bare pink house in the village. The Burmese jungle where he had become a Colonel at the age of thirty-one, where death and the smells of death and disease and wounds and flowers had shrouded him, took a further step backwards in his memory. He moved luxuriously between the idea of lighting a cigarette and the idea of kissing Slaney again. Vaguely he was thinking: I won't kiss her yet. I have time on my hands again. I have to-day and I have to-morrow and more. I have for ever. I'll take my time.

She had turned away, looking out at the sea. He could see the bones in her thin childish neck, a winter bird's bones, and the young stiff breasts under her blue shirt. Her endless legs lay as dead as a doll's along the rocks. She had red hair, and the pale acid skin which belongs to the rather frightening generosity of red hair. She had a forehead as full and high as a white sugar Easter egg and a chin as frail and pointed as a long-tailed tit's egg. She dreaded spots which her acid skin invited. She had less than no belief in herself. She imitated what she admired. She had loved before, of course. Her heart had been flung over her shoulder, once to the games' mistress, twice to bus conductors, now to Chris. To-day she had been kissed for the first time in her sheltered life. She had crossed that chasm, deep as it is narrow, between the kissed and the unkissed. She was really translated. She was beside herself, and so, she supposed, was Chris.

So, when he found a piece of chocolate in his pocket and gave her half, she murmured:

" Isn't it a miracle? "

" What, darling? "

" That we should eat chocolate like this after that."

" Well, we're hungry."

" I haven't ever loved you before."

She gazed. He was good-looking in the best way. Lean and dark-haired. Clean-minded, long-limbed, simple. She moved closer to him again, revived perhaps by the chocolate. He was anxious to behave with exemplary restraint. He said:

" I hope I'm not going to have hiccups."

Slaney leaned nearer: "You're my mouse," she said, " aren't you? "

He felt his reserves slipping. " No. You're my mouse."
How weak to admit it.

She could beat that one. " You're my mouse—touse—
touse."

This moved him to contradiction. " No. You're my
mouse. You're my touse. You're my tiny little house.
You're everything, actually."

She knew it. It was love triumphant. The Why we Are.
The place where stars for ever burn.

" Oh," she breathed, " how I wish we were two little
bears."

He too, leaned close. " Do you. Why?"

" Then we could hibernate all the winter months—wouldn't
it be lovely?"

" Rather lovely." His resolutions seemed quite purposeless.

∗ *3* ∗

JULIAN HELD Sally's hand in his own under the rug.

She was a tiny Scandinavian blonde, dressed with the
exquisite correctness that only Americans maintain on long
journeys: little crooked hat with diamond clip, pale tweeds,
vast handbag, manicured, sunburnt hands with many rings,
sweet mouth and grey eyes as hard as cat's-eye opals and set—
like Bambi's—endways in her head.

The expensive taxi climbed a hill. They were coming to
the place. She was going to see it, she was going to be thrilled.

" Look," he said.

" Where?" she said.

" Slievenamon," he said.

" Speak English, Toots," she said.

" The mountains."

" Oh."

The mountains rushed into their sight in great galloping stretching lines. She saw his eyes, eating their distances.

" This is them," he said. " They always look like this when you come home."

" Do they? " she shivered.

" It's my own view. Round the shoulder of Slievenamon and the other side goes down to the sea and Owlbeg, where we live."

" Where we live—— " She recognised vividly how near she had come to this foreign life of his. The day before yesterday was past. Italy, the war, the sun, the sea, their meeting and loving lay behind. This stony road and grey mountain ahead, and beyond, a strange house, a strange mother, strange seas.

But she wasn't scared. All her life she had dealt with strangers. You learn the technique young, or go under, in the show business. The thing to remember was how deeply this kid needed her. That was the essential fact at present. He was a fine boy. She had found him, shaken and uncertain. She had made him whole again, and she knew she had done a good job. One certain job well done in the shifting muck of war. She was here with him for as long as he needed her. Marriage was what he wanted. Very well. She had been his refuge and his security—he offered her back those very things. A lifetime of both. The long prospect appalled her faintly. She wanted reassurance of that live love there was between them. She wanted his eyes back from the famished mountains.

His eyes came back to her after the shadow of a delay.

" What do you think of my mountains? " he asked.

" They make me think of Austria."

" But you didn't like Austria. And you know you have to love my mountains, don't you? "

" I'm going to adore them."

His eyes went back again. He was on that familiar road, every passing age of his that had travelled it. Every age but that of the moment, which is always the unknown, the unfinished. Now, when a horned mountain sheep popped back across pale stones to the heather, he was the little boy returning to Birdie the Nannie, to teddy-bears and biscuits and milk, with the dentist and the Zoo behind him. Where the dark lake with its flowerless rhododendrons lay for ever out of the sunlight, his thoughts went for cosiness and reality to the stamp collection and the Meccano set of middle years. And when they climbed towards the sun again it was the lobster pots, the boats, the sea-trout in the river that came unbidden to mind. He had never yet worked at Owlbeg, it had always been holidays.

And now what? There was an unbridged place between the boy who had gone up this road to the war and the young man who returned, with some glory (which the sixth form cynicism of his age decried) and with this first love, sophisticated and decorative ticket of new experiences, by his side. The young must boast on their way to maturity. She was his present absolute boast.

She moved away from him that fraction which provokes fresh contact and spoke to her servant, who sat in front with the driver.

" How do you like the mountains, Walter? "

" Adore them, Mrs. Wood. Gorgeous big things." He adjusted his scarf (pre-war Charvet) and looked anxiously at her over his shoulder. " I do hope we arrive before my headache."

" You can't have your headache till you've unpacked," she told him briefly. She lit a cigarette for herself and one for Julian, neatly and expertly, with the exaggerated decorative gestures which enhanced her least activities.

He took it and looked deeply at her.

" I am excited," he said, " aren't you? I can't wait to show you everything. I can't wait for them to see you."

* 4 *

" TRUST, OLIVER, is a lovely garden with its gate locked to all cynics." Angel brought out this fearful aphorism with a tremendous air of originality.

" Fancy," he breathed. " Just fancy."

" Anyway "—something more dependable than trust and less arbitrary than coercion thrummed out—" I know my Julian, and I can't have my Slaney wasting her beautiful youth in some awful hill station in India."

" Young people do have a trying habit of preferring to waste their beautiful youths in their own way," he pointed out reasonably.

She answered reasonably: " No. If they are handled tactfully, firmly and lovingly, one may do with them what one pleases."

" You're so full of tact and the wonder of mother love, that one filthy day you're going to pop."

Instead of answering back, she accepted, she surrendered. She asked the reason for his unkindness.

" Why turn on me like this, Oliver? Why choose to-day when I'm so happy? When my Julian's coming back and my sun's shining and my sky's bright blue. Why choose to-day?"

He answered truly: "Because I love you."

Always delighted with a situation she murmured: "You love me? My dear, you too?"

"Oh, only in my own quiet way, of course." He could not have been more disappointingly deprecating.

"Oh, just in your own quiet way. Oh, I see"—Angel recovered poise as easily as a tree gives and regains itself in the wind—"well, of course, as you know, dearest, my love is all for my children."

Now for a flash he was serious.

"That's why I'm afraid for you. You love too much. You give and demand too much. Julian will want to play in his own way and work in his own way. Slaney, too." Would she take it? Would she perceive, even dimly, some of the perils of reunion. Not her.

"Don't worry. I think I may say I understand my children. Don't forget my husband was killed when they were babies, so all these years I've had to be——"

"Don't say it. I know—father and mother, too. A hopeless combination."

"Thank you. It worked out."

"And what would happen if you stopped being an understanding adoring mother and went to bed early with a headache and three aspirins and left Julian to welcome himself home?"

"Don't be silly." She was not so much impatient at the suggestion as at his idiocy in making it. "Why, he'd be lost without me."

"Would he?" Oliver sighed. "Have it your own way. It was only an idea, of course." He gave the whole thing up and sat down again at the piano with an air of irretrievable idleness. Idle, and at three o'clock in the afternoon. That Angel couldn't take.

"I rather wish, dear, you'd remove yourself and your ideas to the office and take a look through the farm accounts. After all, which are you? My spiritual adviser or my land agent?"

"And who made me her agent, when frankly, darling, I didn't know a bull from a cow. What made you pick on me? A solicitor with only one lung and very little knowledge of the countryside."

She loved remembering. It peeled back time, like skin off a lovely banana.

"Well, you were so sad and sweet when we found you, that last lovely spring before the war, all alone in the Austrian Tyrol—*and* a gentian in your hat."

It was these small accuracies that tied her charm to life. The gentian in his hat ribbon gave him back that very day . . . The lovely swagger of the child, just come from mountain places, who threw his sack of gentian and alpenrosa down before the wooden guest house. The way the sun shone, lighting the height beyond height of lichened tree stems to primrose and white. The chocolate, the cream, the glass of water. The well-made empty road. The milky-green snow water in the violent river. The dreadful solitudes of bright woods . . . Then Angel's arrival with Julian and Slaney and Tiddley, a glamorous absurd party. Lovely woman; lovely, gay, absurd children.

"I do remember," he said, and smiled now, "giving my remaining lung and my broken heart a breath of mountain air."

"I never guessed about your heart."

"Do you remember the mountain ash, like sour whipped cream?"

"I never guessed about your heart."

23

"Oh, all right. I'm more than cagey about my heart."

"It must be better now. Six years gives the worst heartache a chance."

"It is better now."

"But what was she like?"

He would not have told if it still hurt. Ignorant of such a grief, Angel had ministered to him till he knew the blessed air of unconcern again.

"Must you hear?" He enjoyed the sensation of trifling over what had once mattered so much.

"Don't pretend it still hurts."

"Just a twinge." He said it to provoke the face she made. How she grudged any unshared bit of life.

"Well, she was American, small, blonde, tough, and utterly fascinating. She had left her husband in Prague."

"Her husband? How nice. Really, in Prague, did you say?"

"Yes. But this is the sad, awful part; she left me in Innsbruck to go back to him."

"Well, Oliver, I'm delighted she left you. She can't have been a very nice type of girl."

He agreed heartily, Angel's reaction delighting him in its brief senility: "That's quite certainly the last thing she was."

An indulgent warmth of reminiscence was apparent to Angel in his tone. She hurried briskly away from it.

"Like everything I do, it all turned out beautifully. You came back with us to Owlbeg. Your lung healed, like I said it would. Your heart healed because—because I like to think you're happy." (Here again was the same true flash as in her memory of the gentian.) "And oh, Oliver, what a help you've been to me, keeping the place right for Julian."

"Not really for Julian," he said, "but because I love it.

I love working and I love the sea, and my good health that you gave me."

He looked out over the sea and he remembered how she had brought him here from Austria in a vaguely bullying way, saying, not very hopefully: "People do recover from T.B. quite often. There's terrific iodine in the air, and you can have Aunt Gwenda's cottage. She had such a nice double-pink climbing geranium—you must look after it, a net in the frost, you know. I think you'll get better. I never let things die."

That was how he came to Owlbeg in the legendary last year before the war. And it seemed to him the kind of contradiction of which his life had been made up that he should live and work and find contentment with the whole world reeking of young deaths. Absurd, that his condemned body should recover health and his sharp mind light the way of a fool like Angel.

For five years now Oliver had checked up on her spending of the money that should be for Julian, if Julian lived. He had deflated schemes for the luxury plumbing of Owlbeg and had led her enthusiasms from the expensive redecoration of her house towards a sober and educated afforestation of the small, almost treeless, sea-blown estate. Under his tutelage and influence she was now as thrilled with a combine harvester as she had been with the all-electric scheme she envisaged for Owlbeg in 1941. And the overdraft that had loomed against Julian's twenty-first birthday was considerably reduced by three years' honest slaving on the farm. Angel called Oliver her land agent. It sounded good, and gave him authority, but working steward would have described his position on the four hundred acres of Owlbeg more accurately.

Oliver had found in himself a latent and overmastering passion for this land that was not his. The three-year-old trees he had planted yielded him a satisfaction nearly of the flesh. The fields that he had limed and marled were like thriving children to him—abortion in the cows brought him to the very verge of a letter to the *Farmer and Stock Breeder*—and his was a most reserved nature.

What name could he give to all his enterprise? For whom and for what did he lay him down tired at night? Endure and indeed enjoy the idiocies of constant association with Angel? And attend to-morrow and to-morrow and to-morrow with impatient interest? It had no unliving name like gratitude. No name either to connect it with Julian's dangerous absence. Indeed the hope that Julian would ever return to his small inheritance seemed most often like crazy optimism.

Oliver had worked first for forgetfulness and then for the happiness he found in work, and for the unreasonable love born in him for this place where he had lived, not died, where he had forgotten love and its hurtfulness, where sympathy had swollen his dead heart again (though it never softened his tongue). Sympathy for Tiddley, so easy to ridicule, so wildly sad. Sympathy for Slaney, so wooden-headed, so untried. Sympathy for Birdie, who to him typified all love denied, whose frustrations took, in her daily work, those sky-roads to hope, those wild flights upwards, without which we die. For Angel, too, his benefactress, he felt some tenderness, but here sympathy was barbed to an endless macabre diversion at her extravagant absurdities, and weighted too by a knowledge of Angel as dangerous, as a force to be played expertly.

"We all love you," she said now. It was like a pat on the back of the hand. "We all depend on you and confide in you. Even Birdie——"

"Even Birdie." He lifted the words from her. "The old gipsy."

"Now, Oliver, no!" Angel was all indulgence and denial.

"Just leave Birdie alone. My babies' dear old cosy nannie."

He thought of Birdie's dedicated life, and the wild hopes like February's false springs, and he said, rather sharply: "That's the way you look at it. Actually she's younger than you are and no cosier."

"Well, of course"—she would let that one go—"Birdie will cut the cards and read the teacups for lovers till she dies. That's her."

"She should have had more babies to look after. She shouldn't have stayed here after Julian and Slaney outgrew her."

"She's terribly useful."

"There's far too much unconsumed passion going into Birdie's dressmaking and cooking, her knitting for starving Europe and her loathing of Finn Barr."

"She is tiresome about my Finn," Angel sighed. "Once a nannie always a bully, and butlers aren't made in a day."

"Especially when they start life as poachers," he reminded her.

She flared back, as every woman will when her domestic struggles meet with unconstructive criticism:

"What do you expect me to do? In spite of our deplorable neutrality, I haven't seen an able-bodied manservant for four years, and all our cooks are earning fortunes in England. We're terribly lucky. Birdie can and will cook, and is Finn Barr's reformation from a starving poacher to a respectable young manservant my job or yours?"

"My dear, it's so typically yours." As though to illustrate the argument, the door from the drawing-room to the hall opened and a blond, sunburnt boy came into the room. He carried an enormous parcel and waited silently while Oliver rose and finished speaking, one hand on the door to the steep garden and the sea.

" It's the kind of job you revel in. Would it be exaggerating to call it a life-work? "

She gave him a look with a kick in it and turned to the blond and the parcel, not without a consciousness that there was probably something in what Oliver said. Something to the point and unpleasant. What was wrong? What code of domestic custom had her young viking violated? He was standing in a correct silence, his blond hair as smooth as a canary's wing, his tie neatly tied, his house coat as clean as a whistle. Her eyes travelled on downwards. No. She could not hope that Oliver had missed it. His dark trousers were held high on his legs by bicycle clips. There were sand-shoes, sand-shoes with the toes out, on his bare feet.

" Finn," she said, all the sorrows in her voice, " Oh, Finn Barr, how often have I told you? When you come into the drawing-room, down with your trousers and on with your shoes. Your black shoes, Finn."

" Excuse the slip, madam." Finn made a kind of retreating movement of apology. " My stalking outfit; I was after Miss Tiddley's carnation rabbit."

" Did you get her? " Oliver asked. Tiddley's carnations were part of the loved estate. The destruction of vermin, rabbits, rats, grey crows, weasels, was his link with Finn Barr. From such destruction Angel had lately removed his body, though not yet his spirit, to the service of the house.

" Ah, if we had her corpsed we were well away. Popped down a hole, sir, when she heard the station lorry bringing this——" Finn tendered the vast parcel again. He burnt with curiosity as to its contents. "Excuse the liberty, madam, but URGENT's on every label. Will I unpack? " His speech varied from the slippery ease of a poacher's to an uneasy formality which Birdie had imposed on his charming savagery.

Angel said, " Please," in the pleading voice through which her most rigorous orders were conveyed.

Oliver came out from the lighthouse window. " Really, I can't be grand and stand off any more. What is in that awful parcel, Angel ? "

That was the thing about Angel and life with Angel. Always some surprise packet appearing. Some crisis or delight in which to share. Some extravagance to condemn or some bargain to praise.

" My dear, I couldn't think myself for a moment," she admitted. " The water-skis of course. I ordered them when he wrote about what fun he had aqua-planing somewhere in the Adriatic. Won't he be thrilled ? "

" Thrilled and chilled to death, dear, absolutely." Curiosity satisfied, Oliver turned to her with exasperated indulgence before he went on : " If he'd written home about fun in Egypt you'd have tried a lovely camel, I suppose ? "

" I would."

" Oh, you're so dependable."

She accepted this with a little smile.

" It's terrifying," he shot at her and left.

He stepped out into the sun and went round the house by the hot flagged path under the windows. Its stones were dusty with the lavish sprawling of catmint and bright with the small frigidities of pinks, very nice, very gay.

The other side of the castle (the side where its monstrous entrance porch, minareted and gargoyled to the last, was built) looked inland and to the north. Grass grew up to the windows, dark green and neatly cut near the windows and stretching away tautly over the plump-cheeked mounds that bulge all fields near the sea, marking them even to a blind man's feet as sea-board fields by their rotund spring beneath the footsole. This space of grass succeeded the cut grass and reached to a belt of trees. The flowerless grass gave an Aucassin-and-Nicolette feeling of desertion and romance. This northern side of the gothic towers held all the dark poetry and anxious denials of its false and splendid date.

This was Oliver's favourite side of Owlbeg. He had planted syringas on the sheltered side of the blown trees, and hoped to see their sickly stars bloom there one night in July. Now he walked down the short, well-gravelled drive (gravel is cheap and handy by the sea) beneath escallonias and fuchsias and terribly healthy palms, out by the entrance gates (covered generously in stone tonsils and adenoids) and down the steep hill to the village. The village sat like a cat in the sun, well below all baronial extravagance. The village belonged to a more acid and dignified date.

* 5 *

FROM THE lighthouse window Angel looked after Oliver, her friend, her creature, the sardonic attractive man whose interest in herself and her children and Owlbeg, the neighbourhood envied and questioned with a satisfactory lack of charity. "Dependable," she murmured. "That's what gets them."

Then she looked down into the healthy garden where she and Tiddley slaved—how she loved it. It was like a villa garden in the south of France, and most unsuited to its wild situation and to the castle that swelled above it. But there was something very pleasant and reassuring about its trim lushness. Angel still longed for a swimming-pool, with water pumped up from the near sea (only thus is sea water ever warm) but so far Oliver had bullied her out of this. For her part she ceaselessly pointed out to Oliver how little he had approved the building of the sun parlour. This was a delightful round, pool-like excrescence, which bulged out against sea and sky, exquisitely sheltered from the wind and open to the sun; here the very best garden furniture (copied, at Angel's direction, by a village carpenter, and covered by herself and Birdie in the sailcloth of local fishing boats) sprawled its inviting lengths, and canvas mats for more ardent sunbathers were faithful copies of the pre-war models at Eden Roc.

" You were entirely outraged by the idea of my sun parlour," she would remind him, " and now it's one of your favourite spots. Especially at twelve o'clock on Sunday morning with a delicious drink beside you."

" And another one inside me. Darling Angel, you're so hospitable and magnificent at twelve o'clock on Sunday morning." He would melt in the memory and the prospect of these Sunday mornings.

Angel turned again from the window to Finn Barr, who dreamed among the wrappings as he gazed at the absurd expensive playthings he had unpacked.

" Now, Finn, tidy everything up. Don't dawdle, child. Time is short." Kindly and brisk she would deal with him now for a moment.

" Jakes, madam, pardon and excuse me! These yokes have me bet. What would they be for?" The innocent savage raised his gentle eyes and got her as usual.

"Water ski-ing, Finn—a million miles an hour behind *Julietta* or *Silver Gull*."

" Imagine." Suddenly he flung himself into position as if cutting his ecstatic way on the sea's extreme surface. " I saw it on the pictures—oh, Jesu, madam, give us a chance at it——"

" Now we don't want Jesu in the drawing-room," she reproved as over the black shoes, " but if Miss Birdie gives me a good report of you—then perhaps, we'll see later on." But his enthusiasm had caught her. " Oh, I do wonder if the bay would be calm enough to try them out this evening."

" There's ugly breakers out by the Golden Head, madam, and an east wind would skin a crow." He spoke with the assured pessimism of the sportsman who knows the sport is not to be for him.

" Nonsense, Finn, it's a perfect day." She was impervious to suggestion. " Now, listen to me," her mind skated on, " did you tidy Mr. Julian's tool-box? "

" Miss Tiddley keeps that under her own bed, madam, everything sandpapered and vaselined to the last little vice." It surprised Finn that Angel should be ignorant of this.

"Does she?" Angel thought: Touching little creature. Little gnome. Aloud she said, " Yes, yes, of course," pretending she had forgotten for the moment. "Well," she went on, " did you look through his fly-tying things and make sure his best feathers hadn't flown away, or been eaten by moths?" An arch suggestion of small thefts, for Finn was a distinguished fisher, too.

Finn countered the direct assault: "Wasn't I up before the crack of dawning to take a pluck at the perching peacock and knock a jay-bird for the sign of blue in his wing. Mr. Julian will never want feathers to dress a fly while I'm around Owlbeg."

She accepted this. " And did you give his school cups a good polish up? "

" Down to the little one for the egg and spoon race." She loved such small detail. "Well done, Finn. You'll make a wonderful butler one of these days."

" I do break my heart after the fishing, madam." It was a wistful cry, and a manifest opportunity to improve the moment.

She took it.

"You're learning to be a butler now, Finn. And that reminds me, when you were handing the lamb cutlets to Colonel Hawke the other day and he took only one, you hissed in his ear, 'Take two, sir.' Now that's a thing no keen butler would do."

"Oh, excuse me, pardon me, but such a hungry young gentleman and the cutlet no more than a bee's knee."

"All the same, Finn, it's not done. And don't ever join in the conversation either."

"I will strive and remember, madam. But oh, there's times it's very hard. Imagine last Thursday—your gentleman sitting there at the lunch-table, putting every lie out of himself about the salmon he killed. He disremembered I was on the river before I was in the pantry—and I never spoke a word to deny him."

"Well, I know it is difficult, Finn"—how gently she could yield—"but you must try. For me."

"Oh, madam, I will. God helping me, I will. I'll do everything to please you."

So these two played each other up and down. They really had quite an emotional contact. He understood and she understood and slyly they would work their wills on one another. It was Queen and Pretty Page.

"I know that, Finn." The Queen drank her little cup of homage. "And it means so much to me. Now"—a housekeeper looked out from under the Purple—"clean up all this mess like a good boy. And, after tea, see if you can't shoot that beastly rabbit. It's eaten half the carnations in the border. Don't forget to give the dining-room table a good polishing. And be sure to unpack for Mr. Julian."

"Mummy"—it was Slaney at the window—"what are you saying to Finn, darling?" She had heard and she was in a state. She was always getting into a state. " Mummy, you know Birdie always unpacks for Julian."

Angel looked over to the window where Slaney stood with her back to the sea and the light—rusty hair drained of colour against the sky, cheeks as pallid as that anxious, soaring forehead, eyes dark with anxiety; she would fling herself into a situation like a swimmer into desperate seas. Chris was behind Slaney, leaning prawning nets on the wall, sunburnt, complacent, slow moving, here to stay.

" You know it, Mummy, don't you? "

Angel gave her a quick, hooded glance. Emotional, she thought. Very well. Temporise.

" Well, Finn, you must help Birdie. He's got to learn, you see, darling."

" Very good, madam." The page bowed his platinum head, and withdrew from the presence.

He went out through the room's third door which opened into the dining-room.

" The Nannie-Bird will be simply furious." Slaney still despaired of the situation.

" I can't pretend to understand why." Angel took the matter plaintively into her own keeping. She turned to Chris who had come in now and was standing over Slaney, a little silently, perhaps.

" Oh, Chris, dear, when did you arrive? " Cool and sweet, there was no edge yet in her voice.

" I sailed across after lunch."

There seemed to be an extravagant quantity of male shoulders and tweed coats glutting the room. Some men do this. Their masculinity possesses too much of the atmosphere. Angel grudged this freedom. Not consciously, but because so many frailer importances had taken the place of men in her own life—and taken it while she was too young.

"Really? After lunch? And I haven't seen you yet."
He did not seem quite awake. She added gently: " And where
have you two been since then?"

"Prawning in the rock pools and lying in the sun." Slaney
spoke richly as though she lived a moment over again in its
telling. Was there a foreign ease in the way she threw herself
down in the corner of the sofa? Something a little less taut
and childish than usual?

"We got some wonderful prawns for tea. Whoppers. And
Julian does like prawns."

Was Chris going to share the sofa? There were a number of
quite comfortable, quite empty chairs about. He chose the
sofa.

"How nice." Angel was genuinely pleased about the
prawns. Any sea-spoils or hedge-spoils pleased her. But there
was more to know.

"And where did you do your sun-bathing?"

"On a spring mattress of bell heather. Oh, Mummy,
how gorgeously blue the sea looks against the bell heather?"

"Does it, darling? Wasn't it very damp?"

"Oh, no. Simply grand. Absolutely first class," Chris
reassured her.

" I *am* glad. And now, as you sailed over, you must hurry
back, I suppose." She handed him a cigarette, she gave him a
light, elaborately emphasising her solicitude. " Between the
tides and the currents where is one?"

"Oh, the tide won't be right for hours." He leaned farther
back on the sofa.

Slaney's thin body had drifted into an unfamiliar ease, the
voice came from the same new place:

"You've got to wait and see Julian," she said; "he'd be
heart-broken if you didn't."

" I'm sure you're longing for a good talk about your wars,"

Angel threw in heartily. "Julian soaring on wings, and you creeping about in your Burmese jungles—so splendidly."

Chris answered her simply: "Actually I want to talk to him about this new lobster ground I've found. We ought to work it together. It's terrific."

"I know he's going to be thrilled about that." Angel had to admit it. Then she came across, confidentially, sweetly: "Chris, what do you think—would he rather love to have just his own people on his very first day at home after—three years? . . . probably I'm all wrong."

Chris got up quickly—he was confused more than hurt. How slow he had been. "Of course. I can come over any day. Good-bye."

"Do, Chris. Any day." She held his hands. "What about Thursday? Not this Thursday. Next Thursday." She wanted Slaney's reaction, and got it.

"Mummy"—a despairing wail—"that's years away. Come to-morrow, Chris. I'll be waiting at the boat-cove. Three o'clock."

"Of course it's always lovely to see you." Angel halved the invitation with her child. She smiled—not even a tight-lipped smile, and swirled away from the subject: "Darlings, what do you think about these water-skis? Aren't they a good surprise for Julian?"

They agreed. Thrilling, they thought. And pretty good. They got up from their sofa and poked curiously about the skis.

"We must think up lots and lots of fun for him," Angel's voice was pregnant with generous plans. "He's got to forget his three years Dicing with Death."

Chris looked up, faintly startled by this extravagance. "Excuse me, what's it with death?"

Angel repeated icily, "Dicing, I said." Then the lights

36

went up in her eyes and warmth came into her voice as she went on: " I do think this is going to be the most wonderful time for him and for me. I'm so excited. There's so much I've planned and done here for him while he's been away. There's so much for us to do now together."

Chris hesitated, then spoke with real shyness. " You don't think he'd rather be let alone for a bit? He's had rather a doing. It takes chaps in funny ways——"

" Perhaps I'm the worst judge of what's best for Julian." The correction was gentle and cold. Then beguiling: " Am I really such a silly old cow? Be fair——"

There was a commotion while Slaney embraced her: " Oh, darling, you're not a silly old cow. Who ever said so? "

" Didn't Chris rather imply it? "

" Good God, no." He was shattered at such a translation of his words. " You know how wonderful I think you. Always have. Who taught me to sail a boat, after all, and how to light fires at picnics, and all about out-board engines, before I was thirteen? "

" Darling, you're so sweet to remember all the silly things we've done—and, oh—could you take a look at *Silver Gull's* engine for me? Dear Chris, could you do it now? I'm going across the bay to meet him, and it would be stark tragedy if I was held up, wouldn't it? "

" Of course I will." He went over to the window for their prawns. Chris never forgot things.

" I'll help you." Slaney's insistence was obvious. " Wait for me." She swung across the room like a mating bird and joined him.

Angel waited till they got to the door into the hall, the buckets of prawns between them. Then her bright blade fell cleanly. " Just a moment, Slaney. Only an instant, my precious. No, Chris, I won't stop you——"

"I'll give these prawns to Birdie," he said. "Julian must have a pukka, Owlbeg sea-food tea to-day, mustn't he?"

She had parted them. He stood alone.

* 6 *

CHRIS STOOD alone in the hall. The drawing-room door was shut behind him. He had always thought the hall very lovely when he was a little boy and came in a pink suit to Christmas trees. He still thought it very lovely. He liked the marble pillars that sprang up in groves from the marble floor to support the balustraded gallery circling the bedroom doors on the next floor—the dome above he liked and all its coloured glass, and the pompous white stone staircase with its ice-cold marble banister as clumsy as a tree-trunk, and as grand. The fireplace was very right, too—a remarkably good specimen of its date; carved, crested garlanded stone, swelling magnificently upwards above its open hearth, its crossed yew logs, its pack of brass-balled dogs, and its finely representative collection of iron rushlight holders and ships' lanterns.

Not one of the narrow mullioned windows of stained glass looked towards the sea. They looked northwards with the cold restraint and dignity suitable to an entrance hall. But their rose and amber and yellow glass sentimentalised the light coming through, so that it fell in coloured quarters and lozenges on tiled floor, oak tables and Knole sofas, and shed a nice pantomime transformation effect upon the two mixed flower groups that Tiddley arranged religiously every Thursday. Even should Tiddley's mood be for grey and white flowers, or cold, stripped lime blossom, the light sanctified and cheered such austerity, without relieving the proper gloom of the atmosphere.

Chris knew his way to the kitchen as well as any child of the house. He threaded a path through the marble banyan tree of pillars to the door leading into the back passages. He went down the long passage with the unseeing eye of custom. Since he was eight years old it had been the same.

The pantry door always stood open opposite the service door to the dining-room; always the same quiet smell of damp walls, limp but clean dishcloths and unknown things put away. A little farther on in Angel's flower-room the tap had dripped for twenty years, and medicines for long-dead dogs were on the shelves. Here flowers were steeped in buckets, for the house, for Dublin flower market, or for funeral wreaths (Tiddley was a wonder at their contrivance), and the damp stone passage would smell like heaven with mimosa and freesias, and like death and grave-clothes with narcissi, and the discreet disinfectant for a corpse of chrysanthemums. Farther on still, past the vast brushing table where men's suits and suède shoes were cleaned, two black boys in starred white hats leaned perpetually together in a wall alcove meant perhaps for a clock—they had been squeezed and jostled in there and forgotten. On the shelf above their hats Birdie kept her precious hoard of spaghetti, because the alcove backed on to the hot-air cupboard. She would take it out of its blue paper wrapping and sun it on a dry day, and brush off the bits of spore and fluff that clung to it. She had been so careful with her spaghetti that there would still be plenty left on the shelf when ships sailed again, when the glory and boast of Italian spaghetti and tomato sauce in a reeling world was a thing of the past.

At the very end of the passage came the kitchen and its offices. The kitchen windows looked out over the untamed cliff beyond Angel's flower garden, and on to the sea. The back door opened into a yard, the wall of the yard continued to surround the kitchen garden farther on. This wall was niched and castellated and turreted, too, so that it looked just like another wing of the castle and lent it a false air of size and grandeur when seen from the sea, or from the inland side either. The architect had done an extremely cunning job here, but there was neither thought, cunning, nor care evident in the layout of the kitchen, sculleries, larders and dairy, all situated at the farthest possible distances from the cook. Birdie must have walked many miles in the year between one place and another. However, it did not occur to her, or to anybody else (except Oliver, who kept his mouth shut about such an expensive improvement), that a couple of sinks and perhaps a frigidaire in the great open spaces of the kitchen would have pretty well halved the labours of the cook. Of course, the kitchens had been designed in the days when boys turned spits and dairy and scullery maids slushed about in twos and threes, and the reigning cook practised her elaborate arts in a luxurious leisure.

There was no luxurious leisure about Birdie's life in this kitchen. But leisure Birdie neither knew nor needed, and the rich life of her imagination went far beyond any reality.

Oliver was right when he called Birdie a gipsy. Her outlook was highly coloured, she was loving, suspicious, wildly prodigal of energy and life, enormously generous, desperately resentful. The woman and the gipsy in her looked for magic, believed in hauntings and the fall of the cards and changes coming at the turn of the moon.

At forty-four Birdie still had looks, and very strict she was in their preservation. In youth there had been a softness of skin and hair, despairing blue eyes and a certain silly charm —the attraction of an exquisite milk pudding with summer fruit—in her abundance of sweet and healthy flesh. Such a figure should have had its pleasures and its ease, and gone to bits its own way, but Birdie—in faithful imitation of Angel— pursued each stringent diet and course of exercise which in Angel's case gave the effect of a brittle leopard to limbs past youth, and in Birdie's hardened muscles to clutches of ostrich eggs, and to breasts like sleeping rabbits gave awful iron springs which practically went ping at a glance.

Birdie had been caught and tamed young. After Julian's birth Angel had seduced her from her maternity hospital, from births and babies and the gossips of gay dramatic days. There was some affectionate biddable quality in Birdie, some- thing easily englamoured, that made her yield up her life to Angel's charm. She would have left after Slaney's babyhood, but then the death, in a car smash, of Angel's husband, had weighted Birdie's importance to Angel even more heavily. An attractive woman of strong personality has an astonishingly powerful hold over a lesser creature such as Birdie. She can spoil, confide, and slave-drive with endless success if she possesses the secret of imparting glamour to trivial things, and can tip with colour everyday importances and deal out sympathy like cake. Angel employed every trick of the kind without even the consciousness that she was using tricks.

There had been hours and moments when Birdie had almost escaped. She had her admirers, but her position was so ambiguous—neither servant nor yet quite of the sad order of governess—that courtship was set about with difficulties. In the early days, Angel had laughed off more than one suitor as beneath her Birdie's consideration, and of late years Birdie's status as old maid became an established thing with everyone but Birdie herself. For Birdie still had dreams with new hats at Easter-time, lied about her age, read of love sometimes with tears, and for all of herself that she spent on Owlbeg, there was a reserve within her still for that dark man the cards foretold. She had always loved and given desperately, and she needed a definite object and anchor for such love—there was a hidden wild regret in her for the man she had never had, and an unstated resentment against Angel who had so ordered her life while the years fled by, that now the genius and gift in her for easing birth and giving life and love found its main outlet and fulfilment in her exquisite dressmaking and cookery.

In cooking, as in all birth and creation, there is mystery, difficulty, pain. When Chris came into the kitchen with his prawns Birdie neither saw nor heard him. She was disentangling a new-born cake from its caul. Her anxiety was desperately manifest. Her hands seemed slow behind such a concentration of will. A light-scented breath from the hot cake hovered about her hands.

Chris said: " Prawns, Birdie, prawns for tea." He rattled the can. He had no possible contact with the terrific wedding of her hands and brain to this moment. She tore off the last shred of baking paper. She performed some dangerous sleight of hand that turned everything upside down and inside out and left her achievement, her dream, exposed in its perfection.

" I prayed to Holy God," said Birdie, as she stepped back from it, and her blue eyes filled. It was a true emotion, an exquisite spasm, and passed unshared. It was between herself and her flesh and God. "It's an Austrian—" in a word giving the confection breeding and personality. " It's a terrible recipe they brought from the Tyrol. I didn't chance it since the war—I wouldn't risk my almonds on a flop."

" Oh, Birdie, I wish I was staying to tea."

"Why not, then?"

"Julian's first day and all that. I thought I'd better fade out perhaps."

" Who put that idea in your head? "

" Well I rather guessed the form. His mother would want the family to herself, wouldn't she? "

" You're wanted all right, child—unless there's a very queer change in the weather." Birdie had a nannie's skilled nose for trouble and a nannie's encirclement of untold hurts. She looked at Chris keenly across the Austrian's crisped whirls.

Birdie had known Chris since he was eight, when the little boy (one parent in India and the other remarried) came to live with his aunts in a house across the bay from Owlbeg. It was first as a playmate for Tiddley, and then as a watcher and assistant instructor in outdoor sports to the younger Julian, that Angel encouraged Chris to spend all his time at Owlbeg. He was pleasant and useful, so she seduced him charmingly from his aunts' home with its smaller interests, and because he loved her, made him her silver-collar boy.

For Chris, in all these early years, Owlbeg was adventure. Angel was Romance. She taught him to sail boats by day, and took him out fishing for white trout late on summer nights. They set lobster-pots and trammel-nets together. He would light the fires at picnics, spend half a day ambushing the bullfinches that ate the peach buds against the garden walls, or bicycle twenty miles on any message. When the war tangled him in ugly absence Angel was his interest and contact at Owlbeg. He had left Slaney a little girl, spoilt or ignored at their grand pleasure by Julian and himself, and he had come back to this strange creature newly kissed to-day.

How far Birdie envisaged the situation it would be hard to tell. But some outward-going tide of sympathy in her raced towards an understanding with Chris's hesitating tide.

" Honey-my-love, I never said what was wrong." She leaned confidentially nearer across the cake and the crowded table. " Go your own ways, and keep your mouth shut." She

43

took the prawns from him and rattled their death-pot into place on the range, then, turning from the execution, " Will I cut your cards ? " It was as though some completely physical act was suggested. To Birdie life and the cards were a part of each other.

" Birdie dear, I haven't time. I must look over the *Gull's* engine for Her." Chris spoke of Angel as " Her " with the same reverential fall that goes with the " Him " of God.

" Oh, you're in the tweezers, too ! " Birdie turned to attend to the death of the prawns.

Chris went away. He did not understand what there was to be gained from Birdie and her obscure suggestions. To him, her fortune-telling was an old, and not very funny joke. He had no possible appreciation of the mysticism and power that were in Birdie's character, or of her importance as a person. To him she was the nannie who had once made him wash his hands, and now the nannie translated into cook and housekeeper.

When Chris had gone, Birdie went over to the windows and pushed one up, letting great salty puffs of air into the hot room. She opened the second window, too. They were both in the same end wall and looked straight over the cliff edge, and were all filled with the sea—this end of the castle curved out to the very edge of the cliff. The table where Birdie ate was in one window, her arm-chair and the table where she sewed were in the other. She hung spot muslin curtains, crimped and draped and freshly ribboned as a baby's basket in each window, and she ate off fine china and made her tea in a china pot.

Away from this windowed place, the kitchen ran back as far and high as a church from its altar. At the opposite end was an old-fashioned coal range, which now consumed a tree of timber and a couple of hundredweight of turf daily.

But Birdie and Angel cooked with inspiration on its varying moods. They recognised a quality in food cooked on genuine heat absent from food cooked on most modern labour-saving contrivances. Grills from this kitchen had a fresh underdone crispness never to be achieved on slower heats. Toast was the carefully made toast before the bars of childhood. Potatoes still bore that brown vaccination mark toasted into their skins only by such old-world kitchen monsters.

The monster had her moods certainly, but coaxing and skill dispelled them, and the cold sulking potted heat of fashionable successors was unknown to her natural generous appetite. On her either side great bins had been built into the wall to hold her fuel. Their semi-circular mouths opened on to the stone floor and blocks of wood spewed out of one and sods of turf out of the other.

Tall dressers reared up their gaunt maiden figures against the high walls, soaring into the upper gloom and dust, insanitary and grand in the same way that the old coal range was grand. Unlet and unhindered by any complexes about cleanliness—the dressers carried, like flowers of a different generation, surviving pieces from glorious Victorian dinner services—their pinks geranium pink, their gold-leaf solid and intact, their blues as dark and bright as wet mussel-shells on sea-washed rocks. Some shelves were for bottled fruit, coloured globes neatly dramatised behind thick bottle glass. There were copper shells, too, and moulds of every fluted shape, dusty baskets of garlic and dried mushrooms, and lime flowers from last July, with peppermint and other herbs in paper bags. In a deep centre drawer there was an armoury of spoons and knives, palette knives of various widths and suppleness (Birdie's favourite was worn as thin as paper and would bend to a delicate bow, an artist's instrument and unsurpassed for running between the pan and the omelette skin, or lifting glazed strawberries from a slab), butchers' knives for killing ducks and lambs, scissors for game-birds, knives for filleting fish or for opening oysters. Spoons, too, for any work—wooden spoons worn as smooth as cream, spoons shaped for skimming soup, flowered china ladles, and a silver spoon for jam-making with a handle nearly two feet long and a pointed bowl worn half away after a hundred summers' stirring.

* 7 *

FINN BARR came into the kitchen with a gun in his hand. Coming into Birdie's kitchen like that was as inappropriate as if he came with a leopard's skin over his shoulder, a sling with a stone in it and a grape-stained mouth—there was the same swagger in his entrance.

Finn put down the gun among the china on a dresser and clattered two carefully covered plates of sandwiches on to a tray. Birdie swept them off the tray.

" When I tell you, please——" Her eyes blazed. " It's an hour off tea-time yet."

" And who bade me get forward with my work? You'll excuse the question, Miss Birdie."

" Is your work eating the drawing-room tea? You'll excuse the question, Finn Barr. I know how much would come out of your pantry on these plates."

" Eat these. Boys? These is rank."

" Rank, how are you? My Gentlemen's Relish."

" Oh, a very rank thing."

" Rank ignorance, and kindly shift that gun. I want to get a spoon from out of that drawer."

" Well, my gun won't mind you, Miss Birdie. My gun'll take you easy."

" Take up that gun."

" All right. All right. All right. I'm off for a stroll with it in any case."

" Stroll into the pantry now and scrub your tables. They're a disgrace to Mr. Julian's return."

" I have other things to do for Mr. Julian besides wetting my hands at this time of day. Personal things."

" You have anything to do for Mr. Julian? And what exactly, I wonder."

" Unpack his suitcases for the first go-off."

" Unpack—are you mad? "

" Well, if I am, I'm in good company, for these are madam's orders, and in the course of the meantime I'm to walk the pleasure ground for the carnation rabbit." He took up his gun with the easy poacher's gesture, loose and quick. He turned back from the door. " But I'll not tire myself, Miss Birdie, I promise you. Ta-ta." He was gone.

Birdie leaned her hands on the table where she stood. All the weight of her anger was in her leaning hands. The muscles stood out in the round forearms. Angel had done a madly foolish thing in this slight, malicious act of arbitration over Julian's unpacking. The occasion and the crisis were not the moment in which to pass lightly over Birdie's sense of love and possession, or Birdie's responsibilities, as old exactly as Julian's life.

47

* 8 *

IN THE drawing-room, when Chris had gone, Slaney's rapture overflowed a little wildly.

"Fancy remembering the prawns for Julian. I'd forgotten, and you know the water was so cold he almost paralysed himself."

Angel smiled, this time with tight lips: "Only 'almost'? Really? Pity."

But Slaney never felt the breeze. She was expanding like a plant after rain. "What did you want me for, darling? I'll do simply anything, I feel so grand and good-natured to-day."

"Really, darling? Why, I wonder?"

"Julian coming back, I suppose. What fun we'll have. Listen, Angel." With a rush it came out. "Ask Chris to stay for dinner; I know Julian will love to see him."

It was typical of Angel that she should sit down and light a cigarette with ease and grace at this moment of crisis. If there had been a tray of drink in the room she would have mixed one for herself and made a gesture of offering one to Slaney, who hated alcohol. The "we're women together" atmosphere. She said: "Tell me, do you tremendously want Chris to-night? Of course I'll ask him if you've got the smallest thing about it."

"Oh, I don't mind." The startled hind peered through the shaken fern—Slaney's first reaction was to hide her truth,

48

however awkwardly. "It's only Julian and Chris have always been such great friends, haven't they?"

"Yes, quite good friends." That light and faintly frosted difference. She went on: "And while we're on the subject, sweet, I'm going to say something terribly frank to you about our dear old Chris."

The hind swirled from the unknown danger, its white flag topped the high fern as it went. "When you're frank you're awful," Slaney said, and laughed uncomfortably.

"I'm going to be awful and get it over." Her voice fully charged on the girls-together battery. Angel said: "Slaney, darling, are you, just ask yourself, a weeny bit flinging yourself at the poor chap?"

The whole light of Slaney's day was changed. Some integral aspect shifted in her vision of herself, her lover, her joyous peace and comfort after kissing, for kisses do content the young. She was shattered by the speed with which her secret had been read, or half her secret, and doubly so because Angel should have seen her as the more eager lover.

"Mummy, what an indecent idea," she shouted, confused and indignant. "Can't I spend an afternoon alone with Chris? I've known him since I was six."

"Must I say something, darling? Out loud? Slaney, you're no longer six, or even sixteen. You're eighteen, and you're not unattractive—let's be fair to you, beautiful! Still, darling, take it from me, if you really want any man don't, my little one, my sweet, be quite so eager. Darling, you know what I mean, I'm sure."

"I don't, I don't." It was completely a cry of pain, of wounded vanity.

"Oh, well, 'beds of purple heather' and rushing to help change the wheels of cars. That technique never got a girl anywhere."

The light bright wisdom of Angel's words, her exact memory for what Slaney had said, reproduced the situation in a scorching ray of truth—because she minded so much Slaney doubted herself pitifully—she was ready to believe in any diminishing reflection of herself and ready to clutch despairingly at any attitude that was handed to her. Now she covered her face with her hands, her blood raced, sweat boiled out through her.

"Oh, don't say I was like that. I wasn't, was I?" she questioned the loved oracle.

"Darling, you and I are on the level, aren't we? I went through it once. It's all on the way to experience. You want to attract and keep men just as much as I did, don't you? Very well, truth then? Yes. The littlest bit. Yes."

"No——"

"Sweets, never mind. The dear old boy couldn't matter less to you, could he? *Au fond* a titsy bit dumb, *n'est-ce pas*?"

"Oh, I don't know——" She did not defend, and so denied him, and cried out like a child who has fibbed and must escape the heavy memory. "Oh, Angel darling, this is the most ignominious thing that's ever happened to me—was I throwing myself? Help me out of it."

Angel became so gentle her bones seemed to get softer within her flesh. Her eyes melted. Her neck looked as fat as rubber, and her pretty hands dropped, as if a sigh relaxed her. "You know I never interfere, Slaney—after all, whose young life is it? But as you put it to me, all I'd suggest is, perhaps, just a *soupçon* less vibration when he's about. The coolest little breeze. You know how much better than I do."

Slaney's hands clasped together till the knuckles stood out white as picked bones: "Oh, I'll be icy, icy."

"Sweetheart." Angel bent and brushed her cheek with a little finger. It was like a giggle made of a feather. "It's not

all that, really. You do just what you think. And now "—
her voice changed to a fuller more immediate meaning—
" Oh, Slaney, change those filthy trousers, pet—full of holes,
smell of tar, old boats and very old fish."

" Oh, Mummy, what does it matter? "

Angel gave her a brief look. Had anything gone deep? Of
course not, nothing inconsolable. Secrets and surprises in her
voice, she said: " You run upstairs and see what's laid out on
your bed—just the smartest thing in pale-blue wool."

It was not anticlimax, it was stimulation—curiosity, the
smartest stimulant of them all. Slaney started for the door,
then turned and rushed to Angel and whispered closely: " Is
it lovely, darling? Will it give me confidence to be terrible
to him? "

Angel laughed. " I won't have you being unkind to my
poor old fellow. Hurry and change, and I'll tell you how
much harm you'll do in it——"

" You're a wonderful mother to have." Emotional, eyes
light with tears, Slaney kissed and fled.

Angel, looking out at the sea, felt her heart full of adoring
tenderness and spared herself time enough for this delight.

All day she had planned and worked herself and driven other
people to work—she had cooked with Birdie and gardened
with Tiddley. By superhuman effort and exertion of personality she had got the new engine installed in Julian's boat
and everything in it scrubbed and polished and hitched up
or coiled down. She felt like somebody with Christmas ready,
silver ribbon on the parcels, lights and groups of candles palely
awaiting the flame; faint pastel sugars scattered in star-dust;
everything planned with romantic craftsmanship; everyone
suitably provided for. Crowns of laughter and gratitude
and praise ready to tumble down about her feet. Now she
looked out towards the summer sea and found air and water

changed and intermarried in that lilac-coloured warmth which
she had ordered from God in those punctual evening prayers
of hers, for which she knelt each night when face and hair were
done. The prayers were an equally punctual exercise.

Had there been time to spare, she would have brought that
little problem concerning Slaney to her God, but it had been
expedient to act quickly. And how well she had dealt with it,
lacking divine advice. Some breath, between a chuckle and a
sigh of content, went out of her. She was deeply pleased at
her easy success with Slaney, and all that was hers and all that
was coming to her seemed very good.

* **9** *

BIRDIE CAME to her, and before the sea-coloured moment of
self-communing and congratulation was spent; Birdie, very
smart and sanitary in her well-cut white coat with its short
sleeves. Birdie posed a little defiantly on her best medium-
heeled black pumps. Her stance was that of an exasperated
white pigeon. She shut the door and stood just inside it, silent
and knitting savagely away at one of the minute, rabbit-soft
garments she contrived with a passionate energy and applica-
tion for starving Europe's newly born. "They must have
something lovely," she would say as, with blazing eyes, she
unpicked and refluffed the wool of an exotic bed-jacket.
"It's something lovely they need now, not something
useful."

Angel turned from the window and cried out: "Birdie,
not my peach angora! Birdie, my favourite, my softest, my
pinkest, my almond blossom."

" I don't like pink on a baby, either," Birdie misconstrued the objection purposefully.

" Then please why? I got a whole pound of white wool last week."

" Too harsh."

" Harsh? Nonsense."

" It's as rough as a jackdaw's nest. It's only like knitting up a wreath of thorns. It's——"

" Oh, all right. I give in. I must start off for Julian in a minute. What did you want me for, dear? "

" I just wished to ascertain whether it was on your authority that little—what's this I'll call him?—is to do my Julian's unpacking—that little——" There was a nauseated exasperation in her voice which ought to have signalled danger to Angel—" that little—now what *will* I call him? "

Angel felt smooth, every wheel in her running sweetly. Another gentle victory she knew would soon be hers. So: " Suppose you tried calling him Finn, Birdie," she suggested with affectionate archness.

" That one to do my boy's unpacking? That little jumped up Jackie, that poaching little fairy off the mountains," Birdie hastened on unheeding.

" Dear Birdie, please, please——" Now the personal stop. " I know you don't want to spoil things for me, not just to-day. But when you're upset, I'm upset, too."

Birdie continued her indictment. " The fish in the river, the grouse in the heather, the woodcocks by the springs is all troubles my lad, and he lashing and dashing our good silver and glass round the pantry. Believe me, he's no fit servant for Owlbeg."

" Oh, he will be, dear, when you've finished with him." Angel's voice held more commiseration for her page than compliment to Birdie, who was not assuaged.

" Every young girl I get in to help he has her tantalised and turned on me, and now his wits and his thieves' fingers are to play away among my baby's things while I stir the pots— me that packed my boy and unpacked my boy since he was born."

" Yes, Birdie, I know. What would your boy do without you?" A magazine page expanded in her mind. " But it seems so much more important that you should plan his food, balance his diet, tempt him with your graceful, lovely cooking, build up nerves, and soul and body . . . is there any feeling stronger than that we have for food—nothing more living than the gratitude we feel towards the artist who prepares it. Oh, Birdie, and it's you he loves—you, and you know it, you old darling! He depends on you just like I do—and oh, dear, I've lost something vital, the list we made for dinner. I know we'll forget a bit of gala if we don't find it. Where, Birdie? Oh, where?"

Birdie could find any missing thing. It was one of her special faculties. It did not matter what the lost thing was. Or how far from her domestic domain—the bolts for the combine harvester mislaid by Oliver, the grey hen's nest stolen in the brambles, the borrowed library book, the store-room keys dropped in a cornfield, the bracelet seven tides had washed over, the place in your neck where headaches start, the rarer sorts of cowrie shells in a bank of shingle, the packet of negatives from Will R. Rose—she could trace them all and with such practised concentration that the effort spent seemed slight.

This challenge was nothing to her divine gift, but it served as Angel meant it should, to break her mind away from Finn and her grievance. She clipped across the room on her medium heels, opened a seedsman's bulb catalogue and laid a scribbled sheet of writing-paper in front of Angel.

" Not," she commented, as she did so, " that I don't know it backwards."

" Oh, you wonder—have we time to check through it? First the historic tin of caviare—then soup with the whisper of garlic and the baby onion foundation and all the tomatoes Tiddley can give you."

" Night and day the child's reddening those tomatoes for him."

" Bless her. Then Madame Prunier's lobster *pilaffe* with our own improvements—our cookbook page, 19. I'll come down, we'll do it together."

" Don't worry, I have all the whole trick of it now——"

" Darling, then that wonderful business with the infant chickens—cooked in butter in the shallow black iron pot and the border of tiny vegetables—peas, baby carrots, *fonds d'artichauts*, mushrooms and the most wasteful new potatoes. Do you think salad before the soufflé? "

" I do."

They were together. " I do, too—sharply dressed. Then your strawberry soufflé—I know he will love it."

" It's cooling on the slab now, and there's a scent from it like a field of clover."

" Oh, Birdie, did it rise over the paper? "

" *Foamed* over."

" I feel so happy. It sounds just lovely."

" Quite a change for Julian after years of bully beef." Birdie's needles took up their faint rhythm. She was soothed and lifted by the thought of cooking and giving.

" Now Birdie, don't date yourself—don't be so 1916—he never had bully beef."

" Army rations is bully beef and the R.A.F. the same —I know—I have friends in the Army—several men friends."

"Well——" Angel let it go. "I'm aching to hear everything from him, aren't you? All his adventures."

Birdie's instinct spoke when she said: "Will he let on to you about anything? To you or to me? Do you think he will?"

"Of course, he'll want to tell me all the marvellous things he did, that baby—that child."

Here was something Birdie could take hold of. Some place where her protective sense could exert itself. "Child"—she smiled the slightly annoying smile by one who knows— "Childhood's farther off at twenty years of age than ever it is at forty-five. 'Child' how are you! Ah, my poor baby boy!"

Angel smiled the smile of disagreement, but there was not time now to open every window and air it out of existence. She just pleaded, "*Birdie*, couldn't you leave out the 'poor.' This war is over, and haven't I thought of everything to celebrate our reunion. Now, is it time to start across the bay?" She looked at the clock, a chiming-piece, and sailed from it in triumph; a complete illustration of her union with Julian had been put neatly and tidily in her hands. "Look, Birdie, even that clock he was for ever tinkering and couldn't get right, there it is—I've had it mended, and it's going perfectly."

Birdie finished counting a line of her knitting before she answered: "And God help us all the first wet Sunday." It was one of those prophetic comments that induce pessimistic memory and forecast. "He's been mending that clock since he was fourteen years of age and he won't want to stop now."

"I don't understand." Genuinely at a loss again, Angel took another lovely present out of her bran tub: "And a new engine in *Julietta*." She produced it triumphantly.

" Madam "—this time Birdie was genuinely shocked—
" the child's heart and soul were in that old engine. She was
the same as a box of tricks to him, she was plasticine and a
Meccano set, she was his little all-in-all." The nursery meta-
phors came tumbling out: " His baby-baby monkey."

" Oh, nonsense, Birdie." The idiocy of the defence set Angel
right with herself immediately. " After flying fighters for
three years, *Julietta's* engine would seem pretty silly, I know.
And six lovely new lobster pots in her, too."

" Well, I say no more." Birdie rolled up her knitting.
" But his old pots were lucky pots. He'll miss his old pots,
the lamb. He's a child no more; he could choose new pots
the same as he could choose a bride, if it came to that, and we
may all clear out of his way then I suppose—people come out
of wars very different to what they go in and I wouldn't
wonder he'd have some scheme would knock us all silly—my
boy always had such a brain. Will it be marriage, I wonder?"

" Perhaps not quite yet," Angel laughed.

" Oh, marriage is a fright, indeed. If you thought of it
you'd go mad," said Birdie with a hidden simper, for indeed,
she thought of it often.

" Well, he's just a boy still, Birdie." Angel, always a cool
blonde, swept the marriage question out of sight. " My
darling boy." She looked again from the window.

" My gorgeous boy," Birdie asserted, looking out of another
window.

Angel kept her gaze fixed, her pose deaf. " My——"

But Slaney rushed in, eyes alight, cheeks flaming, nose
over-powdered. The new dress pleased her. It fitted her
moment. It required immediate tribute. She ran forward.
" Darling, it's lovely," she said. " Do I look heaven?"

" Yes, indeed, heaven," Angel said, sipping the sight of
her daughter.

" Glamorous? " She was urgent.

" Yes."

" Just the top? " She must know.

Angel made a noise between a bee humming and a pig grunting, and Slaney was satisfied: " I can't thank you, Angel—you do think up the best surprises—kiss and kiss and kiss."

" Sweet one, you're lovely when you're pleased." Angel accepted the embraces. " Do you like it, Birdie? " She must get praise from every mouth.

" Ah," Birdie sighed, " it's lovely, it's right." She never withheld her genuine agony of pleasure in pretty clothes. " Only—turn around now, dear—is there a faint little dip on the tail? "

Since it was too late for anything but praise, Angel missed the full contentment she should have had. " You'd find something wrong with it, Birdie-bee, wouldn't you? "

" And could you put the Molyneux satin on your back till I got at it? Could you now? " Birdie's retort was pertinent to many expensive models of the past.

" No—hopeless—just a big bag." Angel's memory and gratitude jumped back and her eyes met Birdie's in triumphant memory and affectionate acknowledgment. Birdie knew she remembered accurately—it was the same tie that held her and Oliver.

" Heavens! " Angel came out of the past. " The time, sweets, the time! Oh, if I was late! Oh, I must fly. Birdie, I leave it all to you—anchovy toast for tea, remember, and the peach jam. Slaney darling, bundle these skis away, surprise for him and all that, you know. And kiss me once, and Birdie, Birdie, where's my bag? Come and find it."

Alone, Slaney climbed on to the sofa to see what she could of the back of her dress, in a round diminishing glass with dull golden globules ringing its dark lips. In its changing perspective her skirt trouble lessened to a blue point of nothingness. She got down—she sat down on the sofa—she arranged her hair, her legs, her hands, her face. She froze into a position of preposterous sophistication, while her heart beat itself against herself like a rabbit in a trap, thumping and plunging. Chris was going to be shown something when he came back—if he came back? Oh, God, if he didn't come back? She was up and at the window in despairing anxiety when he came in, so for an instant he took her off her guard, his voice warm and not completely calm: "How lovely you look."

She moved forward: "Oh, do you like me?" Then, recollecting herself she sat down and tried, trembling, to rearrange her frozen pose. She started again, her voice shook: "Oh—I thought you'd gone home."

He missed any chill implication and sat down beside her. "Not yet. Slaney, you look pretty adequate. What a jolly colour." He meant, "You're beautiful and you've upset me very much."

She withdrew a little way into her arrangement of indifference. She crossed her knees, she leaned away, she fixed her eyes, smarting with emotion, on the straps of her white sandals.

"Oh, so glad you like it," she said. "It's just an old rag you know."

"Actually," his voice betrayed him, "it's thrilling."

She caught the note behind his silly words and eager pleasure overcame her. "Oh, do you think so?"

He looked puzzled and tried again. "What about all these cunning pockets?"

"Well, what about them?" She plucked defensively at a handkerchief above her breast.

" They're driving me crazy, that's what's about them."

" Are they ? " Enchanted, she met his eyes and leaned towards a kiss, then breaking contact, flung herself desperately into isolation. " Do," she said, her voice strangling and drowning, " go and get yourself a drink," and she swept a hand towards the dining-room door.

" To hell with drinking." He caught her hand, he laughed and his arm went round her. And they had both laughed on the heather in the sun. But since then, laughter and any assumption of ease in his wooing had become subtly insulting, supposing her so much too willing. Words, horrifying, appropriate and wounding were put into her mouth as she pulled awkwardly back. " Oh, don't be such a pouncer," she said, querulously, " it's so monotonous."

" Pouncer ? " he repeated, incredulous. " What a horrible word. What's the matter, Slaney ? "

Half elated, half in tears, Slaney got up and still keeping her smart voice answered, across her shoulder, " Absolutely nothing."

Chris said with great reasonableness and restraint, " It's girls like you calling chaps like us words like pouncer that makes chaps like us too nervous to take our hands out of our pockets."

Even then she could not see that she had said enough. The young can never bend and give again.

" You mustn't miss the tide, must you ? " she suggested, and this time she spoke only to the air.

" Listen "—he was urgent—" come back a minute."

She gave an ugly little laugh.

When emotion is tense and unspoken, very little tips the balance towards disaster. Chris was furious. " Oh, all right, don't come back," he said. " You don't know what you want, do you ? You blow hot and you blow cold, don't you ? "

" How *dare* you say I blow hot ? " She sprang round on him, eyes blazing, really angry.

" How dare you call me pouncer ? " He faced her, white, ridiculous and determined. " And you do blow hot, very hot, indeed."

" Shut up! Shut up! " Back in the Fourth Form, words left her for a moment, then came in spate: " I may blow hot and I may blow cold, but when I blow cold, I'm sincere."

" Thank you," he said. " Thank you very much."

" Chris——" On a flash she knew she had done a terrible injury to him and to herself.

" Don't bother to say any more." His dignity was a bit preposterous. " I've had it."

" Chris," she whispered, but he was half-way to the door. It was like being in one of those dreams when there is that awful block between fear and outcry. She tried again: " Chris——" but he had gone.

She sat down on the sofa neatly, with no affectation of abandonment, a little girl too early at a party, and she seemed to shrink and grow plainer like a nervous child, there was the same deflowering of her looks.

As in earlier years, Birdie had rescued her with mellow easiness from any spiritual difficulty, so now she returned, her heels clicking on a softer note, the starch in her white coat less defiant, and her hands not knitting but in her pockets, almost suggesting that she was tired.

Slaney got up, wavered across the room and fell into Birdie's arms in floods of tears. They sat down side by side on the sofa. " Easy now, child, take it easy." Birdie's voice was neither over solicitous nor yet too calming; she patted for a moment before she said, " Is it Mr. Christopher ? He's off to the boat cove now a mile a minute. He passed me in the hall and the two eyes jumping from his head. Whatever ails him he looks gorgeous."

"Does he?" The tribute went to Slaney's heart. "Birdie," she raised her head from that shoulder which for the first time in existence seemed less than heaven for comfort, because to-day she had touched so new a height of easy bliss, "Birdie, I was awful to him, awful to him. We've had such a row."

"Oh, Slaney, child." Birdie took the situation in the round piece and remarked saltily, "That's the way to lose a fellow, and quick, too."

"But Birdie"—Slaney began to feel the help of discussion creep firmly about her heart—"But Birdie, Mummie said I was being much too eager and girlish—that is if I wanted him."

"She did, did she?" Birdie turned the thought round, holding her comment back.

"And you know," Slaney went on, "she's always right, Birdie. I had to show him I wasn't, but I've over-done it somehow. I'm frantic. I must ask her what to do next."

"Those who love us best meddle us worst." Birdie said it in the reserved bread-and-butter-before-jam voice, but the criticism and the warning were there. Then she changed to intimate girl-to-girl curiosity: "What did you say to him, child? Tell Birdie."

"I was very grand, and I was very cross and I sat like this— look Birdie——" She threw herself into a position even more grandly frigid than that achieved. "And *don't* you think you'd better go?"

"Oh!" Birdie was greatly shocked at such daring. "Pity, pity! Take care would he ever come back—take it from me, child, put no dependence out of fellows."

The point of view changed and panic dawned. "Would I

catch him and make it up if I went down to the boat cove ? "

Birdie clicked smartly over to the window and looked out, shading her eyes. She turned and shook her head: " He's sailing his boat away now and the wind is with him." It seemed desperately final.

" Birdie, what shall I do ? "

The occasion seemed serious enough to Birdie, too. She sighed and took refuge in a generalisation: " Love's a fright and men are wayward."

" Are they, Birdie ? " Slaney slipped unconsciously into the disciple position, a natural one to her.

" A look will lure them and a look will lose them." Birdie was thinking it out.

And Slaney was drinking it in. " You know so much about men, Birdie. I do wonder you never married." There was no taunt or teasing and Birdie saw none. She responded with simple vanity.

" Oh, I could count down the names of lovers on the fingers of my two hands and only for my well-wishers I'd be settled in a little home of my own years ago. Ah, well, my day for such notions is over, I suppose."

" Indeed, no." Slaney supplied the contradiction readily. Actually she thought Birdie most attractive and lovable and any man's fancy.

" Well, indeed." Birdie accepted it gravely. " If you seen what I seen in my teacup last night (never mind the dark medium-sized man up to me any day I'll cut the cards) you'd say I had my last chance before me yet. And when my last chance comes, do you know what I'll do ? I'll grip it, and you should do the same with your first."

Slaney drank in counsel and advice in such gulps that she could hardly wait to get to the telephone. " Oh, I just know you're right. Shall I call up and leave a message for him to ring me? As soon as he gets back. The very instant would you say?"

"I'd wait till he was there himself, messages get twisted, and it's half an hour to sail the bay."

"Half an hour—it's forever."

"It's a flash—and all I have to do yet." The starch seemed to recreate itself in the jutting bird's tailed coat, as infinite business reasserted its tyranny. "Look at me, wasting my time, and my Julian's bed to be made yet. Three blankets and the new blue blanket, two dogs and a hot-water bottle. My lamb was always chilly in bed." Birdie started for the door.

But as children cling unashamed, Slaney clung. She needed, and towards Birdie she was still almost in the pre-natal position; her mental hands were flippers up to her chin in a panda bear attitude. "Wait, Birdie, wait. What's your hurry —tell me something. Do you think, when Mummy gets Julian back, she'll forget all about me and Chris, perhaps?"

Birdie could always put a good gossip foremost: "Julian is her only son, Julian is gold." She turned the words in her mouth, making him sound more precious. "But she'll forget nobody."

Slaney said with the wisdom so easy to find for other people's situations, "Of course he can't still be her little boy, the same as when he went away, do you think she knows that?"

"I wonder, too." Birdie on a low note was very near some deeper confidence, then checked herself. "He's my own baby Julian," she went on, "but it's Mister Julian he'll get from me now."

"Birdie!" The protest was astonished.

"It's to show him we all start fair again, no cuddling. And not one word"—Birdie's eyes snapped with resolution,

" about brushing his hair or washing his ears shall pass my lips."

Slaney made a further readjustment of attitude towards the coming stranger. " And I'll shut up about the stamps and the egg collection and the rabbits." A shade of uneasiness clouded her. " What shall I talk about, I wonder? "

" Oh, you'll think of something." Birdie quite saw the difficulty. " You won't be shy long."

" Of course, I won't." Slaney took stock of possible topics. " I'm grown up, too. He's got wings and decorations. But I've got my first permanent wave and I've lost my first man."

It was then that Sally and Julian came in. He looked lighter and younger than when he had gone away, and strange as a man in a restaurant, with the white scar of the burn they hadn't seen on his dark face and his hair bleached pale as a field of wheat. He was wearing a very nice blue suit, but not the kind Angel would have chosen for him. There was a sparkle about it somewhere of which she would not have approved.

Before Slaney and Birdie a chasm dropped open, but a chasm into which they threw themselves with kisses and cries of welcome and desperate curiosity halved between Julian and his companion. Sally spoke the first coherent words—spoke with the definite husky drawl and restraint, in the tone of one used to an audience and an amplifier: " How about introducing me. Give out the good news, honey. Ring a few bells."

Julian stepped back to her and took her arm with rather an enchanting air of protection. He was very proud and a little deprecating. " I found this in the American Red Cross. She's going to marry me one of these days too. Mrs. Wood, my nannie."

" My Baby's Bride——"

Birdie took the hand held out, a thousand emotions shook

her. Unashamed, joyful, with tears, she stepped back, still holding hands, to add, on a low note: " Oh, Holy Hour." It was wildly right, this serious acceptance.

The unpremeditated prayerful comment put the matter right up where it belonged.

Sally's eyes lit. " I've heard such lovely things about you, Birdie," she said.

" Oh, he didn't forget me then," Birdie glowed.

" Never." Julian's other arm pulled Slaney into their circle, " and this is Slaney, Sally. Darling, haven't you got fat ? "

" Oh, how dare you, it's my new figure." It was their antidote to Birdie's emotion.

" I love it "—Sally was in their current too—" they're swell."

" Thank you. Can't he be terrible? Are you really going to marry him ? "

They were still in a ring, there was something foreign to the room in the group, like the sound of children broken loose from nursery restraint galloping through some unaccustomed part of a house.

" Yes, she is. Say it, Sally." He was insistent, they were to be very sure about this.

She broke the ring and sat down, opening her great big bag on her knee with studious perfection of gesture. In no matter do women differ so widely as in the management of their handbags.

" Don't fuss, sweets." She looked up, the cigarette case and her smile snapped open together. " I was just going to."

His eyes made rings of possession round her. " Isn't it terrific ? "

Birdie gathered herself from a gloating appreciation of the stranger, her clothes, the thought of love—she had an Elizabethan's pleasure in the thought of loving—there was nothing ashamed or sneaking in her vicarious delight—but now she judged it time to organise a little formality. She loved a bit of the right thing. "And may I, Mister Julian, offer my most sincere congratulations." She pitched her voice to the correct old nannie formality.

"Nannie-Bird you may "—he was laughing at her—" but for God's sake forget the mister, it makes me feel so funny."

"Ah, Doatie, you're lovely——" All her resolves to Slaney melting. Her hand longed for the little boy's head. "You're just the same, bride or no bride." Then, recovering from the baby-day lapse, "But I do congratulate you, love. I think your bride is wonderful—wonderful."

This warmth made Sally feel confident, sheltered, cosy. She could afford to play herself down, to allow herself the liberty of self-depreciation. "I'm not wonderful, Birdie." She put out her cigarette, she was a little tired at last. "Just a suitable cutie for Capri—blue seas and relaxations." She glanced up. Would Birdie take this point? "After far too many operationals—that's how it was." She had not said so much to anybody yet. It was something in Birdie that matched some part of her own loving, faintly giving weight to a blindly protective instinct. She got up, escaping from emotion, and walked with her dancer's adjustment of shoulders and hips to the window—the lighthouse window—and looked out and down and back to them all, with a stranger's eyes again. "This sea looks colder, sweets, and still and always mountains—you should have told me. You know I can't take mountains."

Julian was beside her with an arm round her shoulder. "It's a neurosis. Keep your eyes on me." His own eyes drank the sea. "Darling, think of all we planned, fishing-fleet—

everything. But we'll have fun first—sailing and lobster-pots."
He shook her. "You are going to love it all—every bit,
aren't you? Mountains, too?"

"Of course I am."

"And wait till you meet my mother. Where is she, Birdie?
I'm so excited seeing you and Slaney and the sea again.
Darling, I'm all nowhere, too."

Slaney answered him. "She's gone off across the bay to
meet you at the station."

"Oh, what a nonsense. I'm sorry. Sally took one look
at the boat train and said no. So I hired a car. I should have
wired. But I wanted to keep my surprise. Birdie, what will
she think of my girl? How will she like her?"

"Like poison, I should say." Sally said it reasonably. "I
wish she'd come back home, the dirty old stay-away. I'd
like to get the meeting over."

"Oh!"—Slaney was shocked and a little thrilled at the
daring, the non-comprehension of the unknown Angel that it
spelled. "You're not to call our wonderful Mummy a dirty
old stay-away—is she, Julian?"

Julian joined somewhere in Slaney's reaction, some navel-
string tugged. "Darling"—he turned to Sally, serious—
"we've got to keep everything pretty clean—fresh as a daisy,
you do understand, don't you?"

"Oh, I'll clean up the conversation, Toots," she reassured
him; then added doubtfully, "but there's a lot of me left
after that."

Slaney gazed at the strange painted picture and all the
implications of the unfamiliar, the indifference, the absolutely
allergic to the known code, seized on her violently: "Do you
know," she said, "I'm going to ring Chris and get him back
to cocktails—he'll be thrilled."

Birdie saw the opportunity too. "Now's your chance,"

she encouraged. Slaney was at the telephone, her air of nervous urgency unmistakable.

" Is that her gink she's calling? " Sally asked, knowing the question unnecessary, but Julian telegraphed it on to Birdie, amazed. " It couldn't be. Slaney? " His eyes said " Baby stuff, kid-business, bobby-socks," but Birdie emphatically nodded her head off. " Well," he shrugged, " that's news to me."

A wail from the telephone underlined the reality of Birdie's nodding. " Line engaged—oh, well, put it through as soon as you can, and ring me." The effort made at the telephone stabilised some feeling of independence in Slaney. She said grandly and lightly, " Isn't that sickening? I was just getting ready to call him toots like you say it, and I couldn't make a contact."

Pleased at the imitation Sally relaxed, " Oh, toughers," nice kid.

" Well, shout for me when the call comes through." A big idea had taken Slaney. " I'm going to shell the prawns for his tea. I want to." A woman spoke, a woman who would mend socks, and turn on baths and give a great deal. " You did cook them, Birdie, darling? "

" Never fear—cooling in the window. I'll call you." Birdie understood the instinct perfectly.

" Shout loud." Slaney had gone.

" Chris? " Julian said, eyebrows raised to Birdie's explanation. " She's awfully young for that, isn't she? "

" Seventeen," Birdie reminded him.

" And you can't play baby forever with that figure," Sally said agreeably. She and Birdie were on the same side. " Besides, seventeen—she should marry."

" She looks more than she is," Birdie explained. " It's all the swimming."

" Did she say she'd been prawning? " Unaccountably, Julian shied away from the subject of his sister's developments. " Prawns are what we need—a great big vulgar tea after our trip. We're all in, and, my dear, if we didn't forget Walter."

Sally was stricken.

" Julian—he'll throw one of those real temperaments if he's left alone in the car too long."

" Birdie, let's go and get him."

" Is it a dog, my lamb? " Birdie was mystified but calmly realistic.

" Walter—listen, a dog! Once he was my husband's English valet, but he followed the little madam through the rough red cross. He's a wonderful boy, but he has his own little ways."

" Another boy in the house," Birdie said despairingly. " Is Finn not enough? "

" Oh, he's not one for out-door sports like that frightful Finn," Julian was reassuring.

" Out-doors? " Sally laughed. " Why, he's just a hot-house plant, and he's no boy, he's forty-six."

Forty-six, a door for Birdie opened, opened into wonderland, opened into possibility. Breath came faster, a hand had gone to her pretty hair, and then he stood in the doorway, elegantly in the olive arch of the door, draped a little towards his own hand on the handle, his sad unselfish face looked pinched and tired, his forehead steep under the thinning hair.

" Forgive me, madam," he was saying to Sally, " but where are the suitcases to go? "

" My dark medium-size man "—for Birdie the cards were talking, falling, turning and clipping into place. " God send me luck."

" Oh, Walter, got the suitcases off already? That's just swell." The easy and friendly recognition of service pleased

Birdie. Walter's status seemed sure and true like her own. She made a little surge forward when he spoke.

" Well, I ran into a very nice boy with a great big gun " —he had a swift rippling way of talking—" had them off in a flash. Just too quick he was, but he doesn't know what rooms they're to go into either."

Ah, the ace of spades had crossed a meeting, but there were bright hearts to follow. She must possess the situation. She moved forward, paused, deliberately taking charge. " Trust that Finn to shove himself into an unpacking. How well he wouldn't ask me where they were to go." She radiated authority.

" And where are they to go? " Finn, behind Walter in the doorway, shadowed the meeting as the cards had foretold.

" Excuse me, pardon me, Miss Birdie, but I have my tea to get yet, and my rabbit to shoot and my table to polish and only one pair of hands on me, God help me."

" Just a moment, Walter." Sally was with them. " I don't need all that junk up. I'll show you."

" I can't do without my wardrobe trunk." Walter followed her dispiritedly into the hall, but Finn, seeing Julian, advanced, with duty forgotten in greeting.

" Mr. Julian—welcome home."

" Finn——" Julian shook hands. " Birdie has smartened you up." His mind flew from the neat house-coat and dark trousers and sleek hair to the little boy fishing with a string off the pier, cropped head and runny nose, then the older boy who knew by inheritance how eeltraps were made and willow baskets and the right height in a hop to set a rabbit snare, and the kind of worm for fishing in a flood up the mountain; whose disregard for rain and wind and sun and times of day were unimpeded by any civilised prohibitions. He passed through life handling it hour by hour. He leaned on a boat tilted in the sun and the sand waiting for very little but enough to give meaning to his ease. He got ready to go fishing with a tremendous sense of its moment. The changing winds, the moon, the morning star had each a message for this boy who lived on hints from a breeze, turning on his cheek, and measured his doings by the stars' doings. And now, "Birdie has smartened you up," said Julian, shocked by this turning of the tide. "How are you? How's the fishing?" Their hands and eyes clasped on this old note, like a bell under water, between them. The years had gone over the hours they had shared. War, for one, for the other this domesticity.

"Mr. Julian, the white trout are lepping mad, every evening after nine, and I can't get to the river for the washing-up— on Thursday the moon will be up early and the take will be off them."

Birdie was scuffling about hurrying things. Birdie between the reality of the river and the necessities of house-life—Julian who had spent so many days waiting for the night missions had very little patience for domestic complications—he shared a small boy look with Finn which met with eloquent answer. "And I have a black and silver fly tied for you, Mr. Julian. We'll murder them on it." It was conspiracy.

Patience ended, Birdie broke in between them. "May Peter the blessed fisher above look down in mercy on our unpacking. Finn, will you kindly go out to the suitcases." She ran him out of the room.

Julian felt deprived—they had more to say—a surge towards the deliverance and gladness of mind in Finn's importances had been interrupted—he had almost got back there, found the place, put his thumb on it, felt it within him, and now he was pushed off again on the flood of grown-up life, a man's life. Here were Sally's white suitcases, Sally's dancer's legs, and assurance, and good sweetness, the things he needed, but for which he had finished, rootless and shaken by every wind. He turned to follow Birdie and Finn, hands in pockets, head stooped; and it was so, going away from her, unknowing, that Tiddley saw him first.

She came in by the window with her baskets, little Ceres, strong-skinned and downy like a sun-burnt peach. "Julian!" He turned again and came back to her, eager and easy.

"My Tiddley, my little one, how's everything?" He picked her up and kissed her, little spaniel woman, darling creature, his easiness.

"Ah, doatie, doatie, put me down," she squealed and wriggled as he hoped she would—no romantic welcoming, nothing strange, his silly pet. "Oh, you're awful, oh, now my best tomato's gone. Oh, darling, the war didn't improve you one bit." She struggled down, pink and giggling, and restored her scattered tomatoes.

"You don't improve either," he said, not helping her, for Tiddley worked always while he sat down, or watched him while he did something skilled and creditable. "Not an inch"—how wonderful it was to tease her—"same corduroys, not a whiff of powder, is there?" He kissed her again, stooping to her on the floor like kissing a dog's head. "Talk to me, Tiddley, forget your tomatoes."

"Forget my good tomatoes!" She kept her head down, blinded by happiness. A little dark well on a mountain road she was to him, closely stone-lipped. But below the narrow depth lay the perfect water which he knew and needed. He was sitting in the sun now, the dust of heather in his throat. He was waiting to dip a cup.

"Ah," she said, picking up a last tomato, "and I've been keeping him specially."

"For me?"

She nodded.

73

" And I know where he grew exactly—I know all your letters by heart."

It was like a hand slipped close under her arm, her heart contracted. " Oh, there's a lie, and you didn't answer me for weeks." She was packing tomatoes into her basket and rearranging them with shaking hands. She over-valued everything he said.

" You know why I didn't answer ? "

She could not look up, his voice played such tricks with her. She had forgotten how weak and dumb she was.

In the little conversations she had invented for this meeting all the time he was away she had been the crisp, welcoming, sophisticated, good sort, a little more glamorous than when he left her, that peach linen perhaps, and a new hair-cut and a frank handshake. And they were alone, no Angel to take her right and loving place of first importance, to commend Tiddley's usefulness and so put her without the nearest circle. They were alone, and she could only bow her head, with its not so becoming new hair-cut, over baskets of usefulness and tough hands, squatting on the floor in the corduroys he remembered, a confused ecstatic animal, licking salt from his hand.

His quiet words undid her. " I didn't write because I had to tell you something my own self, darling. I've never had a secret from you, have I, ever ? "

She looked up. There was a string round her heart, what secret had he for her ?

" I do love surprising you "—out it rushed—" Tiddley, I've brought a girl home—a beauty, she's a dream, I know you'll approve. Now darling, leave your tomatoes alone, and listen to me. Come with me, let me show you."

" Let me show you, let me show you." It was like the new awful approach to life after an anæsthetic. I'll remember, I'll

always remember pain by this—" Let me show you "—by
these words. I shall know absolute pain. The exaggeration,
the absurdity of her emotion would come to her soon, she
was used to quelling herself, to life alone, to unemotional
satisfactions. Just a moment and she would be right. Only
give her a moment. Her hands were among her tomatoes,
the things she had grown for him, where was her help?
She stooped down and his arms were round her. " What
is it, my Tiddley? Do tell me. Why don't you talk to
me? "

She broke one of her tomatoes moving away from his arms,
and it made a reason for her dreadful tears: " Oh, look, he's
ruined, he's ruined, he's ruined."

" Well, of all the babies! " He was relieved and delighted
at the true reaction to herself, the Tiddley he understood.
The Tiddley who cried when the seeds she sowed didn't come
up, or if he lost a fish. He had known her eyes to fill when
he missed a bird he had fired at. He was back beside his little
stone-lipped well. He patted, he gave his handkerchief, he
laughed with real pleasure—" Shut up, sweetie—of all the
babies—what will Sally think? I've told her so much about
you, and now tears over your tomatoes, you silly billy."

" I'd kept him for to-day." She seized blessedly on the
reason, dabbing at tears, stuffing moss in a mortal wound,
gathering herself with folly still secret, back to where she
belonged, his loving friend.

He patted and mopped and laughed. It was so right that
she should cry. " I wouldn't like you any different, darling "—
his affection for her delighted him. He wanted to show her off
to Sally, as much as he wanted to throw Sally's star-dust
in Tiddley's eyes.

They came back then, Walter and Birdie, small pieces of
expensive baggage hung about them, pausing in the doorway

for Sally's instructions. She planned and worried very much
about packing and unpacking and knew just how inaccessible
she could make all her effects. Her back was turned to the
room, explaining where the white sunsuit might be found.
Tiddley had time to absorb the pale exaggerated shoulders
with blonde hair falling, the long sweep from waist to
knee, the bird-boned legs and small emphatic feet. She turned
round. She had taken off her hat and pushed its diamond
clip into her hair as if it was a tin slide. Her tilted painted
face was set like flint. " It's underneath the shirts in the largest
white case."

" Madam, you are wrong."

" Very well, try the lot."

" Look, look Sally, here's my Tiddley."

The preoccupation with Walter, his obstinacy and her will
to defeat him, left her face dramatically—her eyes blazed into
a smile, she went up to Tiddley, her ringed hand out, sure
of her welcome. "Tiddley, you're just like Julian said and
you do know what a lot depends on your approval?"

Sally was unafraid of greetings. Here was a pretty speech
instead of a dumb how-do-you-do. The Chinese politeness
without sensation that Tiddley knew. Tiddley's reaction was
blind despairing reception and acceptance of the poise and
glamour which were Julian's due, achieved like his decorations,
setting him farther apart from the grubby, happy importances
they had known together.

His polished tools, his oiled gun, his treasures saved and
stored and breathed on in loving care sank, by their own
useless weight, into the depth of nothingness where they
belonged. . . . What were they but nothing beside this
radiant companion he had chosen? Quite empty in her heart
and with hands emptied of their offerings to him, Tiddley
faced his beauty and with an effort that wrung her like the

pains of birth she raised her head and cried, " Sally, I'm thrilled," and to her Julian, " Oh, doatie, she's gorgeous."

That achieved, she turned from them all and ran out through the window, down the flagged path, past the formless glaring of her successful flower borders. The sea on her left hand, the castle wall that extended to the kitchen and vegetable garden on her right, she ran through the green wooden door of the wall garden and up a dark path inside the wall to the little hovel of a toolhouse, corrugated iron, a linesman's hut which she had once bought herself, her own house where she could turn a key and be alone. It was so ugly it had to be hidden. It had no glimpse of the sea. Laurels and flowerless bushes dripped on it darkly, it was Tiddley's tool-house. Even Angel did not make free of it and did not know that she kept Julian's letters here in a box with her rarer seeds. Her paintbox was here, too, and her Bentham and Hooker where she painted in the wild flowers she found and never cheated once—the good garden tools worn and clean, all of a low size to suit her, were propped round the walls, and boxes with oily rags in them held her garden scissors and pruning knives and oil stone for edging them. This was all her property, her things she had bought. She kept them carefully and a little righteously and lent them to nobody. Here Tiddley stood, holding on to the ledge of the little high window, arms up, trying to drain herself of the strength of her feeling.

* 10 *

IN THE drawing-room Sally said to Julian, "I'm going to like that kid a lot—but I'm bothered, why the tears?"

Julian said: "Oh, she always cries. It's one of the things she can't help—she had an accident with her tomatoes—isn't she grand?"

"Tomatoes, how do you spell it?" Sally's irony struck a note with Birdie—wisely and nodding she chimed in, "Ah, the thought of love's bitter on a lone girl and don't I know it."

The echo came from Walter: "Oh, me too." Sympathy breathed its first dangerous whisper.

"Love?" Julian said. "Rot, what nonsense—Tiddley's no more interested in love than a Teddy Bear."

"You never knew Teddy Bears were highly sexed? Really!" Sally's hands sketched something.

Slaney, who had been watching the telephone like a dog whose dinner is up on the shelf, said: "Tiddley's not that sort, she doesn't like men. She's twenty-two and she's never had a walk out. Fancy, she's so practical."

"She never thought of joining in the bad world war?" Sally didn't ask it in a condemning way.

"Oh, yes, but Mummy couldn't possibly spare her. You see, she needed her and Oliver and Birdie and Finn to run this place."

"Finn was the helper all right," Birdie sniffed. "If they

needed the likes of Finn to win a war they might as well give up first as last."

Walter who was still hovering to resume the sunsuit combat murmured: "He's a bit of an out-door isn't he?"

"Out-door, he's a tramp and a chancer. You don't care about fishing, do you?"

Walter shook his head: "Oh, I think it's torture."

"Or shooting?"

"It's the end."

"There's a nice refined boy," Birdie told the air. "A very nice boy, very unlike some I know, not a thousand miles from here. What about a cup of tea now, before we start the unpacking."

Finn, with a tray, came turning round the pillars in the dusky hall, like a woodcock in a winter wood. Even the possibility of his opening Julian's cases was less poignant to Birdie now. And when Walter said quietly: "You haven't such a thing as a *cachet Faivre*, I suppose? Got one of my real heads coming on," a light of delighted sympathy went up in her eyes.

"Ah," she said almost dreamily, "you came to the right doctor."

"Ah, me old hurler, well played, keep going, keep going." Finn turned the last of the pillars with his tray into the dining-room.

"Vice-versa to you also," Birdie snapped, her tongue as usual undoing her dignity, "and don't forget the peach jam. Come, Walter."

"Thanks a million." Walter followed her.

"Walter's a marvel to pull that take-care-of-baby stuff. I wish I had half the technique," Sally sighed. She really adored Walter and loved praising him. When the war started, he had left a good job to go back into the entertainment side with her, and that in spite of a very weak heart which he overtaxed in all directions. He had played tiny parts, looked after the wardrobe, looked after her—cooking, massaging, mending runs in silk stockings, tossing up a breathless little hat when the baggage had been left behind, and always with a headache and a couple of aspirins in prospect when he should at last find time for a lie-down.

" You know," she said to Julian, " how he looked after the company, nursed us all through everything."

" I know."

" Well, it will be nice if Birdie nannies him a bit, won't it ? "

Finn, arranging cups on his tray, said: " Between cutting the cards and reading the teacups, Miss Birdie is out like a lion after her last hope."

Sally sighed, seeing the implication: " That boy of mine's a chancy sort of last hope, bless him."

" Anything, if you'll pardon the word, in trousers, is O.K. by Miss Birdie."

Slaney and Julian pounced: " Shut up, Finn."

" Remember you've become a little butler since I went to the wars."

Like a turning swallow he turned from trouble. " Don't mention the wars to me, Mr. Julian. I'm disgusted with the wars."

" Why ? You haven't had altogether a bad war." It was the first note to suggest that Julian had experienced anything different from the rest of them in the last three years.

" Why ? " Finn was a little indignant. " When they couldn't keep going till my eighteenth birthday and save me from my life in the pantry shelf; and oh, sir, 'tis Holy Ireland's cross and torment."

" Couldn't you have gone if you wanted ? " Somewhere,

Sally and Julian's hands joined in joint experience—their eyes had the same look.

Slaney unknowingly joined Finn. "Oh, he couldn't. He promised Mummy he'd stay till his eighteenth birthday."

"And that's not till October"—Finn was reluctantly going towards the door—"and I wouldn't vex my madam for the world, madam." He reached the door and paused there as if he was in the porch of a church with a stoup of holy water at his hand.

"She's so good," he said it like a little prayer, and went.

Some faintly restraining, depressing influence seemed to remain in the air after he had left.

★ 11 ★

ANGEL PULLED her dark blue beret to a better angle, and gave the porter she had bespoke two shillings.

"He'll be on the morning mail for sure," the porter consoled her lavishly.

Her smile blazed out. It was as good as the pearls pulled out over the icy-blue shirt neck and the heather-coloured jersey.

"Of course," she agreed, "there'll be a telephone message when I get back. See you in the morning, John. Nine o'clock. I'll be here again."

The porter walked out of the station and down the steps to the sea and her boat with her, conscious that she needed comforting.

"Every day that boat misses the train. There's a lot of people let down every day."

"This isn't every day, John." Angel paused in her neat contrivance with a rope—she was admirably handy about boats. "It's just one day in three years." She gave her lovely brave smile again, and the porter, properly stricken, watched her push off from the pier—brave, gay, pathetic, beautiful— she had shamelessly, unconsciously, played up all these things to him. "Bloody let-down, God help her," he thought and went back up the steps, turning two shillings for nothing in his pocket.

Angel started her engine and as easily as doing a bit of knitting she sat down to steer her boat the way she knew so well across the bay home, alone. The water was dark and green with as many oily blue eyes in it as in a peacock's tail.

When alone, Angel usually thought of her daily life. Her neat mind was like a little scissors clipping and trimming at untidiness, cutting a neat way through difficulties. This evening her disappointment left her with no sense of direction. She was tired. She had worked very hard, and strung herself up to a nice pitch of excitement over Julian's return. Everything had fallen her way. She had achieved all her results with a dreamlike simplicity, a simplicity the outcome of such scheming that it had left her with a feeling of real power. And now, the object and meaning of her day snuffed out, all triumph failed from her and she felt as sad as a French cemetery —skeleton wreaths and a plump sad widow at evening. Sea- gulls arched their wings as black as church doors over her head against the sky. The engine of her boat beat against the brightness of the day.

To rest her eyes she looked inland to the watery spread and pallor of young bracken on the mountains. She never took time for suffering. Now she breathed deeply. It was one of the physical tricks she had learned expertly and it lifted her out of deep to shallow water and left her in a false peace of spirit. Her mind went calmly to the lovely dinner that she and Birdie had planned and cooked for Julian, and true to the artist in her she decided to keep none of it for to-morrow, but to eat it and drink to his arriving to-night.

* 12 *

JULIAN SAID: " She is wonderful. That's it. One never goes against her, does one, Slaney? I don't know how she had such ordinary types as us for children." His eyes found Sally and lit. " She'd be awfully impressed with me for getting Sally."

Sally smiled and shut her paper eyelids. She leaned back in the sunshine and she looked immeasurably older than the two who talked.

" She thinks you're marvellous anyway, Julian," Slaney was reassuring. " She's so thrilled you got those "—she swept a little chord across her breast with her fingertips— " decorations." Why was it a shy word to say and to hear?

He said quickly: " Both meant for other people. They just dish those things round."

" I don't believe you." She was deep in the wrong current now. " Tell me about your combats."

" Tell me about your rabbits," Julian countered, putting her straight into the twelve-year-old group where he had left her. " Much more interesting."

Slaney said stiffly, feeling the rebuff, "Anyway, I've got pedigree Minorcas now—I happen to be grown up."

Julian suddenly seemed younger again when he said: " So am I. I'm experienced. Look at Sally."

" Just get a load of me, honey "—Sally still kept her eyes shut—" if you want to check up on anyone's experience."

" Angel's going to be pretty thrilled about you, darling," Julian said with unnecessary firmness.

Sally opened her eyes: " Maybe. I'm not building on it."

" She wasn't very thrilled about Chris and me——" After the rabbit reflection Slaney had to claim elder status firmly.

" But darling, you're so young."

" Young? " she jumped at him. " Don't insult me, what about yourself? You come home practically married and I can't ask a man to dinner I suppose——"

" I'm different. I'll never be much older."

" Well, that's the way I am, too." She paused and added impressively, " It's our glands, I expect."

" You must read a lot," Sally said. Again her voice took Julian back to his main preoccupation. He touched Sally with his finger. " Seriously, this is going to throw Angel on her back, isn't it? "

" Absolutely, of course, and instantaneously "—Slaney practically believed it herself. " You know how badly she wants us to be happy," a retrospective generous memory flooded in her mind. Amidst uncertainty, the past seemed liquidly happy and simple. " Just think of all our lovely times together before the war—like our trip to Austria and the little gasthaus in Ergen where we found Oliver."

" Ergen in the Tyrol? " Sally shot up as straight as a rush. She said despairingly, " Why didn't I ask you about Oliver? "

" You did ask me. He's the agent. I told you."

" But you said he planted trees and studied abortion in cows and yessed your mother along."

" Well, so he does, but you'll love him I promise—a bitter tongue and a tender heart and a wonderful way with Angel."

" So that's how it is." She lay back and shut her eyes again. " Well, what the hell, anyway." Everything seemed to go out of her. " Just tell me," she looked at Slaney, " what year were you in Ergen? "

" I was eleven and Julian was fifteen—six years ago last April."

" Six years ago last April—it's a long time." She looked at Julian. " You were a child. Leather shorts, I suppose—*leder-hosen*? "

" Fifteen."

" And I was twenty-two. I hated Austria," she said. " My husband felt so well in the mountains. I hate mountains." She got up from the sofa and went to the window. " This place is silly with mountains, they even come down and paddle in the sea. I can't take mountains."

" Don't look at the beastly things," Julian said. " I've told you—keep your eyes on me. Keep thinking about me."

" My, don't you like mountains? I love mountains—oh, Julian, do you remember the mountains in Austria? And all the lovely flowers we got for our collections? And how we nearly killed darling Tiddley over the precipice and she never said a word—don't you remember? " Slaney was ecstatically recalling. As in old age, youth is enchanted, so in youth childhood gleams far off.

Julian said: " Of course I remember." Since the times Slaney recalled he had had other experiences over those mountains. He turned towards the window blankly. Then his face lit with intention: " Where's my Tiddley gone now? I must find her and dry up these sniffles before Mummy gets back." The power to be sweet, the longing to comfort had got him; lost over a cliff; crying in a garden; it was all the same thing—Tiddley was in trouble as usual.

" Earthing up the celery, I expect," Slaney said. " She always goes for some desperate heavy job if she has a cry."

" I shan't be long."

Sally caught one of his coat buttons and looked up, " Don't hurry yourself," she said; her look was slow, " but don't forget it."

" Forget what? "

There was a note of trouble in her eyes—" That I think you're pretty swell," she said lightly, but as though asserting an unescapable fact.

" Don't be half-hearted, I know you're crazy about me."

The moment of emotion past, she laughed: " You're over-confident."

He stooped to the top of her head. " You underestimate me, but you do smell good." He swung off and as he passed the back of the giant sofa caught sight of the water skis, ineffectually hidden behind its skirts, like Christmas parcels pushed into the guest room on the 12th of December. " Good heavens, water skis, whose idea? I was just getting good when we left Capri—she's expert——" she was always his boast—" I can't wait for Angel to get you in her lights, silhouetted against the Golden Head "—he was off to the window again, still talking. " I'll hot up *Julietta* after tea and we'll all drown together. I hope Tiddley knows where my tools are——" Suddenly full of serious business he went out through the window calling, rather importantly, for Tiddley.

Sally sighed. " He's slap-happy now, poor baby. Who bought the skis for him? "

" Oh, Mummy did, of course," Slaney sighed too.

" Did she? " Sally was thoughtful. " She must be full of cute little ideas."

" Oh, she is—but I still think she's wrong about his boat."

" You make me anxious—what has she done about that? "

The telephone rang. Exploding all importance to dust it lifted Slaney across the room on a shivering wire of intensity. "Chris," she breathed, "Oh, hallo—it's just to say——"

* *13* *

ANGEL, TURNING her back to the sea, walked down the boat quay, past the salt-white nets looped on peeled poles to dry, past a pyramid of dark tarred lobster pots, and went with bent head up the flight of steps that led away from the sea and the village and through a short field of bracken and stones and many flowers in its clipped sunny grass, flowers which Angel did not see, nor ever once looked down and back to the common evening life already entering its nightly movement in the village below; a stirring towards food and leisure and love after the day. The village troubled Angel only in terms of providing it with a maternity nurse. Oliver would have delayed her to dream above the sea and the little coloured houses and the backs of flying gulls, awhile, but only needed to get back into her own garden. Back to her own through an elaborately wrought iron gate. Past veronica bushes—veronica, that consolable brisk widow, favouring parma violet, keeping through any neglect her trim suburban quality, changing into semi-evening dress in darkest Africa, scent as dry and heavy as the worst bath powder; not too much imagination, sensible and healthy, and soon to find her consolation. That was a little parody on veronica bushes Oliver had once made, and it slipped through Angel's mind as she passed them by, although she herself thought of them merely as windbreaks.

Just as the tough gay village brought to her mind only the district nurse, veronica and consolation turned her mind to Slaney and Chris and a sensible little plan about a visit to London and parties with some of Julian's young friends carefully picked over. He would have new friends, of course, and she would welcome them to her house and make for all a lovely holiday, cooking with Birdie delicious food and producing effortless and organised sports and pleasures and repose for them.

She was walking along the bottom path of her deep garden now—lupins, exaggerated their spires and fires, apricot and rose and primrose and blue on her right hand; they grew between hydrangeas, their young leaves primrose green, on her left; the drop to the sea over milky green headlands was steep below. She was conscious of satisfaction in the lupins' health and colour as long ago she had positively obtained pleasure from her children's looks, condition, suntan and healthy greed.

What gentleness was with her as she walked up towards her little castle, turning right-handed and upwards by tortuous flagged paths that terraced the hillside? She did not seize and plan and hold all the time. She was tired, when there is room for a lessening of the major forces. First, she was sad he had not come, then faintly springing into herself again, she dramatised this little loss—straightening her shoulders and walking faster, she saw herself brave and gay. Passing Tiddley's Victorian tin soldiers, the sweet williams, she thought of her replies to Birdie about to-night's food—the caviar? But it's open, it won't be the same to-morrow. Yes, yes, we'll carve the chickens, and of course the soufflé can't wait over. She would ask Oliver to dinner, he would appreciate this brave fling.

It was odd, but never once did she think of Julian, sitting in some overcrowded hotel lounge, impatient and uncomfortable, itching at this last delay. Nor, though the dinner was planned for her children, did it cross her mind that Slaney would be sore and sulky that even now Chris might not be asked. She had not quite the imagination to see this as a moment when she should have asked Chris kindly, teased a little, made more visible the small stupidities and limitations which she had outlined to Slaney to-day with such violently successful effect. She did not think of Birdie either or how, given this delay, she might further smooth the trouble between her and Finn. She did not see that trouble as a danger—each worshipped her and each lamp should have its due portion of oil to feed that flame of worship, and from each she would obtain the maximum of that slave labour which is the expression of such a love.

Far into the future Angel did not look; that Owlbeg was Julian's property and not her own dismayed her not at all. He was a child still, he would not want to settle at Owlbeg yet, he had a career before him in the Air Force. All there was for him to do here was to admire the successful achievements of herself and Oliver—the little herd so exquisitely purified of abortion, the reclaimed pieces of bog land, the dividends reaped from tomatoes and chickens and pigs, and all she wished was to go on with this work for him, this work she loved, into which she had put her strength. Thinking of how she would show it off to Julian, it seemed entirely her personal endeavour. There was genuinely no memory of Oliver's force or direction behind the plump achievements.

She sat down on a bank and flight of steps beneath the house—a favourite place, a stone seat at the end of a rich border —it looked as lush from here as the backs of a thousand seed packets, emphasised and divided by plateaux and canyons of shadow.

Sitting on her stone seat, Angel did some mental staking and planning and rearranging in the borders, narrowing now to a haze of colour at their farther ends. She took a little notebook out of her pocket to write down her commentary for Tiddley or herself to put in practice when the time was right—that was how she got so many things accomplished. The past years were full of closely written little notebooks, names of plants and apple trees, hints on every conceivable subject: cookery, poetry, acidity, colour schemes, books, dogs, children, gramophone-records or fish. To-day the brisk noting eased and slipped, for she was tired and disappointed, and her mind, as she sat on, went back into the past, into the time before she had made this garden—the years when the children had climbed up from the sea through rocks and heather and scabious and fuchsia, when the children had been all her care and all her world and Birdie her serving priestess. She saw things left behind where children had been, wilting bunches of fuchsia blossoms, picked as plump brisk bells, very flat and soft in sunny places; handfuls of shells abandoned, their shining novelty dim; a penguin or a little red engine, undecorative unimproving toys that they loved and carried with them and forgot and cried for. Her mind's hands picked them up and carried them gently back. There had been a very popular turnstile where she had now hung her wrought-iron gate. She saw them taking turns at letting people through, healthy and luscious in the sea clothes she bought for them with an original and faultless eye for childish glamour. She saw picnics and pink mugs of milk, and remembered now that she had told Finn to put Julian's mug on the tea-tray to-day because he still liked milk. With the sharp remembrance a longing to see him, unadulterated by the thought of all she had done and prepared and planned and given, to kiss and know him surely living and young, went through her so that she jumped up to occupy herself and escape its force.

She walked down the path between the light senseless orgy of colour, graded height and contrasted textures that she and Tiddley had achieved and for once she saw nothing, nor praised, nor criticised, an odd sense of being with Julian and yet parted from influence or intimacy with him had taken hold of her. It was because he had not come when she planned and waited so faithfully. Then she heard him calling, calling, so plainly that she stood still. It was not happy, it was a completion of the odd knowledge of presence and loss, because it was not herself she heard him calling but Tiddley. Sometimes in dreams she felt powerless, her guiding gripping brain failed her, and other people smothered her clear purposes. It was the worst nightmare she knew, and now, awake on this bright spoilt afternoon, she was in the middle of such a dream. She delayed on the last flight of steps up to the light-house window to shake herself into reality again; and as she paused the telephone rang, its first ring broken in half by Slaney's eager uncertain voice. A few more steps brought her to the open window and she stood, her hand leaning on its latch, her dream alive, as Slaney's voice hysterically loud and uneven, ripped on, and she saw the back of Sally's head and shoulders and knew that quick revulsion from an unknown personality that many women feel.

"But Chris, you've got to come back—everything's different——" Held by the snake-charmer force of a one-sided telephone conversation, Angel leaned in the doorway suspended in fear. "Yes, Julian's back with a lovely girl-friend, such glamour . . . American . . . yes, full of S.A. and wisecracks . . . you must . . . . you what? . . . You won't? . . . Not if I say please. Not? Not really? . . . Oh, very well then, what the hell. . . . Don't."

Slaney turned from the telephone to the other girl, tears

were pouring down her face. " Sally, he says he won't come back."

" All baloney, sweetie, men are like that." That was her voice, tough, hoarse and gentle; Angel had never been so frightened by a voice. She waited still, suspended, solitary, every fibre of strength in her nature set against this situation. Hands, eyes, stomach muscles hardened to knots and stone. The afternoon air was of fire and ice and loneliness. She was outside, and for the first time.

As near embarrassment or clumsiness as she could ever be, she came forward into the room. They turned, and she saw Slaney's tears and Julian's woman, and stood still again, a further chill adjustment changing in her. Here was no soft girl for her to mould, or silly to expose, but a subtler, hardier type, someone whose beauty and power of living, giving and taking would be within her own knowing discretion to expend or reserve. " Experienced type, not nice," was the phrase which best described Sally—agate eyes, Cartier clips, unembarrassed silence and unready smile—to Angel.

And for Sally, Julian's mother was not a type she could classify. She did not know the insolent simplicity and un- pretending youthfulness belonging to Angel's class and kind. And that hair, growing as prettily as Slaney's, the long girl's legs, the air of entire destruction and easiness that was not afraid to be a little shy and puzzled at a first meeting, these things were cool and alien to any world Sally knew.

Slaney crossed their greeting despairingly, all pose broken. " Did you hear that? Do you know what I've done? Chris won't come back now."

" Won't he, darling? How silly." Angel did not even look that way. It was as if the current of a river had all gone into one channel. Slaney was stranded aridly where once water had exquisitely lapped and comforted.

"I must introduce myself," Sally took another step forward, waited, spoke without hurrying, "I'm Julian's fiancée——"

"Oh——" Four hands met as friendly as steel traps in a frost springing together, and Angel's ready beautiful smile blazed out, obediently to her will, as she held Sally's cool hands in her own, cooler still.

"How wonderfully thrilling this is——" She hesitated just long enough to create a tension, to convey the threat in the words—"I'm Julian's mother."

* 14 *

BIRDIE WENT down the passage to the kitchen, a strutting, flitting bird; Albert followed her, a tired predatory cat. There was gaiety in Birdie and a certain youthful embarrassment.

Walter held himself distinct, apart, important in his headache, his weariness, his beautiful clothes, his strangeness. He followed Birdie and they spoke to each other ceremoniously.

"Lovely old place." Walter paused, faintly sketching a pose among the pillars in the hall. "I'd love to make an entrance down that staircase." His sense of theatre was unaffected and true.

"Terrible place to keep up," Birdie answered primly, but her eye for beauty lit at his faint grace.

"What's the staff?" He chased her over the hall and held the swing door open above her head, holding it open as if he offered a caress.

Birdie felt good as she slipped through. Always she butted that door with some part of her body and always alone.

"One green girl and Finn Barr and myself."

"And your department?"—he was sniffing the old scented air in the passage with appreciation, almost with excitement. This atmosphere was as new to Walter as Angel was to Sally. The long flagged passage, so used and cleaned, so filled with flowers and people and food, alive and dead, for so many years, was strange as a catacomb to a boy from the café life and the rich hotel world, and latterly from war-shattered places. He was an artist with a smell for distinguished things, all that he could not place here thrilled and titillated his curiosity. Birdie he could not place at all, nor a castle with three servants any more than the light lovely smell of old expenses in the passage.

"What's your department, miss?" he asked, sidestepping, with a little dipping motion, as he passed the starry-headed boys leaning in their alcove.

"Well, I was a qualified maternity nurse one time"—Birdie stood aside to let him into the kitchen before her—"this is my department now."

He stood quite quiet, aware of the character and stateliness of this room and the dignity of Birdie's work in it. "Oh," he said, "it's a real kitchen, it's divine." He stood in front of the range lifting and looking. "No gas, no electricity, no frigidaire."

He crossed to the grooved scrubbed table and walked slowly round its exaggerated length, touching a board where parsley had been chopped, smelling his thumb with pleasure. "I can make you a wonderful omelette," he said dreamily. "Have you any dried egg?"

She showed him a deep pink bowl with seventeen pink eggs in it. "I've no experience of that kind," he said, a little shocked at so much nature all at once. "I've only actually cooked since the war, I trained as a masseur——"

The masseur and the maternity nurse faced each other

across the bowl of eggs. " Mrs. Wood's husband paid me a fortune to valet him, but when Mrs. Wood left to entertain the troops I went too. I don't know what I shall do now."

" You won't stay on with Mrs. Wood? "

" Well, I'm not exactly cut out for a country life. I like the bright lights and a dash of colour."

" But they won't live here."

" Not live here. Isn't this his own *château* you know? "

" Yes, but he can't settle down here yet——" Appalled and delighted, Birdie denied the idea.

" Well he's full of plans for trying—fishing fleets and a nice trade in lobsters I've heard mentioned. I'd prefer a casino and a couple of sea-plane taxis if I was him. Is the weather often like this here? " He was standing before one of the high muslin-draped windows. " What an attractive material "—he tweaked it gently and went on—" A small hotel would be nice. What a golf course you could lay out along those shining cliffs."

He was looking across the calm bay and saw a square yellow washed house which had the sun slap on its western face—it looked as round and kind as the sun on a cheek. The same light ran the edges of the cliffs like a narrow garland of careful pointed leaves—it emphasised and outlined the plumper curves of grass, their heart-shaped décolletages, and swelled outwards above the dropping cliffs and sea. Each treeless field looked mature and healthy and the few belts of trees lost their sea-board meanness and found dignity and easiness in the beneficent light.

" Now, who lives in that house? " He was dreaming and turned to Birdie—Birdie quiet and dignified, her hands busy slicing a brown loaf.

" Nobody," she said quietly. " It could be bought cheap."

" Electric light and a nice bar." He looked out again. " A

trained masseur." Again he looked back at Birdie, who was lightly filling her wafers of coarse grained brown bread with a coral and cream mixture of lobster and a hint of jade and pearl in chopped lettuce. " And a wonderful cuisine," he murmured.

Birdie's eyes lifted again from her work, " Will you have a new-laid egg for your tea? " she invited.

He felt strangely as though he had gone back, not to his own mean city childhood, but to a richer, kinder, childhood, back or forwards. He did not answer at once. She put the plate of sandwiches down on the table in the window and carried the rosebud china teapot round the kitchen table to a kettle on the range. Quickly and with a clicking easiness and grace Birdie accomplished the little actions of domesticity which can smell of soured routine when the mind and the hands are divorced.

Walter said, " This is nice." He sat down by the table. The curtains bloomed and rounded faintly in the sea air. He looked down the whole length of the kitchen to where Birdie stood, a white china woman in the distance—just right. The aroma of sea air and kitchen vapours, the foreign perfection and reality of this place gave him an emotion, a lovely feeling of tears and hunger and generosity.

" You'll be busy while we're here," he said, as Birdie came back with the teapot. " You must let me give you a hand. I'm mad about cookery, prefer it to dressmaking really."

Birdie's heart reeled. He understood about sewing too—was this possible? Was it true? " Eat your egg now," she spoke with a nannie's beneficence, all archness lost, " after tea, we'll see."

Finn came in with a silver teapot and hot-water jug on a tray.

" May I, miss," he said, " have the drawing-room tea?

That is, and always understanding, that your gentleman friend is able to top his egg for himself."

Walter looked up from his egg, appraising this relationship and situation. Then he looked into his egg again and his eyelashes swept his cheek.

" Thank you, Finn, that will do. Heat your pot as usual and come back for it in five minutes." Birdie spoke from the calmness of a new place in life, the place of a woman who is admired after the hungry years.

* 15 *

In the toolhouse Julian was sitting on a box that had once held croquet mallets and red, blue, black, and yellow balls, all nice from the Army & Navy Stores, Victoria Street. His trousers fell smartly from his thin knees, his feet were planted comfortably, his arm was round Tiddley's shoulders, and he was cleaning up her face with his handkerchief. It distracted and diverted him to think how he could make her cry and cheer her up and get her cosy again and trusting him altogether.

He did not notice how stiffly she sat against his arm, but had she relaxed and broken down on his shoulder he would have been worried and shocked.

" What is it, pet? " he kept asking her, but she only shook herself in answer. She meant to shake her head but her whole body shook with it. " Stop it," he said at last, " I've got so much to ask you about, I like you to be like you used to be. I was always glad Angel bullied you out of the war. I was afraid it would make you different."

"I am like I used to be." Tiddley said it with a sort of desperate roar.

"Are you going to help me? I know I'm going to want you."

"Yes—yes." A faint circulation ran to her heart like a tide from the sea.

He said, "We have so much to do. All the time I was away I used to be thinking up plans about the fishing—we could develop something good here you know, Tiddley."

"Oh!" She was taken aback at this independent scheme.

"But the first thing of all," he spoke greedily, "we must get our *Julietta* together again. You've got all my stuff in order, I know. You haven't let anything be pinched, have you? All ready for me to fix."

"Yes, Julian—but——"

"That's all right—we'll have a lovely week messing with her. I think we'll start after tea. The poor old girl must be in an awful state." He almost rubbed his hands—a keen young doctor itching to take the knife to an ugly job.

Tiddley ceased to suffer. The apprehension of his coming disappointment melted the glass splinters in her heart. She only thought of him. As a spasm of pain passes and is extinct for a moment so her pain went, dying in the anxiety of love that possessed her. And she could not tell him what she knew. Always the slave, she worked like a mole, a mole with a little gold heart as sound and as neat as a locket. And a brain no bigger than a pea.

He set her on her feet soon, dusting down her neat corduroy behind, and took her hand to bring her back to the house. Before she went she turned the clean worn key in the lock of her door and put it into her trousers pocket.

Again the contrast between Tiddley and all the free and lovely and independent girls he had known in the great world broke on him. Tiddley was the stuffy secret place in the shrubbery where you hid when you were little. This narrow dark path they walked down hand in hand from her locked house was Tiddley. She was the smell of ferns. She was the locked door in the wall. She was moss on a stone. She was not a girl at all. She was the embodiment of things and moments secure in the past. She must not change.

But when they were out in the other garden with the sea, the tea-time sea, beneath, and flagstones and flowers in order standing and a gay breeze in his face, Tiddley's dark reality dropped from his mind completely. Now he was all for Cartier clips and yellow hair, speed and sun and danger and good times and easy good-byes and taking things lightly, as you must if you are to stay whole in mind. And on the other side of himself his mind was all for work. Not watching work in gentlemanly leisure like his forebears—no: he was going to drive tractors himself, and service them. He would see all safe and right about his boats, of which the first was *Julietta*. The quay at Owlbeg would be heaped with catches of fish. There would be tanks for lobsters, and ice, co-operation, science and organisation and transport and all the things not known at Owlbeg before, or guessed at by the fishers or the fish. Julian knew, of course, that Angel, poor sweet, had done her best, and Oliver, good old soul, had given his all. He was going to be wonderfully patient and tactful in winding up their old-fashioned works and ways and exploiting his own live theories. He was a little forced, a little ruthless towards their soft living and circuitous easy ways. There were going to be changes. He was going to make the changes. He would bring discipline, too. It would be very salutary for these non-sufferers, inhabitors of an island that floated in the air for years with the crawling pit beneath.

He said to Tiddley: " This garden is altogether too well

kept—you ought to see the gardens in England." He said it reproachfully. "Of course they've had no men in them for for years."

"Nor here either. Angel and I do all this," Tiddley said apologetically, then added with all truthfulness: "Sometimes Oliver gives us one of the worst dodderers off the farm for a couple of days."

He threw a yellow pebble into the air, up and up, and down there towards the sea. He was completely unaware of the passionate self-denying toil that went towards making so lovely a garden—the ease denied, the forethought, the exhaustion and discomfort of body, the spiritual contact across years of time. The wet hands and cold feet and awkward effort of amateur gardening. He did not know about the radiant hours either, when the workers' minds and bodies dreamed, for the present satisfied with their creation. What had he to do with the sluggish safety of gardens, he who so lately had experienced the extremities of fear, and the sickness and exaltation of its control? He who had satisfied youth's greatest lusts for speed and for destruction. When had there been time for him to lean, and listen and look in leisure in the slow hours of civilised life?

So now he did not pause when Tiddley paused near groups of pansies pretty as coloured silk, or congratulate on the lilies' early springing strong and clean of disease. He saw only the sun-pool at the farther end. "That's new," he said. "How lovely. Oh, wait till you see my girl's sunburn. But what a gorgeous idea—Mummy's?"

Tiddley nodded.

"Does it really keep the wind out?"

"It's as good as under the cliff." There were tears of truthfulness in Tiddley's eyes. She saw her garden in a hard way now, as a mother can see her child when it does not

appeal, immensely defensive and yet its value to herself less
bland and secure, some value in question now that was a
golden certainty. Tiddley's mind rushed back over the time
to when they had had their gardens together, the children's
gardens in a row, beds the shapes of graves and hearts, and
edged with box, yellow, green and trim as pins in a paper
and little paths between and buckets of fine gravel they carried
to them from the shore with enjoyable ostentation. She saw
seed packets and fairy rose trees and saxifrage, six pink
tulips each and whose would flower first, and the unbearable
delight of picking your own moss-rose bud for Angel. And
his garden at the preparatory school which that shade, Hall-
Groves Junior, had shared with him and her. Tiddley had
sent plants and plans for this garden too, and bright seed
packets at the right time. Although she was never taken to
the school's big days which Angel attended so regularly, she
knew where every plant grew, thrived and failed. When
Julian and Hall-Groves Junior won a first prize for their garden
one summer term, Tiddley cried her eyes out with emotion.
But that prize was both the summit and the end of
Julian's gardening ambitions—from that date a garden was
eclipsed by the importances of the second eleven and his first
gun.

Then, as if that vulgar, careful, successful sun-parlour was
a frame and set up for her loving, Angel came out of the
house. Lightly, quickly and unemotionally she met him—
light on her feet and no delay over the light kiss. She slipped
an arm through his as carelessly as she slipped the other
through Tiddley's and so they walked back all three together
—she bent her head against the wind as she walked and looked
up at him from underneath the stoop.

"I've seen her," she said, her first words, and how warm
and gay, "Quite, quite, lovely."

His face seemed to light and curl like a flame up there above his two other loves.

"You do think so?"

"What else could I think? And how exciting to bring her home as a surprise for me."

"Oh, Angel, you are perfect. I told her you were perfect and you are being."

"Darling, I'm so happy you're happy." Her wide and pretty smile lit up like a torch. "Aren't we glad, Tiddley, you and I?"

But Tiddley was aware of the nervous steel in the arm through hers and she knew the little wheels that turned below and within—little sharp wheels biting their tracks into Angel's heart. She was sensible of unhappiness as of an ugly smell, yet she too nodded and smiled and caught her dreadful heart in her will and crammed it back into the great new nowhere it now had all to itself.

* ## * 16 *

TEA-TIME was the gayest business—the silver tray, the teapot, the hot toast, the exquisite cups, the nursery milk jug, for Angel made all her children drink milk. The meal was set on a low table between fireplace and sofa, with a proper Edwardian sense of tea-time's glamour and importance. Here, where the air of afternoon subsides, falling loosely to the end of a day, where minutes drop with the rich, fulfilled detachment of petals from a ripe old rose, here was an hour that Angel knew how to mature and celebrate.

They all sat round the table, on parts of the sofa or stools or in low chairs, the slight discomfort of drawing-room tea making that difference from other meals which gives a faint acceleration to the desire to eat. There is a delicious contradiction between hunger and wafer food, scented tea and the greed they breed between them. Angel leaned about in the coloured group, pouring tea out into cups, handing plates of sandwiches, cutting up the Austrian cake with deadly accuracy. It was all food and flutter and a disjointed account of Julian's and Sally's journey from Italy. Nobody said anything that mattered in the least, and in spite of all the chatter, food and fun, there was an anxious foggy feeling.

" Ah, *petite*, ask Finn for another cup; don't scold him, he didn't count our beautiful extra."

" *Un, deux, trois, quatre, cinq*—yes, he did," Tiddley's finger wagged over the cups on the tray.

Slaney sighed: " Anyway, he probably thought Chris would be here."

" Have a *foie-gras* sandwich, darling—Sally—try one. I won't tell you what we run it up out of, but it's delicious."

" Thank you." Sally's voice was as deep as a well with water twenty feet down. " I never eat at tea-time, do I, Julian ? "

" We've never had any tea-times that I remember—only dinner and breakfast."

" Oh, those foreign breakfasts! Everyone acid with yesterday's red wine and quite unfit to speak to."

Sally's eyes rose from her empty plate as slowly as a bucket being drawn up the well. " I certainly don't have to *speak*," she said.

" And what did you do in your day-times." Angel emphasised the virgin presences of Slaney and Tiddley with a kind of alert indulgence.

" I worked with the company—we put on a different show every night."

"We used to meet in a beautiful dark bar after the show."

"Really, what lovely fun." Angel sat back, sipping her own tea and lifting her eyes from it as prettily as anyone else. "And why didn't you cable your wonderful news to us?"

"We didn't have time, really, the whole thing got a bit out of control."

There was an anxious silence. Everyone in the pretty group was possessed by the necessity for speech, a necessity which extinguished the words in their brains. Only Tiddley could not have spoken if the word to set at ease all these she loved had been on her lips. She was drinking her tea as if it was a cup of cold water, something to steady a girl, and looking fixedly out at the faintly glaring sea, its glare turning to terrible coloured prisms the tears she might not shed.

Just on the moment when the simplicity of discomfort has reached that climax when someone clears their throat, Sally spoke up.

"Well, I'm glad he persuaded me," she said. "I think it's lovely here, just lovely." Her eyes and Angel's met and questioned each other. "I'm going to adore it," she persisted as if in answer to an unspoken denial. She put some jelly on her plate and ate it with her teaspoon, a rather low-born foreign look about the business. "Even the mountains," she went on, "are getting me."

"More jelly, Julian darling?" Angel removed the white china pot with a strawberry on the lid from Sally's vicinity.

"It's a change from our prevailing jams——" Sally seemed to intend to keep on talking.

Julian said: "Trust Angel."

"Darling," Angel said then, a different kind of 'darling,' "Darling, don't eat so fast, you'll choke."

It was Tiddley.

Julian leaned forward. "And you've spilt jam on yourself,

piggy!" He cleaned her up solemnly. Then Tiddley choked.

"What's your hurry, Tiddley?" Sally said.

Slaney, who loved Tiddley, said decidedly, "It's her piano time."

Angel put an arm round Tiddley's shoulders. Everyone was a little demonstrative to her; all thinking, with the absolute vanity and complacency of satin ribbon bows, not at all from their ugly hearts, that they had only to stretch a hand and pat and laugh for troubles to be forgotten. Slaney's comfort got the nearest because she, too, was in pain, and she said again darkly, "Really, it's Tiddley's own piano time, she ought to go."

"Not this evening, darling, please." Angel squeezed the top of Tiddley's arm in loving amusement. "Don't forget Sally comes from the real entertainment world, we mustn't try her, must we?"

"I'd like you to play, Tiddley," Sally said.

"Let's all hear more about Julian's engagement"—Angel spoke in a come-on-children-buckets-and-spades-to-the-seashore voice—"How long have you known each other?"

Sally said: "Just six wonderful weeks."

"Thrilling." Angel looked round the table. "Wake up, Slaney—aren't you thrilled?" The thing got silly at once.

"Other people's love affairs are just eternally thrilling."

"Darling, six weeks is not eternity." Angel was delighted with her baby girl.

"No loitering on the road for this madam." Sally slammed a window down between them. She knew now how things were. "I'm a fast worker."

"Indeed, you look it." Angel's voice melted. "I mean so streamlined—built for speed, aren't you?"

Julian looked up, a sudden flash of dismay, changing immediately to incredulity, but he said, "Suits me, I don't want any dame stringing me down the years like you and Oliver, Angel."

"You awful child." Angel was delighted at this thrust which put her on youth's own ground. It was a hot streak of comfort in the cold and woeful bed where she struggled so elaborately to pretend that all was well—pity and disapproval turned her heart against Julian. She was keyed to a pitch beyond her own controlling and her brain and tongue combined with dreadful ease to destroy.

"Sally, Oliver's just our land agent and dearest friend— nothing more," she built up the situation by this elaboration.

"Some may believe you, but I never would." That meant nothing, but it was offered politely.

Tiddley had thought of a way to account for her emotion and escape.

"Please, Angel, may I have ten minutes at my piano before the schoolmaster gets it?"

"Finished all the little jobs in the garden, *petite*?"

"*Mais oui, ma mie.*"

"Well, ten minutes at the piano, *c'est entendu, petite chou*, and then hurry down to the boat cove for a water-ski-ing party. Have you seen the skis, Julian? Second-hand, wasn't I clever?"

"My dear, you were—it's Sally's chief thing."

A shiver shot through Angel's blood. Was it for this?

Tiddley was standing waiting to say something important when she could get a word in—it was, "What shall I play, Julian?"

"Oh, Tiddley—'Isle of Capri,' of course, darling—your own theme song."

"But I've got a new one for you"—she could not deny herself the boast. It mattered so very much that it was out of her power to be sensible. "I won't tell you what it is.

I'll open the schoolroom window so that you can hear properly."

She shut the door on the end of this, and as her little dark presence scurried away, a certain relief went through everybody's heart as when a sick child is taken up to its bed.

Only Julian's mind was with her still. " A new one? I thought Capri was her only piece."

Angel said: " It's far worse than Capri ever was. It's what really decided me to sell her piano."

" Oh, you couldn't do that." Julian laughed at the idea and as he laughed, Sally saw something tighten in Angel, but all she said was, " Slaney, darling, you've eaten no tea."

" I'm not hungry—may I get down? "

" Finished your milk, darling? And you, Julian."

While they looked into their mugs, Sally wondered if she was seeing things—she had no nursery past herself but she had read about it.

Julian put down his mug with the luscious sigh of a full little boy. Sally began to expect, " Thank God for my good tea, please may I get down," and it frightened her a little, but he only looked at his mother and said, " Me, too. I want to plumb the entrails of my old clock. I'm sure it hasn't gone since I went to the wars——" So it was after-tea-time games, now. Sally felt agonisingly adult and far away.

" Just back from Dublin—mended and going perfectly," Angel rippled at him, and to Sally, " One of my little celebrations for his home-coming."

" How cute." Sally was watching Julian. He stood, hands in pockets, disappointed. " How very cute," he said, so she wasn't so smart as she thought. Into the moment of loss came the heartbreaking false gaiety of Lili Marlene, that tune so full of death to be the silly hymn to the fine and private graves of unspent youth and loving.

" That's it," Angel sighed. " Far worse than Capri."

Julian listened to Tiddley's playing without comment.

" I'll tell her you're loving it," Slaney said firmly. " I'm going up to the schoolroom to do my scrap-book." She sighed and went.

" Scrap-book," Julian commented a little grandly, " Slaney hasn't grown up much, has she ? "

" Just my happy baby still——" Angel tied a little bow with the words.

" Don't you ever fear arrested development?" Sally asked coarsely.

" Did your poor mother have that dread for you, dear ? " Angel's voice was sweeter than jam.

" Oh, no." The agate eyes were one better—clearer than jelly. " I went away to a convent school, that cleared up my complexes. I held down a little job in a Broadway floor-show at eighteen."

" I see—just non-stop." Angel said it as if she could see a lot more than she liked and all the time Lili Marlene beat its death-winged sweetness into the air.

" I've wasted my life." Julian had gone back in time, back to a Broadway floor-show and Sally eighteen years old. " Why didn't I know you then."

" Indeed, darling, why not ? " Angel spoke meditatively. " And you were such a friendly baby—always talking to impossible strangers in your pram."

" I liked my boys older then, sweets." Sally wondered if Julian was really unable to hear these cracks. She would hold on, she would not slap back, not yet. " That's why I married my first husband—let's get them all over."

She smiled towards Angel.

Above them, Tiddley came to a hard bit, and Lili Marlene faltered and stopped.

" Ah," Angel sighed out her relief and gathered up her powers again, " do tell us about your married lives. Were they all blissful? "

" Nothing to what they're going to be." Julian seemed to be absorbed only by Sally and his view of her. He exploited stupidity and all it could do on her behalf.

" Blissful? Well, I don't know," Sally kept on the tough, sleepy note. " My first was Greek and middle-aged. He kept me in mink or sunshine all the year round—oh, we got along."

" Sounds ideal—how exotic, and what ended that? "

" Mutual accord," Sally sighed, " the stuff that kills most marriages——" She knew that she was being as trite and as false as a snappy paragraph or a bit of stage dialogue. Within she was only frightened—entirely off any standard she knew. She saw Angel's power to defeat all that she had done for Julian and eat him and drink him and take from him everything but her own love. She could not see that Angel was as helpless in her own loving as any other woman, as powerless not to kill what she adored.

" How sad," Angel sighed, and as she sighed, "Lili Marlene" began again and Sally sighed too, but Julian seemed pleased that Tiddley had conquered. " And the next? " Angel looked at her watch, it was as if Tiddley's playing and Sally's marriages were two things that demanded so much of her attention and indulgence, so much but no more.

" I'm the next "—Julian struck a note of insistent triumph— " I'm next and always, and forever—I've got this job—twin engines, big brown eyes and all the other wonderful gadgets." He was being as foreign and Air Force as he could. " Angel, have you looked it over yet? Isn't it terrific? "

Angel looked—" Terr-ific——" a prolonged and perfect smile, chatelaine, hostess and mother, masked the word and as she held the note, the door opened and Walter, in extreme distress, swirled in:

" Oh, madam, can't somebody stop 'er? " He indicated the piano. " If she plays B flat once more I'll scream the place down."

More apprehensive than soothing, Sally said, " Now, Walter, don't be so sensitive."

Angel gazed . . . this, too . .

" It's coming, it's coming, I'll have to, I'll sker-eam——" Fingers in ears he was ready when the music stopped. There was a pause, a big anti-climax. Angel said truly, " How very disappointing."

Sally didn't care. " You can shut your mouth now, Walter," she said, loudly to penetrate the stopped ears. She was really used to such genuine coloratura performances.

" All over, Walter," Julian shouted.

It was then that Angel saw Birdie standing easily in the open doorway. There was no hurry about her, nothing tense, no knitting in her hands. She said with a sort of gentle importance, " 'Twas I quenched the piano, Walter."

Angel, very still behind her tea-tray, knew immediately that here was something else she had to watch.

" How you all bully my Tiddley——" Julian got up and walked across to the lighthouse. " Thank God I'm unmusical."

" Oh, I'm so eternally grateful." Walter and Birdie were both used to talking freely before their employers. " And one other thing, dear," he wound his way towards her, through the furniture, " if I could have a bedroom facing south. A north aspect frightens me."

" Of course you can," she spoke in gentle agreement. " Just leave it all to Birdie."

But Angel was up on her long legs and across the room

before they could go together. " Birdie, darling, you try to do too much," she fluted, exquisitely caressing. " Come along, er, Walter, that's right, isn't it, Walter, and I'll see to it myself."

" Oh, thank you, madam." Walter saw the quality of this lady. He had a fine and delicate eye for quality and liked the muscular ease of a racehorse's quarters, and liked blue flannel, exquisitely old. It smelt of well spent money. He stepped back to the door behind his own clasped hands.

" Now, tell me, Walter "—she was all the great lady at her ease—" do you like a view of the sea or the mountains? "

Birdie heard him say, " Oh, I love mountains. I dream about them," and watched him go. It was all so easily contrived, so gently executed, that she was hardly aware of what began within that flying moment, Angel's play was so fast.

Sally made a very common little face. " She pulled a fast one on you that time, Birdie."

Birdie took a quick breath. " Maybe, but I'll win my own again." She leaned nearer. " Take the gipsy's warning, there's a fight before you, too."

A germ of conspiracy quickened between them, they looked at one another with new eyes.

Flushed with the relief of music and achievement, Tiddley came bundling in, Slaney behind her. Julian turned from the window with the resolution of one who looks now for his simpler pleasures.

" Darling, it was lovely, and I guessed it, ' Lili Marlene,' am I right? "

" Yes." She was calm and cosy again. That was what the schoolroom piano did for her. Now she was ready to trench a line of celery, or bear any sorrow. " The water-skis," she said. " Angel said to start, I've got your swim-suit and Walter gave me Sally's——"

" Oh, let's—death or glory. Where's Angel? "

" Angel's fixing Walter. Angel said she'd be down after us."

Angel . . . Angel . . . Angel . . . Sally's eyes and Birdie's met again.

" Sweets," Sally said to Julian, " I'm not feeling like the cold water. You wouldn't take me out for a little walk around instead ? "

" Oh——" Julian stood between Tiddley and Slaney. Her innocent representatives. A fire of dismay seemed to flare between the three. When Julian stepped away from them and towards Sally, the girls' faces had the powdery texture of burnt paper.

" Darling, don't you really want to ? "

" Not to-night."

" Right, a walk for you and me."

" Oh, but Angel . . ."

" She said . . ."

The girls felt something that crept round their hearts, dismay and giggles. A new reaction.

" Tell her," Julian said, " and we'll be back soon." He put a finger under Tiddley's chin. " Don't drown, Tiddles, be very careful."

Sally let go a little breath of relief or excitement.

" Birdie," she said, in a tiny voice for Birdie only, " I like a fight, sometimes, do you ? "

Inside her exquisitely laundered coat, Birdie rustled about like a virile cock inside crisp feathers.

* 17 *

"IT SEEMS I'm with you again," Sally said to Julian, as he and she put their feet on the little road outside the castle gates, "this is nobody's, is it? Let's go to a nice pub. I want to see some common people. I want to hold your hand in public. I want a drink. I'm alone. I want to cry. I love you. I promise you I love you."

"Hush." He took her hand, then let it go again, the reserves of familiar places impeding him. Would his eyes let her know? "First times are hard, aren't they?" he said. "But you're so good at them."

A puff of salty air, a streak of common seaside turned on her cheek. She was back in reality again. She knew what he had meant very well. "When you know about love, there's something a bit ghostly in family affection."

"It haunts me and hurts me rather. It's very strong." Julian had all childhood in these words and the fall of his ghost sandals on the hill, where the same tongues of rock came bulging through the road's surface and houses would soon begin as the road dropped down from the baronial extravagances of his castle to where the village sat, its lap at sea level. The road forked and they took the lower prong. "Now, we pass Oliver's house," he said, "shall I call him?"

"Oh," she said quickly, "let me have you to myself a minute." But her eyes ate up the house on her left hand.

Oliver's house was built into the side of the hill and the

two roads on different levels passed it after they had divided. The upper road was level with the second storey, a door opened into it. The deep road that they were on, going downhill to the village, passed the house on ground floor level. This ground level of the house contained only the kitchen and the cook's bedroom, the window of which looked out over the road, about the height of a man's shoulder above it. Very nice and accessible, Oliver thought, as he decided it should be his cook's bedroom.

A steep austerity possessed the little house. Its two flat gable-ends faced towards its two roads and its full face it turned resolutely inwards to an oblong courtyard, high walled on the sea side and with a steep stone-faced drop to it from the upper road. The house gave the courtyard one of its ends, and an open-sided stone-built shed the other, where Oliver had luncheon parties in moderate weather—vast lobster pilaf straight from the kitchen door, perfuming the salty air as it came, and a salad which he dressed with uncaring perfection. An iron gate as high as the walls of the yard striped high into the sea and sky, and gave a Spanish look to the whole affair, bars for the ladies at evening. And this evening the high gate with its shadow made a birdcage of the place within the cage. The double pink geraniums, frilled and fluted, grew against the wall, extravagantly female and sly among their tough leaves. The house door into the courtyard led straight into the kitchen.

" Do you smell toast, darling?" Julian said.

" No. No," she denied toast desperately.

" Toast for one," he sniffed decidedly into the wind; he picked up her fingers again. " Oliver eats awfully well. He knows. He taught his cook about trout *au bleu*. He's awfully cruel really and he's always pretending things like nettles are good to eat—even bracken shoots and butter for asparagus. It

was cooking that tied him to Angel, I think. He's a bit old
for anything real, and of course Mummy's not interested in
that side of life. She has us——"

"Would she not give him asparagus?"

"He's so maddening, he'd rather have bracken really—like
he wouldn't have any surplus furniture from us for his house."

Julian looked back towards the three flat windows so high
and drearily beautiful for such a little house.

"He's made the whole top of the house into one room.
It's got five windows. He's like an old heron in his nest up
there. There's a door in from the upper road and his food
comes up in a lift, or else he eats across the courtyard."

"Oh, stop about him, he does seem to be an old aunt."

"I'm entertaining you, don't forget."

"I can wait."

They passed a couple of summer bungalows and a clean
hotel before they came to the real town, its single street ending
in boat, cove and sea. The town houses were sleek white
cats and marmalade cats and pink china cats sitting with
crossed paws behind fuchsia hedges, humping unfriendly
shoulders to the sea and looking leanly out on the street,
flat-faced and faintly forbidding in an eternal reservation.

As Julian and Sally walked up the street with the sea at
its end like a garter, an occasional house door stood open and
the door on the opposite side of the house open too, so that
there was a theatrical flash through the cat reserve to the
private world behind. Through some doors the glimpsed
world was of mean depressing hens and greyish clothes blowing on a clothes-line. But through other doors, passage and
again door, there were gardens, as prim and over-full as a
German shoemaker's with currant bushes and patches of
onions, pale lettuces and cabbages with blue hearts and piercingly blue hydrangeas and mallows pinker than soap; corners

full of dusty mint, and hideous begonias precariously arranged in short lengths of pottery piping, the texture and colour of their juicy flowers like slices from Lyons' ices. Into such brightness Sally was looking when a woman came up the passage from the back of the house and shut the front door without a word—the house was a cat again with muslin between its flat eyes and its cold rapturous thoughts.

"I don't know why we expect friendliness," Sally said. "Let's go buy ourselves a drink." They walked on. "Ah," she said, "here's a nice shop."

"It's lovely. It's the bus stop, too. I can talk to the conductor perhaps, if they're on time."

The shop had calm windows with paned glass in them. Behind the glass there was a fine display of little things that come in useful; reaping-hooks and aspro; biscuits and binder twine; packets of garden seeds and farm seeds and hair nets on cards; tins of paint and pots of jam; cards of name brooches for babies and cuff links for gentlemen; and postcards to send home to the children. They walked into the dark, abundant confusion. A beautiful girl who owned the shop welcomed Julian with friendly assurance—her eyes admired Sally without curiosity or bitterness. She asked Julian if he was home for good as if he had got off the bus on his way back from school.

Sally smelt her way round the shop while Julian talked. Ease flowed again where sides of bacon and strings of onions hung from hooks in the ceiling—on the counter there was ten pounds of butter in a lump—it gilded the lovely girl's chin underneath as she leant across to talk to Julian; the motes in the light round it were butter-coloured from its reflection. On the floor there was a box of navy-blue lobsters, surging and clicking faintly, waiting apprehensively for the last bus home. Precious oddments had lingered on in this shop from the time when there was no war—paprika and wine vinegar, black pepper balls and spaghetti, yellow and diminished in its long blue tubes. Each thing in the shop spilled some of its quality into the air and light. Round the full baskets of eggs the light was as pink as a young pig, kingcups under a chin near the butter, pink diamonds round the glass pots of jam; and in the bar on the left, blackberry gloom and the silky brightness of amber. Here Sally sat down and lit a cigarette. She did not call Julian to her or disturb him in any way.

It was half an hour before they left. Julian had a nice gossip to his favourite bus conductor while Sally and the calm beauty got together over those disastrous Paris fashions and starving Europe's babies.

The sky looked good and soft when they came out, and their feet reached satisfactorily from flagstone to flagstone of the pavement; "I always like you better when I've had a couple."

"Isn't it funny, that should sound complimentary?"

"Do you like Guinness?"

"Beautiful. It's like Dublin in the Black Forest. *Zwei Dunkelbier, Bitte.*"

"It's great after a swim."

"It's great anyway."

"What did you buy?"

"A round tower——" she showed him the postcard.

"What a business."

"Mmmm."

"We could go home that way and round by Oliver's house."

"Oh, yes—do you feel steady and happy?"

"Always with you."

"Oh, yes."

"Come on, then, it's lovely this way."

Up the dark hill away from the sea the road was patched damply under trees. A Protestant church sat down, a grey and toothless dog behind its kennel wall, a kind and lonely dog among its bones, non-aggressive, non-competitive, waiting. Farther on again, a square spare house held sea light in its dark windows, a dark air clouded its straight, short avenue of sycamore trees. At the end was the closed door, a strict virgin crowned narrowly, elegant and sad as a doe, stone roses bound her brow.

" And blue lilies do I see?" said Sally. " Wet blue lilies, for heaven's sakes, where have I got to with you?"

They stood still on the hill under the iron gate.

" The clergyman lives here. It's the Rectory. He's a funny old buster, just doesn't care. Mummy tortures him a lot."

" Is that where we tie it on?" she nodded down towards the church.

" No. There's a church on an island about as big as a mouse. Mummy even had us christened there. It was built by my great-grandfather—he didn't like the parson either. She'll lay on a Bishop for our wedding, you'll see."

" Don't you mind her doing everything?"

" Does she? I suppose I'm used to it."

" Well, come on, show me your round tower—she can't interfere with that."

It leaned up into the sky and against the sea—measureless and without reason and without entrance. Small stones had built it and it was as lonesome and ungothic as the sphinx. Stone-coloured goats tore at the close grass round it and looked at one another with dark, slanting design.

" God, it makes me sad," she said. " I adore it."

The road and the evening were empty, so he kissed her.

" How much do you love me, I want to know?" she said. " This place is all yours. They understand you here."

"Not like you do."

"You're itching to get at your boats. I'm a bad sailor."
She said strongly, "I feel everything here just fits into you."

"I don't like this sort of talk. What are you planning?
A walk out on me? But you know this place would be
nothing without you. I want you with me all the time. I'd
be funny again."

"No, not again. Anyhow, you weren't funny. Just a very
tired boy."

"No one's been in love till they've loved you."

"It's inconsequential whom you love."

"Never believe it."

They walked on up the hill and then turned back towards
the sea, along a tiny road with wide grassed edges, high above
the village and the sea below the village again. Pieces of
the evening picked themselves out sharply as they looked
down and into places from above. Three pink houses in a
descending phrase—the treetops of an orchard, long grass,
rank and green, growing between the stems of its apple trees,
but a barer later day is evident, fruit like lemons, and a basket
of washing on a quick September afternoon.

"It's good up here." Sally was seeing the shadows of
gulls print wings on the hot slate roofs, and their plunging
through air to sea slowed by the height; she was above their
backs. Everything was slowed in this moment. Cyclists in
the street beneath kept level with their blue spoked shadows
at an indifferent walking speed, and a man cutting a fuchsia
hedge snipped in slow motion to delay its flowering. The
dark juicy green of potato gardens sulked against the sea
and the grey strips of onions and brilliant unripe peas. Every-
where except in the gardens there were flowers, the long
banks on either side of the road were grown from ditch to
top with tall daisies—the blowing wind moved them along

like clouds. The sandy, sunny turf was gold with coltsfoot, and watery parsley grew, elegant and bloodless, along wet ditches where honeysuckles reserved the unconsolable hysteria of their scent for the later saltier evening chill.

" And then, oh, boy," said Sally, fastening a crown of it to her pale coat, " does she let everything go? She's like some place in music they'll never get to."

" Well, I'm unmusical, I keep telling you," Julian put his honeysuckle in his buttonhole, " but I could cry like Tiddley over this stuff when I meet it at night."

" You're very very appealing when you cry."

" It's funny how I don't mind you knowing."

" It's your longest suit with me."

" Anyway, it's all washed up now."

She threaded wintry fingers through his. " I love your hand on a hot day—I need you more than ever," he said. " Do you know what I want you to do? "

" No? "

" Come on and give a show on the water-skis, will you? "

" It's too late."

" No—come. This is what's going to kill her."

" Kill her, what? "

" Oh, please, Tiddley brought down our swim-suits."

" All right, sweetie."

* 18 *

BIRDIE STOOD among the tea things. God's wounds were in
her hard palms. Her nervous, forceful artistry had created all
this and now her strength ebbed in the desolate untidiness
round her. The numbers of people who ate her food un-
thinkingly, unknowing of her pains, were suddenly apparent
to her, a brutal force, and she who had so calmly stilled
Tiddley's piano a little while before, turned now with the
absurd anger of an anxious woman on Finn, who came with
an indifferent distaste to clear away the tea things.

" At last! And where have you been? "

He looked at her, waiting his chance to strike.

" Playing my melodeon and boiling your lobsters as you
bid me."

Her mind flew to an injury. " And will a certain party
who took my scissors to go gutting fish, kindly return them? "

" If a certain party " (his imitation was gently deferential),
" who lent a certain party her scissors to skin the eel she
couldn't skin herself had the wit to look on the nail behind
the pantry door, she'd find her scissors and save her breath."

" Excuse me, and pardon, mister impertinence, for I found
them with the stinking lobster bait."

" Oh, I'm a liar, I suppose, Miss Birdie." He took the
accusation with nauseating tolerance.

" Well——" she considered this. " I'll not fight with you
over that, Finn."

He said to the air: " What a pity I'm not able to make up to you like another party, till I'd get my tea in your rosebud pot and sugar cakes on a Tuesday. Oh, he knew how to cod a birdie, how to charm a little birdie off her bough, what? "

There was a common chord in Birdie that rang venomously true to these contests with Finn.

" Less chat in the drawing-room, and Miss Birdie to you, please remember."

" And miss you'll live and miss you'll die, that's one thing sure, and certain."

" Out, you pup, will you bet? "

Flushed against the light in her exquisite white, she was a Christmas angel as Walter came in; his arms were full of picture papers and he was singing charmingly, wearily, " They call me Countess Mitzi——"

As a dancer pivots, Birdie changed and whistled the air all for fun behind him.

Blond and sulking in the shadows, Finn murmured and not so low that he could not be heard.

" A whistling woman and a crowing hen, God help the house that holds the two."

" Now, now, now, do stop it." Walter was used to the emotional crisis of the theatre. He had no embarrassment nor saw anything silly in little scenes and passionate exchanges. Childish intensity to him was intense, and that it should pass like a flash was not unreal or ridiculous.

" You make me wish I'd gone water-ski-ing," he said. " Your madam did suggest it."

From the window Finn looked over his shoulder and back to the sea, quick as a gull's eye his glance. " They'd need you," he said. " They'd need expert advice out there—oh, look at Miss Tiddley, she's up, she's down, she's up, she's not, she'll drown."

The other two swept across the room, sports spectators—curious, insensitive, aloof from the unshared effort, critical to the last.

"Aren't they terrible?" Walter sighed. "Not an idea, have they?"

"How would they? God help them, and they'll be perished and paralysed with the cold. Finn, would you kindly pop a match to that fire before you go out to the pantry."

"Oh, I love a fire in summer—and as they're all out—may I?" Walter sank into an armchair. "Haven't had a moment for the new *Vogue*."

Finn looked round to hear Birdie rebuke a liberty, but all she said was, "Are you keen on the fashions?" She was looking over his shoulder. "Mad about them, dear——" his eyes were fastened on the turning pages, his voice absent. After a pause, he added, "I worked with Poiret when I was just a kid."

"Never!"

"Really true—hats are my thing. I can toss off a little hat in a flash."

Animation blazed between them.

"Can you imagine? It's a gift." Then the artist's boast in her supreme over all else she beckoned Finn: "Come here, Finn, till I give Walter an idea of that little dress I ran up for Miss Slaney." As though he were a lay figure, she arranged and demonstrated until the rustle of taffeta was almost audible between them. "Look—see—tight corsage—off the shoulders—full skirt, chiffon over taffeta—as white as a pearl—oh, if you'd seen it coming down the stairs." Everything flowed, the creation lived again. The past moment filled and was borne up on the air of the present.

"Must have looked a dream," Walter said softly.

Birdie's hands dropped to the flow of skirts, her eyes

swayed down a luscious false length of white over white, over glowing flesh.

Then the spell broke. Finn cracked it apart. " S-sh! " he said; he was a cat about to spring. The hunter among artists. Blood forever, and men must kill. " S-sh! " he breathed, " don't stir, I see a mouse."

Walter screamed and jumped on to his chair. Birdie's eyes froze out the same track as Finn's and pin-pointed the enemy; she was nearest to the fire, and in one lightning movement she had seized a brass shovel and brought it down on the mouse.

" I have him," she said with practical triumph.

Walter stopped screaming rather regretfully. " No," he said, " I shall faint—oh, I'm very upset. Really I can't bear mice. Mrs. Wood can't stay here if I'm to be tortured by mice."

Birdie gave him the nannie look, the my-little-little-boy look, deeply understanding. " I'll bait a trap in your room the way they'll not annoy you through the night."

Finn, breathing his tinker's magic on the fire, put in: " They're savage in that room, they're like the lions."

" That's just your mischief——" Walter was uneasy still.

" They'll be no trouble to you now at all, only to shake them out of the trap in the morning," Birdie soothed.

" Touch a mouse? Oh, I *couldn't*."

Finn came nearer. " Did you never catch a mouse? " The inquiry was unaffectedly solemn.

Walter tossed his head a little. " Yes, I did."

" You did not," Finn stated a fact simply. " You did not, for you're not fit."

" All right. And have you ever done any water ski-ing? Can you dance? Can you sing? Can you sew? "

" I cannot," Finn took a breath, " but I shot six snipe with eight cartridges my last Sunday out, and I'm a beggar to catch rabbits with my hands."

"Oo," Walter appreciated a good boast, "that does sound tricksey."

"Don't mind him and his shooting," Birdie breathed. "When myself and yourself can spend a nice afternoon planning hats. And another thing I badly want is some bright fellow to take a look through my bank book and advise me."

"Ah, nothing like a rainy day account, is there?" The secret cosy glow of money was nicely present.

"Oh, there's a little bag in the bank marked we won't say what for, Birdie——" She tossed this out, her point fastened off.

"Ah, the mountain breeze and the birds falling like stones in the heather." All the ecstasy of lonely achievement and the chill unused airs of high places was in this sudden proclamation. "There's the life, boy, come on till we knock up a bit of sport."

"And do you fancy long hours in the bog holes?" Birdie struck in, "and dragging your feet down miles of lonely road? Oh, wait till I tell you the very nasty experience I had one time on a lonely road. Did I ever tell you, Finn?" A gossip must hold all the audience, or lose power.

But he was a subtle non-player. "Oh, you did, Miss Birdie"—innocence only—"oh, you did, miss, the time the man——"

But God sent her words, and quickly: "Now was it your nasty experience or mine, Finn?"

"Oh, pardon me." Defeated, he picked up his tray and went. Birdie turned softly to Walter: "Shall I tell you about my experience?"

"Do." He knew how to breathe out a word so that it meant something.

" Well, I never got married or anything, but, mind you, I made a few great escapes."

" Oh, you've got about, Miss Birdie," he nodded. " Anyone can see that. I've had my moments, too."

Her current bore her on. " It was a long, lonesome——"

Simultaneously memory inflamed him:

" It was the esplanade at Nice——"

"—road——" She could not yield. " Not a house or a gate on it, and I wearing my new green two-piece——"

Nor could he: " *L'heure de l'apéritif,* and I had on my smoke-blue linen shirt—the subtlest décolletage——"

" When a dark villainous looking chap——"

She must hear him: " When a great big friendly——"

She bore through: " When a dark villainous looking chap came up behind me on a cycle—oh, I couldn't look—only when he passed me I glimpsed him and the long ginger moustache on him. Well, it was down across his mouth and it went back to his two ears—and, oh, the meaning look he gave me, well, I gathered myself to keep him off. Oh, I was ready for him—and then——"

" Then ? "

" Then if he didn't ride away."

Walter's exquisite sympathy knew every unspoken implication of the adventure.

" Oh, aren't men awful? " He gazed at the disaster, wide-eyed. " I couldn't sympathise more, dear. Much the same sort of thing happened to me once. It was the esplanade at Nice——"

Absorbed, Birdie gave him back the passionate attention he had yielded her.

* 19 *

OLIVER IN the doorway said: " Good evening, don't let me interrupt you, dear Birdie; just tell me where everybody is and I'll go and find them." Birdie loved Oliver, his constant understanding had long comforted her.

" All out getting their deaths in the bay "—she did not resent the break into her intimate moment.

" Dear, dear, I'll catch cold just thinking about them. Get me a drink, Birdie."

Walter, with exquisite tact, floated towards the door. He guessed he had Oliver puzzled. " Tell you what, sir, I'll stay and mix you a real snorter, shall I?"

" Oh, thank you." This had Oliver guessing even more wildly. " Gracious me "—he turned to Birdie as the door closed—" who's your fairy prince?"

" What would you think of him, Mr. Oliver?"

" Birdie, dear, I think—lovely."

" So refined!"

" Indeed, yes—don't tell me Julian brought him home."

" Not at all, he came with Mr. Julian's bride."

" Oh, that's better. But a bride—Birdie, tell me all."

She had but one thought. " Would you fancy him, Mr. Oliver, if you were me? Wouldn't he look gorgeous on the pillows? Do you admire blue eyes on a fellow—of course I wouldn't give you fourpence for a blue eyes, imagine!"

" Birdie, I don't dare think about it. I know you've clicked —you've got that ripened, magnetic look."

"Look—what's in looks? Did you see the look he gave me and he going out? Oh, Mr. Oliver, it was very remarkable. I'd want to mind myself, wouldn't I, those gay-going theatrical fellows would take advantage of you in a flash—I think I'll set a mouse-trap under his bed. Would that give him notions, though, I wonder?"

"Certainly, the very worst. You take my advice—lock your door and avoid all disappointment."

She smiled at him, not quite understanding. Then he said: "Now tell me all that's happened here since I left."

"And my dinner waiting on me!" Birdie bounced back into her day.

"Come on."

"Mr. Julian's home—all defiance and a gorgeous bride."

"Is he very changed?"

"Changed?" She thought about that. "It's his first school holidays over again."

"You convey the idea absolutely, but the bride?"

"Gorgeous. Gorgeous, and I never unpacked such lingerie."

"Indeed. And how does his mother react to the gorgeous bride?"

"A widow lady, and as smart as herself, Mr. Oliver. How do you think?"

They were getting into deeper water now—old adorations, old grudges of the flesh, spent sacrifices, too clear an understanding of motives, bitter acceptances. Oliver knew how the ripple of Birdie's memories and her present reactions were coloured by the stuff of the past, by the years that had taken her youth, by the love she had given because love she must.

He said quietly, "How she'll hate it."

Birdie added with appalling gentleness: "And break it."

" Perhaps she would be wise? " he suggested, a try-out to see whether Birdie would agree—she knew so much.

" Never," she said. " Let them find their own ways in and out of love—look what she's done to Slaney to-day."

" What's she done to Slaney to-day? "

" Got her fighting Colonel Christopher. Now the sun and moon and stars only shone from him this morning and to-night she's crying her eyes out, and my laddo won't come back to dinner."

" I'm afraid I started something there."

" Mr. Oliver—and why? "

" Something to do with Tiddley's piano, I think it was."

" Oh, that's to go too, madam says, and God help her, now her pal Julian's swept up in a love affair, the piano is her only little all."

So Birdie could place the piano in its proper importance. He would speak fully to Birdie, together they might betray Angel and her dangerous loving; together destroy that bright, terrifying ring banding these children so straitly.

" A bride for Julian, and a beau for Slaney, a piano for Tiddley, and a man for yourself—these things may come to be, dear—or they may be shivered in bits to-morrow and forgotten by the middle of next week. Which is it going to be? "

" Mr. Oliver," Birdie faced him squarely, " what's going to be depends on you."

" On me? What can I do? What does it want—this mother bird of prey? We've all got a price."

" A man of her own and a road towards to-morrow." Birdie still spoke gently, a weary gentleness that had long been held by the limitless power and knew its reason and its strength. " That's her price," she said.

What truth had he called up? " It's too high," he said, with finality, " much too high. I couldn't pay it."

"Ah, Mr. Oliver." Birdie's voice lifted from seriousness to a raillery under the cover of which words could be spoken, suggestions made, taken, or ignored, without embarrassment. "You travel the world alone——"

He took up his cue. "Come off it, you nasty, suggestive old bag."

"Come on"—she whipped up a pack of cards from the sofa table, her hands spread them out like the tail of a peacock —"cut the pack. The cards don't lie."

He had, too, an absolute respect for her integrity with the cards. Indeed he was a little afraid of taking her card demon too seriously.

"Well, I'm trying everything first," he said, and cut the cards in half with pronounced nervousness.

Just to give her mind a turn for the time being, Birdie pursued slyly, "Only for the colour of the idea."

"It's a very dangerous idea—I like things as they are. I don't want everything settled up and tucked in and signed and sealed and delivered. I like to laugh at her and work for Owlbeg."

"You like your laugh, but what about the love she's pinching out from each one of us, the same as I'd disbud a rose." She was laying out the cards then, and their peculiar necromantic flutter made an exciting unknown third in the talk. How long would he tangle words with Birdie? How often before had he done so? Neither of them willing to express all the danger, or quicken love or hate by speaking of it.

"Oh, it's a gift," Birdie said, still laying out the cards. "I never saw the equal, never. The whole pack is tingling with marriage bells."

"Gracious, how sad and awful. You don't mind if I telephone, do you. I'm getting Chris back anyway—we can't have that going wrong."

She ignored him properly. " A bright parcel and money from overseas."

An overture he knew: " Goody goody, swell." He was at the telephone—" Clohaman 3 please—yes, I'll hold on."

" And the very best of hearts up to you—from—look—a medium-aged widow lady."

Oliver replied unmoved across the telephone: " You aren't just trying to make my flesh creep? "

But Birdie's eyes were rapt, intent on her medium; the suggestiveness left her voice. All archness collapsed. She was serious. " Look, look," she said softly, " it's the marriage card all round to-day—gold rings and wedding bells to the house. But the blackest trouble card in the pack to each of us—oh—here it is again. In three short spaces of time you face misfortune and sorrow is your bed-fellow."

" Under the circumstances, hadn't I better keep away from medium widows? " Oliver said, and their eyes met frankly. But on that bridge in time his call came through, imperatively tiresome, and exacting as only a telephone call can be.

" Oh," his brain switched. " May I speak to Colonel Hawke? " As he waited he saw Walter returning with the drinks, saw with grave doubts how Birdie lit as he came towards her and decided on the face of it that this was where Birdie's heart would most likely break. It would hardly require Angel's interference to keep marriage out of this business. In a polite silence a drink was poured, was sipped with genuine criticism and handed to the protesting Birdie. " Oh, Chris, how are you —there's a celebration party here to-night——" through his attention to the sulky careless voice which answered him he saw the two sipping alternately, pretty as birds at a pool, their silence unbroken in deference to him.

" Yes," he answered the stereotyped question, " I hear

Julian's got a six-foot blonde—some people prefer them—
no, I haven't seen her——"

Birdie was making some silent suggestion to Walter.
What was it? A mime of exotic dressmaking, flinging
draperies, snapping scissors—Walter raised an imaginary gun,
shaking his head—ah, Finn perhaps. Of course, an appoint-
ment with Finn—she drooped her wings—sulks again.

"Well, are you coming back? I was told to ask you—
oh, that's really the bunk—nonsense—you've got to. It's
gay here to-night, my goodness——" Before his eyes, Walter
had put a delicate hand between Birdie's shoulder blades and
swirled her towards the door, finger to lips in a very Viennese
waltz—the effect of gaiety was brilliant. "Don't be childish
—right, you will, good—cocktails at seven—I'll be seeing
you——" He put down the receiver and went across to the
table where Walter and Birdie had left the drinks; there the
air was charged with a new and dangerous sparkle. The air
a kingfisher has dramatised and fled. A ribbon of bubbles in
an empty pool. Brief vivid signs of something that has been.

Taking his first sip of a cocktail, entirely alien to the house,
Oliver scented trouble and excitement—he knew quite certainly that odd forces were moving and currents crossing where
the full strength of water had flowed before.

* 20 *

IT WAS Slaney who came up from the sea first. He watched her
pass the two windows, and turned to greet her as she came
in through the lighthouse door. Her hair fell to her shoulders
in an ugly sadness as she stooped a little, sucking in her pale

cheeks—suicidal, that's what it was, in a wet swim-suit. "What?" he said, "no rosemary, no long purples, not a pansy? Come on and go through your act again, dear, it's a disgrace."

"Oh, Oliver." She sat down, soaking a green satin chair with a kind of despair and disregard for consequences. "Oh, I'm in such a do, such a state, such a mess up, such an old jam, what to do indeed I don't know." This Angela-Brazilian speech was typical of Slaney. She had no brain to change her language, and what had served the schoolroom must do its turn for life's emergency. "You can do anything with her— Oliver, help us. Tell her, we can't, you can. She's all out to save us and we don't want to be saved. Julian or me."

On all sides they assailed his pity, he avoiding the thrust near the heart. "Cheer up, Ophelia. Try one of these." He filled a glass.

"Oh, no, darling, Angel says those are the end for the face." Angel's entire control was implicit in her reaction. In the midst of her despair she was still ruled.

"Angel says this, Angel says that. Ever tried thinking things out for yourself?"

Her long meek arms were hung, hands clasped between her wet knees. Head down, she spoke out of her shoulder-blades, "And a nice mess I get into, then. Only to-day, Oliver, I did a bit of thinking, and look at me now. I've lost my man—Chris says he's "—she paused before the dreadful word—" through."

"How funny! Actually, he's just rung up to say he'll be over for a drink at seven, if that's all right for everybody. I said I thought so—I didn't know about this——"

"Oliver—when?" she sprang into life and length to stand in the firelight and sunlight, a newly strung bow, ready for a next shot at life.

"Just before you came in." I'll get her going under her own power, he decided. He picked up the second drink. Things appeared smoother and more workable. Influence streamed from him easily. "Just before you came in."

"Oliver, not really! Oh, goodness, it's too much." Her hands dealt wildly with her hair. "What shall I wear? Would you try a bow in your hair if you were me? A blue bow, would you say? I'd better be terribly casual though, hadn't I? This sort of thing——" She tortured her body into a stone pose, a plaque against the chimney-piece. "*Who cares anyhow.* Or this," a frigid indication of the drinks, "*Martini for you, I suppose?*"

"For God's sake, child," he implored this violent innocence, "that glacier stuff went out in the ice age. Try what you know about love."

"Oh——" she moved towards him. "Oliver"—confidence now—"I know lots."

Her voice dropped. Her eyes chased round the room, avoiding his reaction, but eager to confide.

"I bought a little book about it all. It came on Tuesday."

"Fancy!"

"Fancy what?" She was ready to be insulted.

"Has Chris read it too?"

"Oh, my dear, no, he must get quite a different book."

"Why different, why complicate things more?"

"Now, darling, really, if I thought he was thinking about page forty-two I'd get the giggles and then where are you?"

"Indeed, there's something in what you say"—he felt a profound respect for this sound piece of perception— perhaps the same quality of physical truthfulness would answer again. He asked gravely: "Tell me, child, is Chris in love with you? Truth if you can."

"I did think so. I truly did."

The drowned bell of truth rang up almost harshly, and then was extinguished in the apology of: "But Mummy said it was all my own vibration and girlishness."

"Did she?" Now he had the matter caught by the hair. "So you pulled an icy lady Honoria on Chris and he walked out? Exactly, dear, exactly, and if he walks out a second time he's the type who stays out, believe me, for good. Now"—he bore through a protest—"don't quote wonderful Mummy to me—I know what I'm saying and what I tell you is this—forget Mummy, yes and page forty-two, and when Chris comes back, just let him see—oh, that you're his and you worship him and it's June."

She took the words from him breathless, "Oh, I'm his and I worship him and it's June—oh, I'm yours and I worship you and it's June." She closed her eyes, she surged forward. She did not see or hear Tiddley, who came bundling in like a wet spaniel.

"June," Tiddley repeated, then stopped. "It's like December in the bay—gracious, Slaney, you do look funny. What's wrong with her?"

"Don't rush me, don't rush me——" Slaney held her act still. "I'm yours and I worship you." She was trying another key, and looked questioningly at Oliver, who shook his head, giving everything up.

Tiddley said, "Don't talk such nonsense, darling—go and dress yourself."

Very anxiously and in her own uncertain voice, Slaney asked: "Or do you think, Oliver, a pink bow would be more alluring?"

"Well, I know I'm old-fashioned, but under the circumstances, darling Slaney, I'd wear as little as possible of anything."

"Oh, you aren't much real help"—she was on her way to

the door now—" Mummy will know the right answer in a
flash."

So what had he achieved? The bird hopped still from perch
to perch and chirruped to its jailer. He sighed:

" The poor child's a perfect Trilby," he said desperately.
" Now, Tiddley, you are an independent girl—you have
some—what is it? Guts." He considered the value and
improbability of any revolt from this quarter. She bore too
clearly the stigmata of service. A swim-suit shrunken too
small for someone else, but not small enough for Tiddley, did
not flatter the body like a short Italian boy's, it suggested only
a womanly elegance forever lacking. He just did not think
of Tiddley as a vibrant little female creature. One felt the
soft dark down on her back should have been on her chest.
Nor would sock suspenders have seemed out of place on the
straight, strong legs. She shivered over the fire and the flame
light ran through the down on her back like a torch singeing
feathers—why did she stay?

" You're an elemental," Oliver accused her suddenly,
" indeed, yes, a royal blue elemental at the moment. Have a
cordial, my dearie, let old Mr. Machiavelli mix you a potion."

" No, thank you dear." She accepted the elemental and
refused the drink mechanically. " Have you heard about
Julian? " Looking away from him she said harshly, " Wasn't
it a lovely surprise? "

Of course that was it. " What do you think of her? "

" Oh," the harsh little voice flew up an octave, " she has
such chic, such clothes."

" American style has no more to it than good bath enamel
really."

" Oh," she considered this, comforted. " Do you think
so? But then, she has the rudest little laugh with two coughs
in it."

"Two coughs? Yes, I can imagine that being rather appealing."

"Oh, she spells glamour all right."

"How awful for Angel."

"Let me tell you," Tiddley flared, "Angel is being quite wonderful about it."

"That's an unhealthy sign for the lovers."

"Quite wonderful," Tiddley repeated stonily, "and don't please criticise Angel to me. I worship her. You may despise it but I do."

"I don't despise it, indeed I envy you. You follow a star."

"Yes."

He had given momentary wings to her empty heart. She smiled, consoled, and he pressed on. "When was your last break? I know, don't tell me, before the war—that lovely holiday in the Tyrol, wasn't that it? Washing out the children's woollies in the evening after dinner, while Angel and I danced."

"But the waltzes"—Tiddley looked at him, her eyes dark with remembrance—"used to come echoing up the wastepipe, lovely, through the lather."

"You were seventeen and you didn't mind? You really didn't mind her dancing?"

"Julian and I used to walk such a lot, there was our flower collection, and when I'd done the socks and things, I used to paint what we'd found into Bentham and Hooker."

"Tiddley, tell me something else. Have you ever done any real shopping? Girlish nonsense—a ruinous satin dressing-gown, a pink big sponge, paid for in clean notes out of an expensive handbag——"

"No, of course I haven't, because of the war—and I don't want a big pink sponge. I like little small sponges best."

There was one other road up which he might lead her to a

sense of injury, to a rebellion. " What do I hear about your piano ? " he asked in a nasty old Uncle-Tease voice.

All at once the air was full of trouble: " Oliver, have you heard anything else ? She's not going to really, is she ? "

" I don't know——"

" But she must know what it means to me." Inside her loose black swim-suit Tiddley was panting like a distressed little dog, puzzled and excited by undeserved mistaken punishment from the beloved. " Oliver, Oliver, she must know, don't you think ? "

" She can't know, if you don't tell her."

" I have, I've tried." He saw knots standing up in the muscles of her arms and her knuckles whitened. She was bracing herself to an effort. He waited.

" You tell her, Oliver," she whispered. " She loves you. She's afraid of you."

Birdie, Slaney, now Tiddley, seeking their way out through him alone—what was he bringing upon himself. In what net did he kick ? What bag closed its mouth ? " Listen," he said, " this is awful—why do you all come to me, I want to know —a brutally selfish old satyr like me ? A stew-stirrer. A sour puss."

Tiddley, who felt within herself that a responsibility was shifting to him, relaxed and spoke from the complacent silly woman place within the saddest girl.

" Ah, darling," she said, " that's only just your fun." In her relief, she stood up and even seemed to fill her swim-suit a little more fully.

21

ANGEL CAME, taking the air and jarring it to wild extravagance; there was hurry and despair and joy in the room now, and a flashing of greater importances than Tiddley's—there was beauty and brave clattering of wings.

"Tiddley, Tiddley, not dressed yet? Darling *êtes-vous sage*?" Solicitude and reproof were brilliantly blended.

"It won't take me five minutes," Tiddley apologised.

"A distracting gossip with me," Oliver said a little dangerously.

"So I see, and nothing nicer." He was included in the sweep of her uncondemning generosity, so was the cocktail shaker. She kissed Tiddley. "But you're shivering, my pet. Have a lovely big drink at once—you'll feel quite different."

Oliver said in a small voice, a wren's exquisite note against all this big stuff, "You may indeed—I feel nice and stinking myself."

Tiddley drank, recoiling as from a slap between each delicious gulp. Angel continued to pour beneficence, and at the same time to convey that all this love and indulgence came somehow through a wound in her side. "Tiddley— your flowers," she considered the lilies on a full breath, "they are more than ever lovely, and to-day I need beauty very much. Now darling, how are you? Better?"

"Oh, Angel, I do feel wonderful now, wonderful——" The well-being was unbelievable. A new high.

Angel considered her. "What you need is a good warm

up, dear. Listen, why not bicycle into the village and get the evening post."

" All right, *chérie*."

" And bring back a stone of flour for Birdie, will you, *mignonne*? "

Oliver from out of his own haze added, " And a sack of potatoes and a hogshead of lard while you're about it. Do you good, *petite*."

" Anything you say, what anybody says, is all right for me, I feel so grand." Tiddley flashed her arms and body upwards into a sudden dancing-class pose, a little chunk from a freize on an urn. " Good-bye, *au revoir, auf wiedersehen, Wien, Wien, mein lieber Wien* . . ." She swung herself into the nostalgic passionate tune, and danced all alone on her way.

" What's the matter with her? ". As the door shut, sympathy was extinguished and Angel popped Tiddley back in her particular silly niche.

" Blind on Walter's cocktail," Oliver said indulgently. " Divine, I must say. Try it."

" All right, I need something, I'm, I'm a bit shaken Oliver——"

He looked at her, retaining his sympathy. She sat posed as an experienced dancer sits, cool brown legs crossed, unmoved eyes regarding him over her drink.

" Your baby hero, I understand, has brought you home a new daughter to love." He refused the shaken note.

She answered with awful patience: " A floosie from a New York Nitery, dear. Yes, and ten years his senior."

" Never mind," he said pleasantly, " you'll smash it, won't you? And what's this I hear about Birdie's flutter? "

" Oh, isn't it awkward and ridiculous? " The laugh was boyish and embarrassed. " But I'll straighten her out, poor lamb." Something clicked. " Give me time," she said.

It was these two things, the affectation of non-comprehension and the dreadful putting on of clean boyish embarrassment that shocked Oliver into real antagonism and made the children's cause a cross of fire on which his own piercing gentleness would pin him if it must be, hands and feet.

" Angel," he said, " take care what you do there. The cards are loaded against you and the stars contrary in Heaven—love with a big S is raging through your house to-day, and if you don't believe me take another look at your little daughter. Julian apparently has got what he needs."

" Thinks, dear, thinks he needs," her cry was bitter.

" And Tiddley," he pursued, " is almost in rebellion over her piano."

" All right. Thanks for the gale warning—I'll settle them somehow. I'm a mother after all."

" Mother! A wounded tigress is more like it."

She took that too in excellent part.

" Actually a completely shattered tigress." She held out her glass, smiling. " More, please, it's far too strong for the children."

" I suspect vodka, myself." He leaned over her easily, with the shaker. " Now, dear, just relax, sip, and sharpen up those claws while I tell you something."

She looked at him at last with faint mistrust. " I know we're devoted to each other, but is that quite grounds for all these jungle insults? "

" Have I insulted you? Have I really got through? Well, listen to me, then. Listen while you're conscious."

Hostility dawned at last. " Don't speak to me like that," she blazed, and added " please " with a trembling underlip. Her anger was not womanly, it was like a hurt little boy and its quality was as dangerously attractive, he recognised it and held on his way.

" I'll speak how I damn well like. Angel, you're at the red lights and you'd better know it. You're a robot mother with distortion—an ultra-modern with every Victorian vice separately embedded in concrete—reinforced concrete."

Her answer to the absurd indictment came tumbling out. " My children adore me. Ever noticed that? They must like concrete."

Words like birds flew to him: " Does that make concrete wholesome? Does it make poison wholesome? Honey and vitriol, my sweet, that's you. Oh, you're just a big lovely ice-cream full of steel shavings."

" And you are an exceedingly rude man full of a pernicious vodka cocktail—are you through? "

" No, I'm not through yet."

Oliver felt very tired. What good to go on? Piece by piece to explain the wrongs she did when to her each wrong was right. He had gone to the limit of his powers in the unreal relationship existing between them, where he teased and criticised, and she was flattered and childish. Each knew the frail and lonely limit of unreality, but shunned any absolute relationship. Angel, because service and admiration were all she wanted from him, or any man, and Oliver because the tiger burned so brightly in her and he saw with wild dismay the fearful symmetry of her destructive loving.

But now, " I'm not through," he went on, driven by his pity, his vision of the future changed and lessened. His will to subdue her power notably enlarged by three of Walter's cocktails, he leaned towards her, charming, pleading as only the bitter of tongue can do: " But I'm versatile. I'll stop the scolding. It's useless—only, face it dear, you'll lose them some day, why not to-day? Do it in a big way—exit to music."

She was untouched. " Exit? Really, dear, you know very

little about me if you think I'll give up my children just when they need me most."

"Oh, God, what a woman!" He got up and stood over her, his hands on those unthickened shoulders, looking down into the young and living eyes. "Angel, I want you to marry me, will you?"

"Oliver——" she was enchanted and excited momentarily —how rightly Birdie had judged her needs. A man of her own and a road to to-morrow . . . the possibility of refusing both . . . all her fondness and care for him were in her voice as she said, "I was a pot of vitriol and a bag of steel shavings a moment ago."

"Forget it. I'm immunised anyway."

"And now you want to marry me." She slipped herself affectionately, unoffensively, out of his hands and as his hands were empty again he felt a cool relief, as if a window had opened to nowhere, but infinitely relieving. "Nice going, I must say." She took a cigarette and offered him one.

"Well, dear," how much he liked her at this moment, "I know what a dangerous girl you are, that's something to start on."

"It's a most romantic starting point,"—she looked up at him genuinely touchingly grateful—"and at forty-four, what woman wouldn't purr over a real proposal?"

"Forty-seven, dear, don't be silly." He lit their cigarettes. She didn't mind: "Forty-four, darling, and don't forget it."

"All right. All right." They were getting on better every moment, all he wanted was a firm No to adore her absolutely. "But you haven't answered my question yet, and it's really serious. Will you marry me?"

"Just a moment, darling." She cocked her head, a bird could not have leaned more faintly or listened with a quicker ear, "I think I can hear Julian and the child bride coming up the steps." She slipped across to the window and then turned to him, her face, even her body tautened, and older. "Yes. Oh, that laugh. Suggestive, throaty, unwholesome—did you hear, Oliver—did you hear?"

"I didn't—tell me, yes or no." He followed her to the window, a little drunk, determined to have the answer he wanted.

"What a time for proposals of marriage, even to your oldest friend. They'll be here in a moment."

"Please, Angel," he said.

She was no elderly coquette. Her mind was truly with Julian now. "There they are," she said. "Now, look, Oliver—how could any mother stand for that? Insolent, practically naked. Radiating sex—yes" (the last offence) "even on this icy June day."

Oliver was quite silent and in the length and quality of his silence there was something so dreadfully still, so lonely, that Angel turned to him, her whole mind his again. "Oliver, my dear, how odd you look. Forgive me—I'm awfully proud and elated you asked me this—you know what the children do to me—my mind was out there with him. I didn't realise you were really minding."

"Those things don't happen," Oliver said greyly, his eyes on the two outside in the sun.

"How could I know you felt like this," she persisted gently. "How could I guess behind all your cracks and teasing ways—your hands are shaking, dear, aren't they? Oh, Oliver," a touch of complacency crept in, "you haven't really minded all this time."

"Angel, what's the answer?" he insisted.

"Dear Oliver, give me till this evening." Her eyes left him as the voices outside came nearer, "I'll tell you to-night," she said, planning not to hurt and still to hold him. Then, as Sally and Julian came in, she put her arm in his and went across to meet them, very motherly. " Oliver, my new daughter." Unable to sustain so much goodwill, she added: " Cute, isn't she."

Sally had changed from the blonde tweeds and diamond clips into some sea-and-sun nonsense, designed for summer in Italy, her sunburnt feet were strapped absurdly to thick shoes which tilted her balance like a doll—she looked tremendously common and savagely attractive—rather slowly Oliver and Sally shook hands—a stranger's meeting.

" Very very glad to know you, Mrs. Wood." The American imitation was, from him, quite desperately silly.

She was more composed. " How do you do. I just speak English."

" I taught her," Julian triumphed, " and oh, how pleased I am to meet you, Oliver. I'm terribly pleased."

" Dear Julian—so am I." They shook hands. " Nobody cares if I play the piano, do they? I won't make a sound." He had to escape to find refuge somewhere, somehow to retrieve composure.

" Oliver, you'll raise the dead," Angel protested as the first chords crashed out.

He played more softly. " Or the ghosts of happy yesterday," he suggested with some of his usual affectation.

Sally moved nearer to the piano. " Play softly, Toots—leave those spooks be."

He dropped his eyes on his hands: " It's my accurate memories," he said, " giving me the willies."

Angel's face lit, she had thought of something. " Julian, mix another drink—your poor girl looks as if she needed one badly." She considered the spaces of sunburnt flesh. " All this exposure is very trying."

"She's all right," Julian said, "likes it," but he picked up the shaker and went to the dining-room.

"Do get warm," Angel implored.

"Thank you." Sally moved a little away from the fire. "I'm hot-blooded."

"Oh, so definitely," Angel agreed. "And how wonderful you were on the skis, dear, just like a young girl."

Sally giggled. "I thank God every morning I still have the use of my legs."

"Oh, a little girl I meant." The apology was icy.

Oliver suddenly stopped playing. "Now which do you mean, Angel?"

"Should I say an experienced little girl?"

"No, Angel, you shouldn't." His voice was as chill as hers had been, then he went on playing.

Angel called across to the dining-room. "Hurry up, Julian, Sally needs her drink."

"Not for me, thank you, Julian," Sally called too, richly and sweetly.

"But my dear, you must," Angel insisted; her voice was caressing. "You're cold—you're bright, bright blue."

"On the contrary," Oliver spoke again, softly and distinctly, "dark, dark brown."

This time Sally answered him directly, "Thank you— twice over."

Angel was holding the subject open with gurgles of solicitous dismay when Walter came in with one glass on a tray, a glass full of muddy green liquid.

"Ah," Sally greeted it pleasantly, "here's my private cocktail."

"And what a job to get the ingredients," Walter put in respectfully, pleasantly, standing fairly distant. "Had to peddle off to the village on Miss Birdie's cycle—quite an experience."

" Too bad," Angel said, " that nothing in the house would do."

" Just looking for fun in the village," Sally excused him tolerantly.

He shook his head and prepared to leave, " Cocktail O.K., madam ? "

" Delicious." She took the first sip.

" So glad." His smile finished with Angel. " Just off to pot the carnation rabbit with Finn, madam."

Suddenly Angel glowed. " But don't shoot too close to the windows, will you, Walter ? "

" Oh, I wouldn't touch a thing like a gun," he protested.

" Tell Finn," Angel said, immediately planning and firm, " that I want to lend you my own little gun. It won't hurt your shoulder when you fire it off."

" How fearfully kind." Walter was truly impressed, he loved easiness and accord. " I'll tell you what, madam," he turned to Sally with a sudden rush of pleasant feeling, " you've had a tiring day—I'll excuse your exercises this evening."

" Oh, Walter," Sally accepted the indulgence. " Thanks a million."

At the door he pivoted, " But I'll be back by bath-time—ta-ta," and he was gone.

" What are you getting up to, Angel ? " Oliver put his elbow on a clash of notes. " Lending him your sacred gun ? Weaning him from indoor sports, perhaps ? Dear, dear, I see."

" What d'you mean ? I don't quite understand." She was again up on that bigger, altogether nicer level. " After his unhealthy theatre life, I just want the poor boy to enjoy God's own outdoors."

" God's own upstairs," Sally corrected, " is more his dish."

" Let's talk of lovely things," Angel implored. And as Julian came back with the new drink, she went on, brightly and clearly insistent, " Gay things. Tell Oliver how you two met, darling Julian."

" Must I? A drink first, I think." He took one and a cigarette, and then faintly wandering, on the scout for a match, picked up the book which Tiddley had parcelled up, addressed, and tried to forget. He put down everything and opened it. " Listen," he said, " she gets me just what I want, doesn't she? Outboard engines—oh, enthralling." He was lost to them.

Angel looked over, preparing to interrupt, when Sally, aware and protective of his happy moment, spoke hoarsely and tough: " If anyone wants a vicarious thrill, I loaned him my sun-oil one day."

Angel smiled. " Well, it's as good an introduction as any other."

Oliver said sourly: " No technique should become monotonous."

" But I thought Julian said it was in a dark bar." Angel was going to embarrass somebody.

Sally answered, smoothly, " Maybe I'm confusing him with somebody else."

" Maybe——" Oliver left the piano. All the gaiety had gone out of his slight intoxication. Angry and obvious he said: " After that, I suppose, friendship ripened into love and died—rather slowly and painfully?"

" Oh, we're still more than friendly, thank you," Sally said without her smile.

" Of course." He sat down on the arm of Angel's chair. " Maybe I'm confusing him with somebody else."

Angel gave him a gentle look, she felt antagonism in the air and welcomed it. " Look forwards, dear, always forwards."

" Or backwards, dear, sometimes backwards." Sally drank off Walter's concoction and set down her glass.

"I do admire the way you American girls can drink," Angel offered grimly.

"Monday, tomato juice. Tuesday, verbena. Wednesday, cabbage and onion."

"Charming for you, Julian dear." Angel could not take the pleasant offer of sobriety, nor could she leave Julian alone. "Yes, that's the awful day," he looked up and back again to Tiddley's book. "Ah," he breathed, "glandular arrests—but this is *Julietta's* trouble exactly"—he was away again.

"Thursdays carrot juice," Sally proceeded smoothly. "The stuff for your skin."

"And do you take it regularly? What is your skin like?" Angel's eyes bored the make-up gently.

"Oh," Sally sat up straight, suddenly determined to take no more, "if I had your skin and you had my bottom, what a knock-out we two would be. Listen, why don't we have Walter fix you a diet chart? It'll lift the years right away."

"But I wouldn't deprive you of Walter," Angel smiled dreadfully, "he must be as busy as a bee keeping you so breathlessly young."

"All the same, I do hate to see a dame let herself go to bits," Sally said discouragingly.

Oliver leaned across Angel and said: "I'm always around to pick up the bits."

"Tame cats have their uses in the home," Sally spat at him.

"And roof cats, I'm told"—Angel leaned so that all her background was Oliver, a man—"get their biggest breaks in world wars."

"Oh, do let's not talk about world wars." Julian picked up the two possible words. "We've had it, haven't we? I need a little fun with *Julietta's* engine, now. This book has excited my old engine lust. How did Tiddley get it? Out of print for years." He got up. "Come on, Oliver. Coming Sally?"

"Darling, if it's engines, no."

"A little surprise, Julian," Angel murmured, swelling with her happy importance. "I'll come along." She joined him, and laughed at his look of disturbance.

"What sort of a surprise, Mummy?"

"I won't tell you. You're really going to be thrilled."

"Surprises——" Oliver said, taking his eyes from the bright swing of Angel's departure, "are the thing to-day. Have a real drink."

"Well." Sally hesitated. "It's six years since our last."

"So long?"

"Always cynical, weren't you?"

"My only outlet. Don't start remembering."

"No, for Heaven's sake. But have you been to Innsbruck since then?"

"Since then—oh, please don't be silly—anyway how could I?"

"Let's go on talking."

"All right, but it's all such thin ice."

"Remember our shopping?"

"What a one you were for your shopping."

"Please don't let's go on. And my first Imperial Tokay."

"So disappointing."

"So very, very."

"Bands forever playing waltzes." Oliver was looking for trouble.

"Little tables, Oliver, in beer gardens, glass shades and candle-flames."

"Pink chestnuts in flower—blue trout to eat."

"Red wine—" she looked at him unforgivably over the rim of her glass—" to drink."

"I still can't understand why you left me like that. Away you went on that awful high titty-fa-la foreign train." Oliver's eyes were quite light and bright with pain, the rippling silly words held no connection with that distinct moment.

On a high despairing note Sally hurried on: "I do think foreign trains are so romantic—I always see poor old Marlene standing on the bottom step in a spotted veil—don't you?"

"No," Oliver said quietly, "I see you, in that affected peasant's dress—I smell the indecent scent of those vast lime blossoms, it comes down over my head like a pale bell of anæsthetic, and if you don't mind, I still feel a little sick——"

That afternoon train, agonising certainty of her going, stood still at its departure platform—he was unfairly shifted back to that other lifetime of the thirties (so derided, so despicable now—so nice then). He remembered how the sun had shone on golden birds and church towers green as cucumbers, and on her hair. He saw her wreathed straw hat swing by its ribbon, and re-experienced his twinge of fascinated embarrassment at the dirndl and pinafore she wore so determinedly, where the nice type of girl wears tweed. Years of time lay between them. Still, behind health recovered and work accomplished and the happy, thin, exalted state of mind he had achieved and enjoyed, this only reality endured. The true self was not an improved character, the happy agriculturalist, the collector of furniture and emotions, and shades of feeling. The true self was the young person who had gone to Austria to die discreetly. "Why did you have to?" he persisted.

"Don't you remember? I had to join my husband in Prague."

" But you were coming back—why didn't you come back?"
She said without bitterness, " The poor old bum needed
me."

" You're a big-hearted girl, aren't you?" Oliver's voice
had nothing nice in it at all. " Just too damn big-hearted."

" My husband's very words, Oliver," Sally said with mild
surprise, " the day he filed his petition. Really, you boys
are identical."

" You might have told me you were divorced."

" Well, we'd lost contact——" Her eyes evaded him.

" And you thought I might be dead. I'm not—Angel
managed that."

" Oh, I see, you look wonderfully well," she admitted
coldly.

" And now?"

" Now, Oliver, I'm going to marry Julian."

" Just cut out for an Irish chatelaine, aren't you?"

" That child was in a real spot when I found him." Sally
stated it directly.

" I was in a real spot when you left me." Oliver spoke
on quite as flat a note.

" Listen. Try and understand. That baby with his row
of medals and citations badly needed a change from operationals."

" Do you love Julian?" he persisted.

" Of course I do, haven't I taught him to love me."

" That's not the answer."

" Is that so, well, it's the answer I'm giving you. It's
the answer I want you to take. Listen, I gave him a whole
new break when he was practically out—he went swimming
with me, dancing with me, aqua-planing with me——"

Suddenly angry at the escapist fantasy of the frankest girls,
Oliver said sourly, " Yes—need we have this encyclopedia

of spotlessly clean outdoor fun? Give me credit for a little imagination."

"That's right, be your sweet self," she said, "you ought to know what I mean if anybody does." All fantasy fled. "Maybe I am tough, but I'm standing by this kid just so long as he needs me—I'm not walking out on him. I did it once —not again."

"Please don't," Oliver said with chill distinctness. "He'd be distressingly lonely, as I'm planning to marry his mother quite soon."

"Like hell!" She swung round on him. "That allergic old were-wolf! 1 won't allow it." Her eyes were full of angry tears, she was the kid in a street row, teeth and nails and a brave heart, reason or reality exhausted.

"Unfortunately," Oliver answered rudely enough, "you aren't the only person who thinks of others. I'm kind-hearted, too. Just at this very moment all my schemes are clicking smartly together. Soon, Angel will be alone and needing me a lot—Slaney gone, I hope, with Chris. Tiddley—I've sown some very nasty seeds of discontent in Tiddley's loyal breast. Birdie has found your Walter, and her Julian has you, dear. Tidy now, isn't it?"

"Tidy," Sally drooped her lovely neck, "is right."

Oliver took a few steps away from her: "Why," he said, "did you have to come back?"

Sally opened her huge handbag and practically put her head in it. "Shut up," she whispered. "Shut up, you big, cruel sap."

* 22 *

BIRDIE CAME in then; she opened the door very gently and
brought in with her an air as still as the hour before thunder.
All strength seemed spent and a sadness floated from her and
round her like a pool of oil on water. She said to Oliver,
" He's gone on me—she has him captured." She looked
weary and a little crumpled. " I had the bouquet for my sauce
tied up and ready to show him every trick in it when I heard
himself and Finn in the pantry and I called him. Did he
answer? No—but the other party popped out and, ' Actually,'
he said to me as cool as that, ' Actually, madam has ordered
the two of us out after the carnation rabbit.' Oh, ' Actually '
from that savage was what knocked me."

" Yes, it would throw you on your back, wouldn't it?"
Oliver agreed. " And Walter?"

" The next thing our friend came out of the pantry, and
madam's own gun on his shoulder, right enough. ' Just off
for a bit of sport, dear,' he says—oh the breeze that chilled
me then—' back to our sauce in half an hour?' ' Oh, never
mind the sauce,' I said (I could match any change). ' Away
off you go, and if you do fire off that gun, don't miss Finn.' "

Sally lifted her head from the cavern of her bag. " Birdie,"
she said, " we're all in a bit of a jam. You aren't the only girl
ready for a good cry."

" She's enticing Julian off you, too—oh, I know—tears
before night all round. The trouble card was up to each one
of us in the house."

154

"It's still more complicated——"

Oliver gave Sally one of those hooded lover's looks which connect so revealingly with the muscles of the throat, and Birdie caught it on its flight. The unhappy facility and unerring perception of a hungry or a jealous woman.

She said, "What's this?" Brief and rough, the love of others filling up her empty heart with pain.

"I knew her very well once," Oliver said, "isn't it unfortunate."

"It's not making any difference, Birdie," Sally said, "while the kid needs me."

The friendly look in Birdie's eyes turned into the watcher's look, bright as a stone and equally unsympathetic.

"He'll need you," she said, almost harshly, like a nurse to a doctor whom she disapproves, "for a long time yet. And what about yourself?" She turned on Oliver, accusingly.

Oliver said, "Just to oblige you, Birdie, I've asked the danger to marry me. She hasn't answered yet. But I think she will."

Birdie's eyes filled with tears. "You're very good," she said softly. "Oh, you're very good. But will she best us, I wonder? Will she best us all yet?"

* 23 *

DOWN ON the boat quay Julian and Angel leaned against the sea wall together, Julian aching faintly all through with the blank knowledge that he should be pleased; Angel aching against her smile with the sure perception that he was not pleased.

"Did you sell the old engine?" he asked suddenly, out of a pebble-throwing silence.

"Well, really, darling, she wasn't very saleable. I told young Walsh who fitted the new one he could keep her—but he didn't want her."

"I see. As far as that goes I could have put it in myself. It's awfully simple."

"I did want to have it just ready for you."

He threw away his last pebble and turned to her. "Have I thanked you properly?" he asked. "It's a gorgeous surprise—the very best possible."

Her eyes flew to catch his—they carried no deep reflection of his happy words and she felt cheated of him altogether. "You are glad?" she persisted.

"Delighted, enchanted, madam. It just fits in with my scheme for a fishing fleet. I haven't told you about that yet, have I?"

"Are you serious?"

"Absolutely, why not?"

"Well, you know how the Owlbeg fishermen loathe the sea. They never go out fishing if they can help it."

"Oh, organisation—a combine—a van to market; the fish and the lobsters—I've dozens of ideas."

"Yes, lovely ideas abroad, but the coast of Ireland is awfully allergic to them." And all the time she knew she should be saying: "How good. Why haven't I thought of it all these years? It's a certainty," and other approving noises. But something sticking against her brain forbade it, and her dislike of Sally mounted in her to a sort of horror. Sally seemed prominent in all this change. She typified the unknown hours.

Julian said: "These fishermen here have never had a break. This whole place has never had a break. I've got to change things. I have to work. I need to work, really."

"But," her protest was a little despairing, "look how Oliver and I have worked for you. My darling, we've even paid off the overdraft."

"Darling, how wonderful, but you've just touched the spot I mean, Owlbeg on the top of the wave never does more than just pay off the overdraft. I know I can do better. I'm going to try anyway."

The unanswerable arrogance of his youth shook her confidence. The years of her own and Oliver's happy effort shrank and dried into a drear unimportance. "But it was such a huge overdraft," she cried, looking for the commendation that should have been there, for the unquestioning adoring approval she expected. Oliver would have liked her more for this hurt moment.

"Well, darling, it wasn't my overdraft," he said indulgently, youth piling responsibility where it belonged.

Angel bent against the quay wall. Its height kept the sea breeze off all but her cheek. Its stored warmth crept against the creeping chill of her body. Quite suddenly she feared for all her triumphs and successes. Dear and absurd, the years flew past her mind as she leaned beside that bright and strong son, whose danger had been her suspense and importance for so long, her reason for endurance, for the maintenance of that brilliant struggle at Owlbeg. How little could he know of the relentless struggle through which she and Oliver had paid off that overdraft he passed by so lightly. What did he know of the industries maintaining life through her persistence against the sickness of Irish apathy—mushrooms, for instance? How early in the year would come her cry for horse manure, but manure of the right texture and temperature for the mushroom spawning—it must be thus and thus—and where is the thermometer, that the temperature may be just so and so? Where is the garden thermometer which I told you was to stay in a hollow bamboo cane and hang from that nail? Well, where is it now? Gone? Lost? Where? When? November, when the bull was sick? They took the bull's temperature. They broke my mushroom thermometer in the bull's temperature? Is nothing sacred? Yet she had made seventy-five pounds out of the mushroom beds that year. No struggle too petty for her driving fever, for that wild free method of organisation which achieved her own purpose through the slack currents of other people's endeavour. Yes, she achieved unheard-of niceties. Midnight milk for the *petits poussins*, Chinese extravagance in manuring the strawberries. Never tired, never sad, never a change of mind or heart, her impulses she followed to their final core of being. Whatever the impulse, her quality drove it forward. Moments lived to her against his silence and the sea and the nasty, nodding *Julietta* out there . . . How, for all her work, the luxury of eating well had never become unimportant. She thought of a certain morning when the idea of *poulet a l'estragon* had visited her forcibly. Although the herb had succumbed in February's frosts, had she abandoned the idea? Such flashiness of purpose was impermissible. Tarragon grew strongly in a garden twelve miles distant. Very well. Somebody was vitalised on to a bicycle and despatched for its collection—and if luncheon delayed until mid-afternoon there was an hysterical degree of perfection in its final production. The aroma of tarragon had a subtler perfume for the dedicated endeavour which procured it. She would forget with a superb abandon every normal aid to an Irish luncheon. The potatoes, the vegetables, the sweet, mattered nothing. She ate with delight her chicken and her bread, and a salad, like chilled glass from its long sit on a marble slab in the crypts of the scullery, and went out filled with strength and pleasure to drive her slaves through the rest of the day. Ah, the good days of those anxious years —the present heat of stone against her gave her back drinks in the sun—bottles of soft stout after swimming. Herself and Oliver leaning together on a pink-washed wall, a wall higher than the windows of the pink pub it sheltered from the sea winds, smoking cigarettes, watching squadrons of gulls, piercingly bright-winged in the sun; watching the windy sea, brisk and common-place as a lot of blue dressed hospital nurses with slapping white veils. In the hot shelter where they drank there was an elder tree dreamily, creamily expanding its cat smells in the sun, and at the unlikely smell, her energy leapt: " Oh, what do I smell? Elder flowers— and its gooseberry jelly to-morrow—Oliver, I can't make it without elder flowers."

" Calm yourself, dear, they are far beyond my reach."

" Sissy! A foot here and here—it's too simple. Thank you, dear—and thank you—perhaps six more—lovely, lovely," so she would break into any moment of ecstatic laziness, never permitting luxury to become purposeless.

Looking again at Julian, she felt breath and being float out towards him, but for once no resolution had any direction. She was a thousand years removed, from the poised youngish mother who had waited this afternoon. Yet she could make no admission to herself of failure or the necessity for any new acceptance. He must come back to her. The boy she knew was only hidden from her briefly by alien influence and experiences. If she could catch this cold boy from the distances in her net, she would hold him kicking in her hands until he changed into himself at last.

It was Chris's return that set everything flying and filled her with pure uncalculating anger. Incredulous, she heard the ugly beat of that outboard engine, showing him too impatient for the wind. Almost instantly she saw Julian

quicken at the idea of his coming, and gaiety and life renew
their hold on him as he shouted greetings and caught ropes.
" Splendid. Grand. Of course you'll stay to dinner, mustn't
he, Mummy? Oh, Chris, don't be so stoogie, of course you
have to."

Chris deferred it to her charmingly. " It was awfully kind
of you to send for me."

She said: " Oh, nonsense, dear," and her curiosity flamed.
" I'm glad you got the message all right."

" Yes, Oliver got through."

Oliver. So it was Oliver. He, too, against her. Oliver,
her ally and critic and admirer. Oliver, who quite truly
owed her his life. Oliver who had eaten her lovely food with
gracious greed and understanding and helped her to enjoy
wine and curious flowers. Oliver, her friend and spiritual
love. Oliver, whose extraordinary offer of marriage she had
so nearly refused this evening, so nearly, but not quite.
" Oliver," she repeated, and a determination to vanquish his
disloyalty and hold him her own again rose past any other
importance in her mind.

Chris still stood smiling, a little uncertain on the quay;
waiting as if for her to ratify the invitation; he was her good
boy, he had always been such, her dear, smiling slave whom
she had taught, to whom she had given his importances and
social behaviour. More, such poise as he had, such originality
of purpose. Almost she felt responsible, in a distant, complicated degree, for his war record and his safe return. Who in
the first place had taught him to keep out of trouble sailing;
how to watch for changes in wind and weather; how to
endure the agony of fishing inexpertly until, in place of agony,
an interested patience was achieved. Only to-day, for their
own young sakes, she had fixed the first wedge between him
and Slaney. How delicately she would tap it into place,

hurting nobody too much. She looked at Chris meditatively, measuring her influence on him, all she had taught him, and speaking in her little persuasive voice, said: "Dearest, of course. So lovely. We aren't," she said in an aside from Julian, eyebrows lifted in amused dismay, "quite such a family party as I expected. You two go on up to the house, I know Julian is longing for you to see her." She was aggressively playful towards him and the whole affair. Perhaps it was a little insulting. It drew from Julian, "No hurry, old man—you'll have years to know her in."

But Angel insisted. She wanted to be by herself to get things sorted out in her mind before she drove on to their accomplishments.

"Oh, you two, go on," she said, "actually I promised to meet the district nurse here at seven o'clock."

"Oh, well," Julian relaxed, "we know what that means." They strolled away along the quay towards the path up to the house, heads bent, stooping together, saying little things to each other that she would never hear, happy without her. She heard Julian laugh. Intolerably alone, she ached for any contact, even the idea she had faked of a talk with the district nurse. She wanted to plan her evening. She wanted to make her decisions, and here she leaned alone against the coarse cement wall, longing for comfort, hurt as a kicked dog, while a vast brainless urge to defeat them all somehow of their mistaken pleasures, rose higher in her like the tide that welled and clucked inwards now through the cleft rocks. Birdie and Walter, farcical and easy to account for with the unconscious help of Finn. She smiled tightly. Slaney and Chris, that was under control now. Julian and Sally, here she was uncertain, and ready to strike most dangerously. Oliver's gross interference she could not reconcile with the emotional conclusion of his outburst to her this evening. Her mind flicked away busy as scissors at a seam, and prolific with plans for the redirected happiness of all. She had ordered the conduct of her day so well that there was no last minute activity to fulfil. Now should have been all leisure with Julian, but now alone, she sighed and leaned in the evening air. As she leaned and listened she heard a shot from the garden above, a shot that sounded three times, first in the garden then pounced off the cliff and slapped against the water. The carnation rabbit she hoped, had died, but her hope changed as the shot was followed by hysterical screams of distress.

* 24 *

"DID YOU hear me, I screamed the place down. Oh, I was upset. You know I'm a bundle of nerves and a thing like that shatters me for days. But the shock! Never again, that's what I said to Finn, never again. I've got through a world war without touching a gun and now look what happens when I do—they aren't safe."

Walter and Finn, in Angel's bedroom before dinner, were explaining to her the disastrous shot which had peppered Chris's legs and left him neatly tucked up on the sofa in the drawing-room, reeking of Dettol and dramatic misfortune, with Slaney and Birdie in frenzied attendance.

"They're all right, if you don't aim them at people, you know," Angel said tersely. The affray had complicated everything. Things were out of hand now.

"Well, madam, I didn't, did I? Ask Finn. Actually, I was aiming at the rabbit—never saw the Colonel. Quite a nasty surprise."

"Don't say a word," Finn said. "We all made a great escape, thanks be to God."

"Well, I'm through with this outdoor nonsense," Walter said firmly. "I'm going to spend a quiet evening with Miss Birdie, and I wish I'd never left that lovely cosy kitchen."

"You wouldn't do a real artist's job for me first, would you?" Angel indicated her bed, across which a white dress flowed and glittered. "Finn can bring you up a little something on a tray from the dining-room and a glass of champagne to steady your nerves." She held the dress so that it bent a little towards its trailing skirts and looked at it with a real caress. "It's for Miss Tiddley," she explained. "It just wants a lift here and a nip here, nothing permanent," she added anxiously, "only for to-night—just to cheer her up."

"She'll need it," Finn put in, "if the schoolmaster comes to try out the piano. It'll kill her."

"Oh, Finn, keep her glass full, won't you, at dinner-time. Just keep putting in a little whatever she says. And remember this is to be a surprise for everyone—not a word, boys, even to Birdie—especially Birdie."

Walter took the dress. It was rather like a nurse who must get possession of the baby—none but he had the right of genius.

"It's the dark young lady?" he questioned. "To me that needs something here and here? And a reasonable make up—that's right, I'll have a real do at her after dinner. You send her along. Miss Widdley, isn't it?"

"Tiddley," Finn put in, shocked.

"Well, if Miss Tiddley doesn't get a gentleman when I'm through she never will."

"Ah, no, there's nothing like that," Angel said, hurt, "you don't understand. This is a lovely thing for its own sake alone. And Finn, what are we to do with Walter when he's through with dressmaking—what about the river? It's a milk and honey evening. The sea trout will be on the take—what about a chicken sandwich and a flask of whisky and my own little rod?"

" No, no, I might hurt something else," Walter said firmly. " I'm going to pack into bed early with a glass of hot milk and a couple of aspirins."

" Early bed with all them mice!" Finn's joviality was quite horrid. " I know how you'll spend the night—sitting on top of your chest of drawers."

" Suppose you shot a great big man and caught a great big fish both on the same evening," Angel tempted.

" Oh, that would be my record." He sat down on a two-ended stool and sweetly, unaffectedly took a needle from behind his coat collar and spread the billowing sequined white dress across his knee. " Scissors, thread, thimble," he said, " and I'll be at it—I'll be O.K. in here. I do admire this room."

Angel was pleased. She, too, liked her room. It was a pink room. It had an after-lunch flush—an after-lunch-at-the-Berkeley flush—everything had been arranged as carefully as a page in a Christmas *Vogue*—everything had been arranged, nothing had ever settled down. The bed was as elaborate as a cage of macaws at the Zoo, scattered with little fluttering pillows of muslin and lace and satin, good enough to eat. The bedspread was quilted silly. The window curtains were milky white, but over-hatted in the hattiest pelmets imaginable. The mushroom-coloured carpet ran the walls so close it seemed to be pushing them out of its way, crying *conforts modernes* in Angel's best French.

Everything had got away with her in this room. It was her unrestricted self and she loved it well. She wrapped her chill soul in this pink cloud. Its pantomime glow coloured the snow in her—she was cold and there was a yearning in her to express by arrangement the warmth absent in herself —yet it was strangely an icy pink that forced itself upon her choice.

Now, as Angel placed the scissors, the silk, the pins all so easily accessible, so beautifully tidy and ready at Walter's elbow, a better feeling, an easier sense came to her. He was hers. Obediently. Finn was hers obediently, Tiddley, too. The rest would follow—the day's defeats would soften out in a certain temperature she should create and she would wind round her heart to-night a string of smooth and well-matched successes.

Everyone in the house was concentrated one way now. All a little late for this dinner, they strove against the close of the hour with the importances of their clothes, their hair, their faces. Their minds were already turned a little more Angel's way, for they were warmed at the thought of Angel's and Birdie's exquisite anxieties and pains expended so generously over soup and fish and birds and wine. In the matter of food, Angel's children had reached young a point of appreciative sophistication.

Idle happy tears of emotion and relief and joy of tending her wounded, welled in Slaney's eyes and flooded their courses down, carrying eye shadow away with them. She smiled through the tears. To her glass. And happiness invaded her altogether. She dragged the pale directoire fancy dress that Angel had designed over her head and tied the ribbon of her cameo in a bow round her young faint neck. She seemed a ghost of happiness from another house and place in time, as she flew about this room, so full of well-selected Victorian objects: frilled glass vases, pictures of swans, china swans; tapestry carpet of fat pallid roses; ribbons and bows on the wallpaper; little draped dressing-table and spotted muslin curtains, as crisp as cake sugar, frilled against the oily sea in the window. And not one single piece of furniture or decoration found or chosen by Slaney with her own bad young taste. Now, as she went pounding round the sweet girlish room, every frill quivered, every tinkling lustre shook, every fat rose burst its petals at the quantities of pure womanly sexual emotion which she generated in the unbridled way that only innocence and girlhood can.

Tiddley's room was another matter altogether. It was rather like an extension of the tool house, but not quite so much her own. Here people could tidy up and pry, which necessitated a depressing number of small cabinets as for birds' eggs, with fretwork on them and keyholes, their keys on a ring in her trousers pocket. Under the fumed oak bed there were several neat wooden boxes, lids nailed down as firmly as coffin tops. The dogs' thermometer stood in a china cat on the chimney-piece; pale snapshots of Julian and dogs, dogs and Julian, stood in front of each other and behind each other and curled unframed in each other's frames. Little trays of precious flower seeds dried in humanised bedroom air. Other seeds in packets and twists of paper were pinned by their corners to shelves here and there. Three fishing-rods hung by the rings in their cases on the wall. One cupboard and a chest of drawers, with nursery pictures on it held all her clothes—the chest of drawers was dressing-table, too. Now she wore a pair of navy blue trousers, and a pale silk shirt with a frilly collar, the kind that little boys wear at parties; had the trousers been shorts she would have looked just like an overweight little boy with the wrong kind of mother, and the wrong kind of glands. Actually, Angel was correct in stylising, but the result was not of much help to the indefeatable girl inside the trousers.

Julian came in as she was standing, one foot on a chair,

fastening the gay little sock suspenders Angel had given her on her last birthday. He roared with laughter.

"Well?" Her underlip trembled a little. "I have to keep my socks up, don't I?"

"I wonder what you'd look like in girl's clothes," he said quite seriously.

"God knows," she answered.

He picked up the book that lay open on the chest of drawers, beside the cold cream. It was one of the stories for girls she read standing up, when she was brushing her hair. "This is a new one to me," he said, "is it good? What's the heroine's name?"

"Hero."

"Hero. That's nice, does she have nice friends."

"Yes, and a terrible old aunt—Lady Harriet."

"Oh." He went on reading. He had come in to talk about Sally and the shooting of Chris and his fishing fleet, and here he was snatching bits out of an L. T. Meade just as he had done since he was twelve and Tiddley fourteen. Still reading, he took two little parcels out of his pocket and put them down on the dressing-table.

"Little pressys."

"Oh, Julian—what?"

"Oh, just little dirts."

Hearing no thank you, he looked up from his reading. She opened them, her tears rained down on a pair of silk stockings and a bottle of Chanel 5.

"Tiddley, you're hopeless. Listen, what is it?"

She said quite truly, "I am so worried Angel is going to sell my piano."

"I won't let her, darling—really, I won't."

How could he know how grateful she was to name even this heartbreaking reason for her tears? Almost she felt as if

Angel had stood her friend again, in direst need, as all through life she had been friend and reason and romance.

"Oh, Julian," she said, "don't mind me, please, and of course if she wants to she must—pianos are very high now, very high indeed. They've soared in price."

It never crossed Julian's mind to say, "After all, whose piano is it? It's my little piano." The piano, like the overdraft, seemed equally to belong to Angel.

"I don't think she can really mean to sell it," he said, doubtfully consoling.

"The schoolmaster is coming to-night, though."

"Do you remember," Julian said, "when we used to put our seed cake under the lid? Nothing went no more till they found out and cleaned her up."

Tiddley said: "I wouldn't do that to it now," in an agony of protective love.

Julian said: "No, I suppose not——" He hadn't really meant it. "All the same," he said, "they'd never think of it, and I could get the crumbs out on wet afternoons."

She still shook her head.

"No, I suppose not," he said again, "but it would be fun for wet afternoons."

He added suddenly: "What the hell—wet or fine—you know she's put a new engine in *Julietta*?"

Tiddley nodded, wordless at the magnitude of the mistake.

"Oh, well," he said, "terribly sweet of her I know." Their eyes met in complete understanding. He felt comforted in his sorrow—she in hers.

* 25 *

IN THE guest-room, which usually bedded men visitors and the lesser sorts of female cousins, Sally sat brushing her hair. She brushed it out straight from her head with a small, sad brush, familiar to her hand, and inside her head her mind hopped about like a desperate linnet in a cage. A nervous resolution held her, a nervous depression emanated from herself and struck back again from the magnificently drear gothic of the room—its three windows, strongly pillared and fortified, looking out on the dark north side (Oliver's favourite). Their woodwork was strong and heavy, serrated and battlemented here and there, but they opened like bungalow windows—a thin surprise. A low chimney-piece of imitation marble pillars, frowned above a small Victorian grate and elaborate fender, composed of shields and arches heavily black-leaded. On the floor, in a yellow green carpet of Morris inspiration, tulips, roses and artichoke leaves mingled. The bed was a heavy mahogany four-poster, the foot-board carved, the head swathed in spot muslin over pink. The frill of the canopy was covered in red magnolia flowers grafted on a creeper—the curtains were of the same chintz and none of them quite big enough to fill its window space. The dressing-table was skirted in muslin. There was a large circular po-cupboard with a savagely stiff door and a very commodious and expensive Waring and Gillow wardrobe with a really good looking-glass. The pale green of walls and woodwork—

green slashed over a flowered wallpaper in a 1930 frenzy for flat paint—had deepened and grown solid as moss. It effectively adulterated any character or reality of date the room might have kept without it.

Here Sally sat in the green air, putting a crêpe bandage on her back wave and grease on her face—so much more common in its solemn pallor. She looked like an anxious teacher, getting ready for the half-term party. Only a person of discernment could have seen the lines of face and body ready to spring into emphasis and glamour through discipline and artifice. She wore the washable cotton wrap she always wore for making up in the theatre, and as always at this hour of the early evening a slight fidget and nervousness took her, an uneasiness before the inevitable hour when the show went on, and to-night, though so far from any theatre, there was a part to sustain not quite within her grasp.

This morning, her love for Julian, her pride in all she had achieved for him, had been simple in outline, strong in intention. This country house of his would be homely, this wonderful mother all understanding and kindly meaning. Mad? She had been crazy to take the child's war-coloured perception of either home or mother. Here she sat in a malign gothic castle, far from bathroom or bidet. Instead of the low calm house by the sea she had visualised from his description—it's a terrible house, but we love it . . . just squats on the edge of a cliff—no servants—only Birdie our old nannie, and a wild country girl and a poacher who does odd jobs . . . Mummy's a wonderful cook . . . we catch mackerel and Madame Prunier is nowhere with her . . . There's a dish she knocks up with tomatoes and mackerel and potatoes. . . .

How cosy it had sounded. How normal and unsophisticated. Now here instead, she found a jealous soul-eater, a cold devastator of love's purpose, with the gift, Sally thought, looking into the mahogany-framed glass, of making a girl feel a double-sexed man-eater with he-fever. Then a truthful thought came to her. It's not me she hates so much as love itself. Maybe there's some way round with her. Maybe I could have found it too, but for Oliver. In the ugly glass she saw her pale face, her great pale eyes light at the thoughts she fled. She pinned her hands out on a cross of resolution, on a love for Julian more whole and strict than Angel would ever guess at.

* 26 *

IN HIS own house, Oliver wondered how best he could break with all accepted standards of decent behaviour and have Sally his own again, and as a start how soon after dinner he should return to the castle and continue his siege—his preposterous, his caddish, his absolute determination—to break and disrupt any permanent relationship between Julian and Sally. He distrusted brutally the war-engendered spirit of immolation as a basis for love, above all for Sally's love, whatever restorations she had made in Julian's confidence. However he leaned on her now there must exist between them points of difference that could have no neutral ground, no meeting-place if love was spent. Different absurdities, depths and shallows alternating against each other through everything. This moment, Oliver knew, was the hour for brutality which should stink strongly but briefly to heaven. Now, if she could see it, as she had once seen it, was the time to take a dreadful train out of Julian's life. Oliver, sick and years older than Julian, had recovered from just such drastic surgery.

Oliver was sitting in the upper room he had hollowed out of the scanty house. It was a place on which no decorator's mind had worked its petty powers. It was the little house itself. Five high windows looked out above lower roofs and courtyard wall and grandly, steeply gazed on sea and mountains and sky—overtopping the falling road and its descending scale of houses and steps and shops and people. The windows were steep and sour from without, gracious to indiscretion from within—sweeping like the ladies of their date to show their all. Oliver would think as he stood inside his windows, while rain poured down their cheeks, of the smooth bird breasts of 1780, wet muslins clinging to their skins, and a consumption eating them from within. He loved the exquisite sacrificial taste of the date—comfort or health as nothing to a line achieved in strict beauty.

To Oliver this evening, the room he had filled with such discreet comfort and so much that was beautiful and so much that was nonsense, was as blank of the affectionate aroma of rooms we love as a station is empty of any sensation except an immediate change or loss. Very slowly he had put into this room things that represented to him moments when he had ceased to mind about Sally; moments when bitterness for no good reason was finished; moments too when he first expected to live, when he knew with real exuberance that he was no longer sick and doomed, and celebrated health and life with the purchase of something he wished to look at always. Gradually this room had come to breathe round him. For rooms and houses redecorated, relived in, take their time about coming to any kind of life. It is like the space with the newly-born between birth and life, but with houses slapping measures are valueless. Only after waiting the pulse is there, idea and reality come to agreement and the frigidity of arrangement ceases on the fullness that swells the air.

But to-night all such importances were in violent flight, and with them, for the time, fled his love of Owlbeg, its seed-time, or harvest, its little thriving forests, its bag in the bank, his interest and gentle care for Birdie and Tiddley and silly Slaney and Angel too, who yielded him so many moments of ecstatically brittle amusement; all this was gone, he was emptier of nice feelings than a dry bath-tub of water in a water famine. The worst part of allowing oneself no pretences is in calamity. When all else fails, pretences come as plump comforters and reasons to be.

* 27 *

ANGEL'S DINNER-PARTY, planned so long before and so carefully, had its own beautiful brief existence. In spite of the torments of human emotion pouring their contrary humours on its hour, it was not defeated. As children's parties have their own separate glamour, indivisible from candle-flames on cakes, balloons in matchless festival flight, from the smell of gunpowder, from crackers and the gorgeous terror and cackle of sparklet stars, so this party maintained its glamour as the hoarded champagne released flights of talk and nonsense as gay and coloured as any oily, floating bunch of balloons.

Angel sat in a pleated floating dress, as green-white as lichen, with a winged little angel's head (a little something from a fountain) pinned to her shoulder and a spray of stephanotis laid beside her plate, white and awkwardly beautiful as a china lamb with green feet—its scent, through the soup, fantasy fainter than a clump of bluebells, but by the time of the *petits poussins*, more violent than a cage of lions—a clarion call to untried maidens.

Tiddley's heart swelled as it came to her down the table, this breath from the pride of her hothouse. She had laid the spray by Angel's plate as a child brings the first bunch of primroses, and Angel accepted and adored the tribute but always with " poor little thing " at the back of the acceptance.

The dining-room table was laid in summer-time in a window which curled out to the sea, almost as extravagantly as the bay in the drawing-room. To-night there was no wind, and they sat with windows open to the garden and the sea. There was no salty breeze, only the smells of stephanotis and newly-watered well-tended earth and the changing scents of Birdie's fresh food. So still was the evening that the yellow spaces between the clouds were stationary, and the water was divided into lengths and steady squares of light and shadow, primrose and indigo, and the waves seemed unable to break.

Angel had seated her party with thought for the results of champagne. Slaney and Chris with herself between them, Tiddley between Julian and Chris, Sally between Julian and Slaney. Angel talked to Chris with careful affection, allowing as few opportunities as possible for those heavy-headed talks lovers pursue in public.

Their blonde and gold heads against the striped indigo sea, Sally and Slaney talked. Considering how Slaney was feeling about Chris across the table, Sally held her attention well to nylon, and how to sunburn your legs if you had red hair and how Italians got over their little troubles about shoes. About the moment for the strawberry soufflé, she turned to

Julian, waiting for his eager eyes as for a hand at night; she was floating, she was a little drunk. Julian, also a little in wine, was completely and absolutely immersed in a talk about copper piping with Tiddley. Sally was aware of a glance from Angel flying down the table, side-long swift and frightening as a bat's flight, and that nobody might miss the fact that Sally was forgotten, she called clearly and richly, " Enjoying yourself, dear ? Finn, champagne for Mrs. Wood."

The decision to stand by Julian ate a little deeper into Sally's heart. Reminded, he turned to her, but as they spoke again she could feel that his attention was following Tiddley's conversation with Chris. " How would you," she was murmuring, " get the better of a gasket like I was telling Julian ? You couldn't fix it ? Would you fix it ? I wonder how would you fix it ? " ... Faintly in wine, too, Chris bent to the problem. They drew with their fingers on the table and moved toast crumbs, heads together.

" Julian," Sally said, " that Tiddley's madly attractive."

Julian looked aghast. " Tiddley ? " he said, nearly crossly. " Not *that* kind of attraction." His mother might have spoken the words. Sally continued to look thoughtfully at the two heads bent together across the table. " Get your mind off it," Julian said. " Really, it doesn't make sense."

" All right," she smiled. " I wonder if there's any more of that wonderful soufflé ? "

Dinner over, Angel could see no way to prevent the exodus of four to the garden. Their quick return she played for. " Don't forget, darling Slaney, Birdie must dress Chris's leg at nine-thirty. Back soon, darling Julian ? " And to Tiddley: " Precious, I need you."

In the near dark of Angel's bedroom, where even pink had gone cold, the white dress shivered down the bed. Outside the plumed elaborate windows, the tide pushed gently in broken silver plates against the darker land, low voices came up from the garden underneath. The exuberant confidence of champagne dulled any heartache the warm sounds might have brought to Tiddley.

When Walter picked the dress off the bed and posed it with simple care for its line and beauty, Tiddley gasped in a genuine rapture of excitement, " Oh, Angel, but why for me ? "

" Well," Angel kissed her, " to-night won't happen twice. I meant you to wear it for dinner, but with everything, I just couldn't manage it."

" Tap on the door when you've got your slip on "— Walter was being rather pixie—" and nothing else please, no knobbly suspenders or fussy brassières."

" He knows——" Angel smiled across Tiddley's startled refusal of assistance, " and he's going to do a little something for your face too, darling. Now I must fly down, come to me when you're ready, I want to talk to you before the others, I want to see you first."

In the dark, trembling and deliciously drunk, Tiddley stripped to her skin; she looked and smelt as sweet as a newly-bathed little boy of eight years old.

* 28 *

THE DRAWING-ROOM was at its best by lamplight. Its expensive comforts glowed and offered ease and warmth; only the most subtle austerity can assert its beauty after dinner; marquetry and luxury go a long way of an evening. To-night, what with lilies and a wood fire and the good silk thick cushions, oily as a healthy baby's skin, Angel's drawing-room certainly had its hour. Through the rich split curtains, sea and sky and faint stars burned like a backcloth for ballet.

Chris and Slaney came in from the garden first, Slaney lacking the sad knowledge that tells how unwelcome the happy love of others is even to the happiest, was full of love's faint aggression; ordering, disposing, with an infinite and terrible gentleness. Chris was to sit so, and put his leg so, and while she went to see if Birdie had everything ready he was not to move, not by so much as so much.

Angel did not speak. She stood in the centre of the fireplace in her pleated flaring dull white, with small, heavy head and big gentle eyes. As Slaney closed the door she lifted up her head and looked across at Chris with a sympathetic smile, a co-operative smile.

" You mustn't let her bully and fuss you too much," she said.

" She couldn't." Chris took a deep breath. " You see, Angel, it's this way. I love her."

" My dear "—Angel's eyes lit—" I love her, too. So silly, so sweet, and so absurdly young."

Chris moved uneasily, he had to get this clear. But she would always understand.

" What I mean is——" He paused in the elaborate hesitancy of real feeling. He looked for little plain words with a horror of over-expressing himself. " How can I explain? To-day, you know, we had a sort of row——"

" Did you? "

" Yes, she hurt me a bit, then I knew I minded horribly."

" Really, about her? "

" Yes." He was so anxious to get everything straight and finding it so difficult to take his emotion out and put it in respectable cold language that her brisk tone slipped his notice. "To-day," he repeated, " we had a sort of row. She hurt me a bit, and then I knew I minded horribly."

" Really—about Slaney? "

" Yes," he had nearly completed the course, "and when I got shot about, not that it's anything, she was so wonderful to me."

" Of course," Angel's nod was very understanding, " she'd adore that."

"What?" Chris felt his first stab of uneasiness. " She was worried to death," he said, defensively, "that showed me."

" Listen, dear," Angel crossed the hearth-rug, all winged sleeves and pleats running out behind her. It was the most completely generous movement. She sat down beside him. She leant towards him. It was like the old days when she had taught him to tie flies and expounded theories about wood-cock and their young—everything must be fresh and of the wild. " Listen dear," she said, " can you *still* take my advice? Or has the war taken you too far from me? "

" Of course." He began to bundle into himself, a young, uncertain creature. For all his lonely war, emotionally he was no more experienced than when he knew and cared only for wild birds' nests. But he did not expect her laugh, her clean, indulgent laughter.

" Oh, Chris, my darling," she said, " lay off—at least for now. She's a proper little minx and who's her first victim? Poor you."

There was a pause.

" Thanks," he said, " but I do think you're wrong."

" I may be indeed "—her agreement was generous—" and at the moment, of course, she does genuinely pity you."

" Pities me? " He was like someone lighting candles in his own darkness, and as he fumbled, she took the match from him with a sure hand and set the light burning.

" Yes, of course, old boy, who wouldn't? You've had a beastly war—you're not right yet, it's pathetic. And you're so plucky about everything, even practically getting your leg shot off. Such a sensation. The whole thing had just tipped her off her balance, momentarily, for that's how I see it and I know you all pretty well."

Chris, forever the boy from outside, the worshipper in this lucky, glamorous family, listened with that wide respect and attention in which he had received Angel's advice since he was twelve years old. " I've always liked you such a lot," she went on gently. " Let the thing go—forget it."

" Is that what you really think? "

" That's what I really do think. And I don't want you to be hurt, you do believe me, still more."

There was a pause before he spoke with the invincible sentimentality of his unknowing kind, putting a monk's hood on emotion, faintly dramatising sorrow, " I don't think, really, I could be hurt any more, thanks very much."

" Chris," she leaned a little nearer, " you've taken this just as I expected. May I say I think it's pretty big of you——" She leant back from him again. " You're an attractive thing, Chris—girls will always fall for you."

Chris lifted up his handsome head and cried from his silly heart; " I wish I had one here now. I wish I had, I'd show Slaney how to play me up."

It was then that Walter's head popped round the door, his sacrifice to beauty complete, he was on the move again.

" Nurse Birdie," he said archly, " is waiting for her patient in the bathroom, and Miss Slaney is, I understand, winding up her bandages."

He came over to help Chris out of the deep sofa. " I'm awfully glad, sir, I didn't hit you in the head—wasn't it lucky? —or anywhere important."

" I wish," Chris said, before the door closed on them, " to God you had."

Angel put her face into a cushion and giggled with relief and amusement and somewhere, pity; but somewhere drowned out of all reality, under flood tides of vanity and power. It was that place in her where generosity throve, gushing from some misused gland to the obedient, to the innocent, to childhood that questions nothing. That place where clean outdoor boys like Chris put their trust; that nest which Tiddley had never flown.

Now Angel looked up at a sound and saw her in the doorway—she gave a start of genuine surprise. Some apprehension took her too, and there was an edge to the, " Tiddley, *ravissante*! Walter—you've done a miracle," falling a little too close to be entirely complimentary.

Tiddley stood there with Walter bustling round her, as much changed from herself as if an expensive photographer had been busy with her portrait. She looked confusedly glamorous. Everything that was really Tiddley had been faintly distorted for the better by Walter's own cunning hand; her eyes newly-deep and sly, the prisoned look of sex set free about her mouth, the boyish hair brushed up to a perched garland, small as a ring. An emphatic nip below the bosoms and swirl of white skirts foaming to the floor.

" Come on, darling," Angel said impatiently, as she still paused. Tiddley moved forward with something that was not hesitancy, something near to a conscious dignity, a rather touching travesty of a dowager's swim across a crowded room. There was something all wrong here. A Koala bear with wings.

Angel put a finger under the chin as a child's face is tilted for inspection. She smiled across the changed head to Walter.

"Yes, I do congratulate you. Off now with Finn and enjoy yourself."

Tiddley turned to him, impulsively, "Walter, I do feel different too, thank you."

Walter answered with emotion. "Feel like you look like, dear, and keep wishing on your heart's desire—oh, aren't I a silly sentimental old cow? Good luck. Good night!" He left them gently, and as he went he hummed with nostalgic charm, "Some day my Prince will come."

"I'm trembling——" The hoarse little voice came out of Tiddley's newly-balanced chest.

"That's no use." Angel changed to strength, to urgency. "No good at all. Listen my pet, to-night I have to depend on your balance, your brain, your discretion."

"Gosh, Angel."

"Yes, dear, on your wits and your looks to——"

"To what?"

"To distract Chris from Slaney, to give him something else to think about."

"Chris? Me? Do you mean me?"

"Listen—we don't want that baby swept off her feet. She must have time to think and he's giving her such a rush. Try, darling. I ask it for her sake, for my sake, to be distracting."

Tiddley considered the business with the sanity she could direct on any problem except that of Julian. It seemed to her rather a hopeless outlook, hopeless to silliness.

"It's like distracting a magnet from a needle with a splinter of wood. Listen, Angel, how do I begin? You know I've never vamped anyone. I'm not magnetic, I'm the bun in the old corner shop. I'm a cosy cup of tea with two lumps. The only secrets they tell me, Angel, are all about some other girl."

Angel had seldom heard so many words coming from

Tiddley at the same time—the piteous cry in them escaped her—she listened only to as much as she could use.

"Tiddley, that's where the mischief starts. That's where the door is open, pet, open wide. Walk right in, little cosy girl."

"Stop please, stop." Something woke in Tiddley and looked out through the new sly eyes. Why did you choose to-night for this Cinderella stuff—you don't know, but it's so dangerous."

"That's right, darling," Angel gave a wild little giggle of triumph. "Feel dangerous—looking like you do, to-night, you could get any man you wanted."

"Be careful with this sort of talk," Tiddley said with absolute seriousness, "it's dynamite. But do you mean it?" She whispered, "Could I? Are you sure?"

"Sure? Positive!"

A certain power seemed to derive from Tiddley then, a resolution and inspiration that belonged to something Walter had freed, something improper to the Koala bear, a kittenish quality, a girliness.

"Promise me something, Angel. If I really try, promise me you won't ever sell my piano?"

Angel was staggered and displeased. Only just playfully she said: "Darling, aren't you being just a tiny bit mercenary?"

"I want it," Tiddley said solidly. "Please promise."

Tired, over excited, Julian's return, champagne, this new glamour, Angel's quick mind ran down the scale of Tiddley's day, as one puts one's finger on a good child's misdemeanour. So she laughed, and kissed a yes. "Now"—she took a little precious bottle of scent from her bag—"a drop of this behind the ears and everything's safe."

"And on my hankie, Angel—I can flap that about—he

mayn't get near enough to notice it anywhere else———"
Tiddley was all honesty and business.

For the first time in life a faint tremor of respect for Tiddley
shook Angel, just a little.

"Now don't think defeat"—Angel dabbed economically
with a glass stopper—"all men are the same. Just study their
habits."

"But I've only studied Julian's habits," Tiddley said.
"Truly, would they work out for Chris? Julian's only really
happy making wheels go round———" She was thinking aloud.
"You couldn't hold Julian on a honeymoon, I don't think,
unless you kept on breaking your wrist-watch."

The wisdom of this escaped Angel. "You concentrate
on Chris to-night, Miss Psychology." She was still kind and
explanatory.

"I don't know how Chris works."

"You don't have to."

"Angel! A girl must know her man, and one thing I'm
sure of"—strange intention dawned—"Julian would rather
mend a broken clock than make love to Lauren Bacall."

"Oh, dear—it's just champagne on vodka, I suppose,"
Angel gushed indulgence, "but you're clear which man you're
out for, aren't you, pet?"

"Yes, Angel," Tiddley spoke the words like a vow, "quite,
quite clear."

When Angel had floated out of the window to summons
Julian and Sally in from the most unnecessary moonlight,
Tiddley moved over to the chimney-piece and took Julian's
clock between hands, strong and quick with intention.

* 29 *

THE ROOM, so seldom left empty and alone with its vulgar luxuries, over-made pelmets, marquetry and gildings, and mirrors and too much comfort, seemed to stoop and bundle itself kindly round the sinning Tiddley. She turned and faced the windows, just before Sally and Julian came in. The silver-blonde head floated like a cold moon against the evening sea light. It brought a frost in around it to the warmth. There was frost, too, in Julian's eyes and the scar of his burn looked stronger and tighter on his cheek.

"Baby, who's magicked you?" Sally came forward warmly. "You look like a double white lilac and a Chopin waltz."

Angel close behind them purred, taking the cream. "Yes, doesn't she?"

Julian looked a little crosser and a little colder.

Tiddley said, "Do you like me, Julian?"

"Not a bit, darling," he said with sour conviction, "You look all awful and different. What have you done to yourself?"

Tiddley's neck flamed—she tried to laugh. "And I even did my nails," she said hopelessly. She looked at them. She had to look somewhere.

"I like you best with chilblains," Julian said sulkily.

"In June—it's just a fetish." Sally's crack came from the place Angel could not go.

Julian looked down, sat down and opened a book—Tiddley's book.

" What's the idea ? " he said, looking at Angel, " Tiddley's dolled up worse than poor *Julietta*."

Unfocused, empty-eyed, idle-handed, Julian sat turning the pages of Tiddley's book. All his plans, all his small warm occupations that had lived so lately were sterilised. He was the child on holiday again, his boat a toy for pleasure, his Tiddley tarted up into this absurd reflection of sophistication. There was something in this copy of the girl he had been so vain to bring home that turned him sour. All that was grown up and real died round him, leaving him a little boy, kicking out the toes of his boots on some endless summer afternoon. This war might never have been ; he was groping for gentleness, for gratitude, for forbearance, where he had thought to find only contentment and happy occupation and a wealth of safety for body and mind—but they did not know about anything. Here, nothing joined on to anything. Deceitfully, coldly, doubt took him ; doubt of happiness, doubt of his own ability to choose and follow any way. He did not take into account the simple thing that he was tired and very much in need of sleep.

When Angel said to him, " Darling, shall we try out the new engine," he answered only, " No, don't let's this evening."

Determined to keep things going and busy, she went on, " Why not dash across the bay and show Sally our island and our little church ? "

Julian went on looking at his book. Sally said, " Ruined churches aren't my kind of uplift," and settled her shoulder straps.

" Ah, it's not a ruin," said Angel, her eyes on the gesture. " It's the little family church where Julian will marry you, perhaps."

" And bury us both one day, perhaps." Sally's smile said,
" You first."

The brittle state of the air frightened even Angel a little.
She tried another line.

" You're tired, darling, Mummy knows. Just sit back and
tell us some of your adventures in the skies. God, how I
used to think of you, hovering like a young hawk. What
were your thoughts ? "

" One great thought upheld me "—Julian spoke strongly
—" how to make my base quickest."

" Of course, that's how you got the decorations."

" Actually," he said with despairing coldness, " the right
types never get the gongs—they only get strips torn off by
the high-ups."

" You're too modest, aren't you ? "

" Modest ? " he shouted, quite in despair. " Listen " (Sally
should save his secrecy), " while I shoot a line about this
piece."

" Keep it, honey, keep it," she whispered. " It's a long
bed-time story."

" Bed-time " (that perfect word when sleep is easy), he
said, looking at the clock: " It's not even nine yet."

" Nonsense," a hoarse urgent voice came out of
Tiddley, who sat huddled in her fineries. " Look at your
watch."

" What a funny thing," Julian got up from the sofa. " My
clock must have stopped again."

" Perhaps it's run down," Tiddley suggested; her urgency
could be felt.

Julian opened the back of the clock and peered, his hand
followed his eyes, and Tiddley's burning eyes never left
him.

" Look at this," he said, life and excitement in his voice,

" the whole thing is out of alignment." The joyous absolute obsession of the mechanic possessed him. His eyes went blank as he explored with delicate attention.

Angel merely said: " Damn those people—twelve pounds they charged me too."

" Where are all my small clock tools ? " he asked, a bit of the old life joining the new, " my pincers, my little vice." His impatience waxed.

" I do hope they didn't get to the church jumble with the Meccano." Angel's anxiety was faintly jocose.

Tiddley said, " They did not. They're under my bed."

The whole business grew in importance and association. Without question Tiddley and Julian joined each other now— together in this they left the other two outside. Sally smoked and yawned, then looked surprised at herself. Angel purred indulgently, trying to make it all seem a bit more childish than it actually was. The two odd job experts paid no attention. They muttered and prodded and at last said with surgical satisfaction, " There's nothing for it except to take her to bits, and then I think," Julian lifted the clock off the chimney-piece, " a good deep oil bath. Here Tiddley, take these." He handed her a coil of awful springs.

" Don't get it on that dress, Tiddley," Angel's voice sharpened. " And hurry back, remember."

Something chilled her a little towards Tiddley, crystallising her obscure intentions about the piano.

When the two had gone, she turned to Sally, laughing a little to counteract the absolute embarrassment of being alone and together. Sally was looking thoughtfully at the space left on the chimney-piece, and only said, " Happy now, poor lamb," before she put her feet up on the sofa.

Angel said, " He's never really got beyond Meccano."

Sally nodded. " And if you knew that," she asked, " why

didn't you leave his boat as derelict a hulk as possible? Why not?"

From the stranger this was inadmissible. It smashed through all politeness. Sally went on: "His nerves were to bits—you knew that? I've helped him a little, I think."

If gratitude could have seized on Angel just for one moment —while the self may weep for the limits of its own power with the beloved, and where in failure one may glimpse repose —all relationships might have changed. But in emergency, character directs the event. One is forced on by the self that is formed, so Angel's brain, seeing only herself, saw with cold eyes a union between three things, the gapped chimney-piece, Julian's nerves and his future.

"Ah," she said gently, "of course, you've helped him. Listen, dear, can't we be friends?"

"Are you kidding?" Sally spoke, half toughly, half anxiously.

"No, dear, quite entirely serious." Angel felt the first faint twinge of possible power over a new person. "Let's try to understand things." She moved just a little nearer across the space on the sofa, and as she did, Sally seemed to melt like smoke into its extremest corner, an arm as strong and well-designed for movement as the hollow-boned wing of a bird, thrown out across the end.

Angel went on—"Five minutes alone with you, that's what I've been waiting for."

Sally looked all along her arm. "O.K.," she said, and stared at the back of her hand, "O.K.," she said, "shoot."

"Don't make it harder. We love that boy, don't we?"

"Yes, in different ways."

"Different? Just—we're different women—different lives —ages—worlds—blood, different blood. You're fresh blood from a new world, Sally, that's what this old family needs for its children."

"Oh, please." Behind her mock coy line, Sally resented the biological angle. "Wait till I tie it on before you embarrass me like this."

Angel drove on. "Some things you ought to know, dear, before you tie on that veil. Listen, you're bright—tell me, what you think of that face."

Sally stared up at the portrait of an old man, an old man with Julian's eyes, three chins and a stomach. The portrait of anybody's forebear and badly in want of cleaning. "Homely," she supplied the adjective briskly.

"Homely—yes," Angel raced on grimly. "Built himself a home in the big beech tree on the back avenue before the end. Thought he was a monkey—you see." Her eyes lit as new detail joined in her mind. "Poor Grannie did have a time—he used to let her up and down on a rope pulley——"

"And lay her in a basket, I suppose—the fresh old man." All the same, Sally felt a little uncomfortable.

"It isn't only the eyes," Angel said softly, "that are so like my Julian's; the passion for clocks is the same. This house is full of clocks—he bought them all. Obviously, my children, his grandchildren, know nothing about this. It's so much simpler to believe he was a little eccentric, amusingly so, and died of drink. But here are the clocks, and the iron rings and supports for his house are still in the beech tree."

Clocks and eyes, the two truths were there, clocks and eyes.

"I don't want to say any more," Angel said. "You've brought Julian home. You're tremendously young and lovely. Dear—don't feel you must give up everything. I can't help seeing how wrong all this is for you, can I?"

They were looking at each other silently. Angel leaning forward, a wonderful curve of generous understanding. Sally leaning back, a little breathless with dislike, when Oliver came in—he had dined alone and had changed only into another shirt of the same family. It made him seem unkempt and a little wild. He said: "Good evening, girls," and went across to the piano. Angel, glad of a break, purred and nodded to him to continue. When he strummed gently, "I'm falling in love again," guying it a little, she raised soft eyes saying, "Six years since you played that, Oliver."

"It's a damn' silly tune." He went on playing it. "Much better left to Tiddley."

"Oh, that Tiddley." The flow of thought and energy joined and Angel was up and away. "Why hasn't she come back to me?" She was gone.

"Drunk, or just looking for trouble," Sally said, as Oliver went on with his tune. He went on with the gentle broken tune as they talked, as though something, however little, had to hold him away from her. "Both." He frowned at the notes.

"Be careful, she's smart."

"Finding that out." He spoke absently.

"Listen honey, it takes something to give me the willies —she's succeeded——"

"She's mesmeric."

"You've said it, so is a rattlesnake."

She shivered in her warm corner. "I can't take it," she said, suddenly pitiful.

"You'll have to take it and like it, remember." The grave, harsh, sweet, sweet, sweet of the little tune went on, picking at her strength.

"Oh, for heaven's sakes don't make trouble just for the hell of it." It was easier to be angry with him.

"All right, I'll go on about my own love affair, shall I? Where was I when they started shooting?"

" You'd just announced your neurotic, quixotic——"

" Erotic perhaps, is the word you want," he suggested.

" Idiotic, sad and idiotic, that's what I mean."

" That goes double for you," he said with maddening triviality.

" Thanks, I get you—you don't really like my marriage either? " She was on her feet with her back to the fire, savagely defensive.

Oliver stopped playing and came over to her. " Frankly," he said, " I think your marriage is the most assy-tassy God-awfully silly business I've ever heard of."

" Ignore my marriage if you can. What about your own."

" For God's sake forget it." He was too near her for comfort.

" Forget it! Oh, go sugar yourself."

He spoke low to the shoulder she had turned to him, to the top of the primrose and silver head: " Don't tell me we're quarrelling," he said.

" Feels familiar."

" Take care "—he still kept away from her—" remember where our quarrels always ended."

" Listen. Once a day is past, it's dead, and the hell with it."

" You're afraid," he said distantly.

" Don't kid yourself."

" You're afraid my darling."

" Don't say that either."

" Why not? "

" Oliver, please, haven't we headaches enough without——"

" Falling in love again? "

" We won't—of course we won't."

His hands were on her shoulders, but he still spoke to the air above her head. " Miracles don't shiver the air twice in a lifetime." His hands dropped down her arms, " Or do they?

Do they ever? Why are you trembling, Sally, you aren't cold?"

"No," she gave it all up, "it's that miracle again." She was lost, all courage spent and only the immense comfort of their well-matched loving alive in the world. When they kissed—"Then we aren't lost any more," Oliver said. "There's only you and me after all. It's really as simple as that."

They stood away from each other, they knew what could be again. They did not wish to contact each other in any lesser way.

"Simple?" her voice broke. "Simple? How cruel you are."

"And you don't have to tell me you're tough, my sweet. I know it."

"That's right—so what do we do?"

"There's a train we could take—what's wrong with to-night?"

"Not to-night."

"It had better be to-night. Come down here later, I'll be waiting in my blue suit, and a gallon of Angel's petrol in the car."

"Oliver, it's not possible—I can't murder for you."

"You know exactly what's going to happen if we live on here together, don't you?"

"You can go."

"Oh, no, I shan't go, darling," he said coldly.

It was then that absurd awful scales and arpeggios and sounds like porpoises splashing and horses galloping came cascading down into the evening from Tiddley's piano—sounds compelled by some hideously expert hand—the strain between Sally and Oliver was taut to a point when absurdity became part of the terrifying sincerity of their struggling wills.

"You will?" he held her mind across the tumbling din, the shaking air.

"God knows. Maybe. Yes, if I must. I'll be no good. I'll be no good, though. Oh, darling, don't you understand why I'm here with that kid? All these years I've wanted to make up somehow for what I did to you—to appease my vanity maybe. No. No, it isn't fair to call it little names . . ."

"All the same, you'll come."

She looked terribly tired. "Yes," she said, "but you'll be holding air. You'll have a haunted doll in your bed."

"I'll chance that." He looked through her. There was nothing kind left in him at all, only complete certainty of purpose.

* 30 *

SLANEY BROKE the moment. She came flying into the room in a tempest of rage, and through the open door the bubbling scales trebled in volume. She flung herself on to the sofa. She seemed all arms and eyes, like a bird flung out of its nest. "I'm through, Oliver," she said. She took a cigarette from the box and lit the cork-tipped end with three awkward matches. "I'm through with men."

"Oh, God, aren't you lucky to get it over so young," Sally said, with desperate appositeness.

"Take it easy, pet, what's happened." For once, Oliver was the kinder. "You were doing nicely at dinner-time."

"Yes, I know, wonderful. And after dinner, but all the same, he came up to the bathroom like a couple of icebergs."

"Two icebergs? Really, it's an insult—don't you take it, toots," Sally advised.

"That's right, I won't," Slaney grasped at the attitude. "I won't take it. 'Chris,' I'll say, 'I'm sorry, but I think you're insulting.' How's that, Oliver?"

Oliver sat down beside her and took her hand. "You couldn't try a more subtle line, darling. Take him quietly. Remember, it's a bit anti-love to get shot in the legs."

"I don't know where I am." Slaney looked a little sick. "I can't think through this awful noise."

Sally said, "Can't it be stopped."

"No, it's the schoolmaster. He's trying out Tiddley's piano."

"My God, poor Tiddley, where is she?"

"Picking pellets out of Chris, if you want to know"—the submerged boo-hoo almost burst out of Slaney—"and he wouldn't let me touch him."

"For heaven's sakes——" Sally was really shocked. "He won't let you touch him—Walter shot him below the knees, didn't he?"

"Listen"—Slaney's head reared itself from sorrowing, her eyes blindly inattentive, but to the one thing, flew towards the door—"Do I hear him? I don't hear him. Do I hear him? Yes, I do hear him. Please, please could you, could you"—she suddenly went grand as the page of a very old book—"could you leave us alone together?"

"My dear," Sally was at the window before the child had finished speaking, "I'm with you all the way—Messalina couldn't make her man in this crowd."

"Easy does it, pet," Oliver heard Slaney calling. "Oh, my heart's off again. Oh, I feel so no-how—oh, what was I going to be——" as he followed Sally into the garden.

* 31 *

IN THE children's bathroom, her operating over, Birdie
fluttered briskly, putting away forceps and bandages with a
faint hospital flourish.

Walter sat on the mahogany edge of the bath that had
always been repainted and never removed. It was deep and
boxed darkly in mahogany, and there was an extravagant
quantity of copper about its fittings. Once it had been a
plumbing gem of comfort, dignity and expense. The walls
were covered in a shiny paper which had survived half a
century of steam, its pattern a veining of blue veins as intricate
as Crewe junction and frightening as the inside of a fat woman's
arm. A hanging gas bracket with two arms had been transformed for electric light. There were enormous laundry
baskets held shut by their steel rods where Birdie stored
nameless treasure. There were no glass shelves, only painted
wooden cupboards, no weighing machine. The lavatory,
like the bath, was caged richly in mahogany and had a blue
and white pattern in its china bowl, and a charming plug that
pulled upwards. There was ivy round the window, a coconut
for birds outside, and a gathered muslin curtain across its
bottom sash. The curtains were thick white chintz with a
red and white and grey pattern of tulips and keys. On their
linings a slight mould from rain, sea mist and steam had
washed out in little rusty spots.

In this bathroom, remote and mysterious enough for murder,
Birdie had bathed and dosed and adored her children

through nameless lengths of time and youth. Here now, Walter sat with her, smoking a cigarette against the faint cloud of Dettol and Slaney's bath essence. He had a gentle delicate quality, a little-boy prettiness of behaviour that was exactly what Birdie had always been in love with. He was all her babies grown up, while his charm, his elegance, his knowledge of clothes, was meat and drink to her mind. To Walter, this bathroom, like the kitchen, was the first real bathroom he had ever been in. He had known squalor and absolute luxury, but the care of old and cherished things he had never known, nor the unfashionable aristocratic odour round things bought long ago. His eyes dreamed round this bathroom, and rested on Birdie and her last business. She yawned faintly, and as she clicked a cupboard shut, she ached to put him to bed as simply as any other little boy of six, to see him bathed and warm, to dry the hair at the back of his neck and tuck him up just right and fold his dressing-gown on the foot of the bed and say good night and go—yes, really go, leaving him to his bed and a star-filled window.

"Now," she said, turning to him, "I'm straight at last—a hot drink and a hot bath and early bed, what about it."

"Just what I'd like myself." He got off the edge of the bath. "But your madam has fixed me up for an evening's fishing. Too silly, fancy me, but I can scarcely refuse, can I?"

All the happy fields in Birdie's heart that had so lately flown with red sweet clover, turned immediately to sand and salt.

"With Master Finn, no doubt, as instructor and guide," she spoke with shrill bitterness.

"I suppose so." He turned aside a little too gaily.

Birdie looked suddenly older and sillier. She said in the voice in which she had yielded her first child to the governess, "That's right—enjoy yourselves."

"Well, ta-ta dear, for the present," he was gone as the children had always gone. She stood alone in her bathroom beneath the two white globes of light, and her angry heart blamed all the loss of her life on Angel only. Unnamed by her were the stone urns full of bitter unshed tears, the sour white grapes of young maids loving. By the inescapable flowing of our love all our sides are wounded more or less. For Birdie, love had always flowed, passing from her in her will to give, her deep prodigality of self. In this evening of crisis and emotion she knew how little she had ever had back, but she did not see that little embodied in Walter fluttering from her like a gorgeous moth to the evening honeysuckle and the summer river.

It was not Birdie to stand idle or thoughtful long. Through all suffering, something to be done next drove her back to sanity. Now she opened the bathroom door into the gallery that ran round the pillared hall below and looking over its banister saw waiting, shy and lonely, the grey schoolmaster, weak and little in the rich religious air and dimly improper with Tiddley's lovely flowers. The scent from their sticky tongues came strongly up to Birdie. She went down to the little man below.

"It's very late, isn't it, Mr. Macentee? It's very late for you to be cycling home with your asthma. Can I take a message?"

Mr. Macentee turned to her gratefully. "Oh," he said, "thank you, it's about that little piano I've been trying . . . 'Tis very bad, I'm afraid. . . ."

* 32 *

In the drawing-room, her heart pounding, Slaney threw cushion after cushion into an arm-chair, as Chris and Tiddley came across from the door—Tiddley an efficient angel in her flowing white, and Chris yielding to her guidance, less impersonally than he might have done.

"Here, darling," Slaney called from behind her chair, "wouldn't here be cosy?"

"Please don't bother, Slaney." He sat down with unforgivable pomp beside a distant light. "This chair's quite adequate, thanks."

"That's right"—Tiddley fussed over him—"and here's the new *Horse and Hound.* Have you seen it?"

"You think of everything, don't you, Tiddley." He gave her a bright look of gratitude—she was an object for his change of voice and he was more than grateful to her as such.

"Tiddley," Slaney improvised hoarsely, "Julian wants you —he's in the garden."

"Oh, no, darling, you're wrong." Tiddley spoke in a sudden flush of girlish success, unconnected with Chris, but the old female implication of knowing more about the boys than the other girl does was nearer the surface than it had ever been with Tiddley. "He's not in the garden, he's very busy with his clock. Actually, it's quite a big job—it's as big as sabotage." She paused; the awful power of little women grew in her, she sat down, arranging her skirts, then turned again to Chris: " Did you see the runners for the Irish Oaks, dear," she secured a new grip on his attention.

" No, where? "

" Page seven."

The pages rustled. Tiddley pointed. They ignored Slaney, who drew in some deep breaths of drawing-room air before she found voice enough to say, " Did you hear that awful noise, Tiddley, that piano noise? That was Angel selling your piano to the schoolmaster."

" She simply had to let him try it, after walking three miles, poor Mr. Macentee." Tiddley was still in the position of knowing best. " But I do know she's not selling my piano."

" You'd better go and make quite certain," Slaney spoke above her pounding heart—anything, anything, to get Tiddley out of the room and—" Oh, give me a chance," her eyes said, " Tiddley, Tiddley, you're my friend, I must have now with him, I'm lost."

Tiddley met and recognised in the air a piece of anguish such as she knew. She got up from the arm of Chris's chair and as she did the noise ceased, leaving behind a violent silence.

" Perhaps," she moved towards the door and the silence, " I'll just take a peep."

Chris raised himself on the chair arms and said urgently, " No, Tiddley, don't go, Tiddley."

" And why shouldn't she go? " the idiot crescendo of love ran Slaney's little wit up its silly scale. " Why do you want Tiddley? What can Tiddley do I can't do? "

" Plenty," he told her in fierce defence of the situation Angel had built in his mind. " She's sweet and sensible, anyway."

" Sensible! " Slaney gasped for fatal wounding words.

" Dressed up like last night's bunch of gardenias—at her age it's awful."

Age and its disparities, woman's ice-axe to woman—Tiddley swung low under the blow and came angrily back to stand near Chris. " I'd rather be an old twenty-one than an idiotic *ingénue* half-wit like you, anyway. And my dress is lovely. And you know it's lovely."

" Yes, it is——" Chris reached out rather awkwardly and pulled her down on his knee. " You smell like a big lovely load of hay in June too, don't you? "

At the window Julian, furiously surprised, stood waiting for Tiddley's angry answer and swift escaping. That she should giggle, that she should wriggle and worse again, say, " Oh, let me go! Oh, you are awful! " shocked him so that his temper flew out towards the crackling group within the room. There was Tiddley, female as a housemaid on holiday, pretty as a young cat, and Chris laughing and kissing her, while true to the everlasting type, he talked about something else—" . . . help me sail my boat home on the early tide in the morning, won't you, Tiddley? "

" Start now." Slaney swayed and turned to that refuge for all dropped heads and clenched hands, the chimney-piece. " Start now and drown yourselves, who cares? " The head went down, the tears ran on hands and marble.

Julian did not really share any part of Slaney's pain, but her tears put a welcome note of seriousness in the picture, justifying serious action. He came quickly from the window.

" What damn silly nonsense are you getting up to, Tiddley? "

Some inspired coquetry slowed down Tiddley's departure from Chris's embracing; that, or a remembrance and gentleness for his wounded leg, but the delay left Julian flaming, an angry policeman awoke in him—he caught Tiddley's hands and jerked her on to her feet.

"Suppose you were to mind your own business," Chris struggled out of his chair, "because if you want to know, I'm in a funny mood to-night."

"Well, I don't like your mood to-night."

"I don't like your damned interference."

They faced each other furiously, an old world quarrel, a slap in the face with a pair of gloves tingling on the air. The scene needed some sense and balance. The two girls awkward and frightened, came yammering between them. It wasn't graceful, it was ugly. The boys had shaken them off, they were just going to hit each other, unreasonably and now rather unwillingly, when Angel sailed like some bright ship into the battle. She laughed her way across the room from the doorway, gay and strong as a bunch of stars on a clear night, she carried an eternal sanity to the silly emotional group, the blind and struggling young creatures.

"Steady, steady, babies." She was between them, invincible, and graceful in word and act. "Chris, sweet, my poor chintz, it's had one cut knee already to-day—Julian darling, wait till he can stand, see." She gave Chris the least push and as he staggered the girls caught him and helped him into the chair.

Angel gave their fiercely joint ministrations a satisfied glance, the pot she had stirred there was nicely on the boil. There was nothing to recall a witches' Sabbath to her mind, no newts' tongues or ivy leaves, only this crying, angry group where such a little while before there had been love, love at its most absolute and destructible stage.

"Darlings, what is it," she asked them, she asked the air, "to-night of all lovely nights? What can be wrong?"

Julian said, "I won't have my Tiddley making a fool of herself with Chris or anybody else."

Slaney, angry, past vanity, burst out, "Chris was making passes at Tiddley, believe it or not, he was."

" Oh, my poor little Slaney," Angel kissed her, murmuring, " Darling, what did I dare to say to you to-day—remember ? "

The afternoon's suggestions crystallised again in Slaney's mind. How right Angel had been. How lightly men thought of eager girls, and yet the exquisite undeniable memory of her loving bowed her in an agony of regret. " He can go to hell— he can go to hell." She threw herself against Angel's knee, the child in grief, in passionate requirement of comfort.

Angel sighed, her hand a triumphant dove, claiming the child's head and shoulders, her happy eyes tucked away secretively—but her voice she could control. " Chris dear, Chris, I was so afraid . . ." she spoke across her envelopment of Slaney.

" I'm through, anyway." Chris lit a cigarette, the unavoidable gesture for the moment—" Finished."

" You see "—Julian still needed a stick to beat Tiddley— " that's what comes of your tarting about."

"At your age, it's "—Slaney raised her head for a moment —her voice broke, a roaring young pigeon's—" laughable."

Tiddley, her back to the chimney-piece, faced them all fiercely, without an answer, until her defence came quickly in from the garden and stood, the wraith of a tart in the window, unpretty out of the chilled garden, but made to measure with such breathless accuracy for her purpose in life.

Tiddley ignored them all, her eyes desperately on the window. " Look at Sally," she said in her deep unhappy, boy's voice, " twice my age anyway." She called across the room, " How old are you, Sally ? "

Sally avoided the challenge smoothly, " Fifty-five," she answered. " Why, darling ? "

Angel, delighted, said, " Tiddley darling, tact please, tact. Sally, you shouldn't tell people, from the waist down they'd never guess it."

"Thanks for the flowers." Sally moved into the room.
"So far I've had no complaints."

"I can believe that——" Julian joined his outlaw, defending
her strange quality, her condemned difference, associating
himself with this foreigner of his choosing.

Angel purred: "Of course, dear, I believe it, too. You and
I are the everlasting type."

"Isn't it nice," Sally came forward, "that we have something in common?"

"You're cold," Julian said, "you've been ages in the
garden. Where's Oliver?"

Sally turned her head away straight as a bird about to
fly. "Where's Oliver?" she repeated. "Home on the piano."

Julian's hands were on her arms: "Icy, come to the fire."

"Please, honey, no."

"Come and be warm, darling, let's be nice and warm
together." They came towards the fire. Tiddley flung
round from them to Angel, who sat still portraying mother
love and understanding with Slaney's lovely head against her
knee.

"Oh, please, please, shall I take this beastly dress off now?"

Another one turning to her. Angel said with quiet meaning, "Tiddley—don't. It was such a phenomenal success."
She joined her eyes and Tiddley's and looked down at her
poor pretty lamb.

"Success!" Tiddley gave a wild little hoot of laughter
before she bent her head and knelt and broke into awful
tears against Angel's other knee.

"*Ah, ma petite, ma pigeon*"—to differentiate in her comforting, Angel broke into her favourite language—"*Tais—
toi, qu'est, ce que vous avez-chérie?* Really, Tiddley darling,
do stop."

Tiddley howled, Slaney howled, Angel and Sally offered

handkerchiefs—Angel's for Slaney, Sally's for Tiddley. Julian dissociated himself from the group and offered Chris an apologetic cigarette—he was bothered and ashamed and very tired.

"For God's sake, let's try and find a little tinsel gaiety," he said, making a desperate effort across the emotion, "where's the gin bottle?"

"Such a good idea," Angel claimed a share of him and it. "You'll find the tray in the dining-room, darling, please do get it."

In the dining-room Julian found no tray of bottles and glasses set ready. He crossed the hall and put his head round the door of the kitchen passage to call to Finn. He was answered by silence and the myrrhish smells of the passage stronger than in the afternoon. Julian stood and breathed in the passage air; his combativeness fell away. In time he was a child again. The association of the passage smells with all those years was so intense that when Birdie came out of the pantry carrying the tray of drink, he did not think of taking it from her any more than he would have done at six years old. And, as at six, one is aware of a grown-up thunder-cloud of unhappy feeling, so to-night, he knew, and he felt the polite nervous small talk of a little boy on his tongue as he walked beside her, opening doors on their way back to the drawing-room.

"Birdie, what a load!" It was Sally's astonished comment. "Where's that Walter of mine, couldn't he help?"

"And where's that naughty, naughty Finn?" Angel, her weeping girls on their feet again and mopping their eyes independently, chose just the wrong moment to put a playful twist in the inquiry.

"Finn," Birdie boiled over, "off to the river, with the pantry the height of himself in dirty dishes, and enticed

Walter along with him. "Yes," her voice rose, "and me with a cup of hot milk for him, and a trap set for his mice, and every little nicety I could lay out." She stood rearranging the glasses with shaking hands.

Angel stepped up to her and put an arm round the taut exhausted shoulders: "Now for your own sake, Birdie, forget this—wouldn't it be an idea? Dear Birdie, it's rather a nonsense, embarrassing at your age, don't you think?"

Age, nonsense and embarrassment. All the witch and all the woman in Birdie caught fire like a great burning skirt. She flared, shameless and fearless: "Nonsense is it? Let me tell you I dreamed last night of tears—ex-cell-ent, a speedy marriage. And only for the hoarded spite in a single card, there's a road clear before us all to double chimes of marriage bells."

The fortune-teller's tent was set up in the room. The drama and tension which the least soothsayer may command were Birdie's. The children went to her, seething with curiosity, ashamed of their credulity, delighted at the diversion she provided. They held out their palms, they laughed, they found a pack of cards, they poured smoothly on the table, and Birdie's hands were on them when Angel spoke, more strictly.

"Bed for you, I think, Birdie dear. You're tired, you're upset, or you wouldn't give that silly boy a thought. Anyway, if he prefers fishing with Finn to talking to you—well, where are you? I ask you?"

"Don't ask me, ask yourself, madam. Who sent himself and Finn off to pleasure themselves, and the pantry up to their knees in dirty dishes?"

"You surely aren't suggesting that I did?" Angel had the awful dignity of every liar. "Dear Birdie, you don't forget yourself, do you?"

Before Birdie could answer, the door to the garden was opened from outside and two fishers, triumphing in a wild success and sure in this household of its instant and absolute appreciation, came in, carrying, curled in a net, the body of a monster sea trout, a trout of epic weight, a moment in the river's history. The moment was translated by Walter, in whom the waters and the wild had found a strangely ecstatic disciple. "Thrills," he called, "thrills, thrills, thrills."

Finn, more explicit but not less excited, produced the body. "The biggest trout ever caught in the river and on a little fly I tied myself."

They all crowded round, all but Sally and Birdie who stood together outside the circle.

"Oh, madam, it was wonderful," Walter said to Angel with reverent gratitude. "A ding-dong struggle—got my feet wet, too, didn't care! And I broke the rod you lent me."

"You see," Sally said, "my poor Birdie, you see."

"I knew it." Birdie felt a new pain that Sally should know so quickly how things had gone between herself and Walter, between Walter and Angel and Angel's slave-boy, Finn. In their elation and in the cold breath of night, river and fish they brought in with them, Angel had linked them. An emotion had been created.

"Oh, what a night's sport," Finn sighed reverently, and then with a change to the butler in his voice, "would there be anything further, madam?"

Madam laughed and indulged: "No, no, that'll do. Just shut up the dogs and put down the rat poison."

"What about a dose for my mice?" Walter suggested.

With childlike politeness, Finn spoke: "Them mice, I understand, were in Miss Birdie's management."

"Can't trouble Miss Birdie to that extent." Walter was a

hunter for the moment. "Give me a trap, chum, and I'll set one myself, yes, I will really."

They were gone—the bond had been made and given between them—Birdie spoke stupidly out of a full heart: "God give me patience," she said, "and grant me a turn of luck."

"You may want it rather badly, Birdie——" Angel's voice was honeyed. "I'm so afraid you may have overestimated your charms."

She committed exactly the right mistake for the situation— a gentleness here and Birdie could have turned again from the new love to old kindness. But the sneer was an outrage, and outraged Birdie stepped forwards: "Oh, there's a slap," she gave a shrill unfamiliar laugh, "and here's another. The schoolmaster, madam, bade me give you this—'Privately' was his expression. Eighteen pounds 'Private.' Would you call that a good price, my poor Tiddley, for your little piano?"

"It's a mistake, Angel, isn't it?" Tiddley's anxiety seemed to shrink her within the white dress, made her seem swarthy and sour inside its froth. "It's a mistake because you promised——"

"Promises," Birdie hovered at the door, "we all wonder why promises are made. I'll trust to my own promises in the future time and I'm off now to trap my mice." She was gone on an upward note of defiant gaiety, wild as a bird's.

"It isn't true," Tiddley pursued, "because you made me a promise."

"Ah, yes, *mais vois-tu, petite, un moment tu seras au courant.*"

"*Hiboux-bijoux-jou-joux :· cailloux-choux-prestidigitateur* and say it with English." It was Sally's ugly interruption.

Angel was silent.

Slaney said, awed: "Tiddley would die without her

piano!" It seemed no more than the truth. Then she sobbed again, "Serve her right, too."

Tiddley found her voice. "If you break your word to me, Angel, I'll never believe in anything again."

This flattery of her supremacy pleased Angel. "You'll see, dearest, I did it for your own good. What's eighteen pounds to me?"

"Just the price of your own way," Sally said, "and you may find it expensive."

Angel put an arm round Tiddley and spoke with awful gentleness: "I won't have people laughing at my poor pet's playing."

Tiddley turned crimson like a child taunted in public. The silence round her held the truth, the hideously magnified truth that her music was funny. Her music itself reeled in its importance under the implication of secret smiling behind hands, the exchange of exasperated indulgent comment. As she got up to run out of the room, even her back looked flushed with this painful indignity.

Julian caught her and held her almost roughly while he turned on Angel. "How could you, Angel? It's not true, Tiddles, don't mind her—I was nasty, too, wasn't I, suddenly I felt mad at your getting up to nonsense with Chris. Chris of all people."

"Oh, you cheated on me, Tiddley, you cheated——" Slaney came plunging in.

Chris came in too, "All my fault, Slaney—silly I know."

"Darlings, do let's forget it all." Angel turned their simplicity of approach into an artificial schoolroom argument. Tiddley was young and more direct than schoolroom: "Angel told me to do it, Slaney—to distract Chris from you."

"Tiddley, are you sure you've got that right?" If Chris

had smoked a pipe, then his teeth would have sunk into the stem.

" Yes, that's how."

" But "—Chris spoke inch by inch—" why should she? Angel knew Slaney's only playing me up—she warned me, and I'm grateful. It hurts a bit, but I'll take it."

" Mummy said I didn't love you? " Slaney sprang up almost with a clash of bells. " Is that true, Angel? "

Angel closed her eyes and leaned back.

" Utter, utter nonsense," she said, rather helplessly.

Sally, watching, silent, thought, " She'll get them—they wouldn't stand for tears."

" But it's what you said," Chris repeated.

Slaney remained on her feet: " And this afternoon she told me not to love you too much, Chris, she did. Isn't that true, Angel? " She spoke stupidly, as if she was spelling her way out of the puzzle.

" Oh, my poor loves, you've got it all wrong from the wrong angle," Angel persisted hopefully; then glad of someone she could wound, she turned on Tiddley: " But, oh, to think it should be you who abused my confidence."

" I don't want your confidence," Tiddley whispered, " any more."

" This—after all my years of love," Angel's voice vibrated, then snapped. " Right—find a job and see how you like that."

" Yes, you're right—I must go." Tiddley spoke from her new world, an unpeopled star and colder than death.

But Julian laughed. " Shut up—my little old silly. You stay here just as long as Sally and I do—you know that, don't you."

" You seem very positive about your future with Sally, Julian." Angel swerved to the new angle.

"Of course, I'm positive." Julian was direct, stronger than he felt, and less gentle because of uncertainty. "Mum, darling, don't be hurt, but really you know, I'm a big boy now. I've had a war by myself and I've found Sally for myself and I'm so proud of her. She's my own little anchor and my own little boat and no one can give her a new engine."

"Julian"—Sally took a quick breath—"do I matter all that? Do you need me so much as all that?"

"Oh, much more." He was all out to establish the theory, absolutely. He said as a kind of shy amendment, "You'll know, you'll love her too, Angel."

"Be fair," Angel spoke steadily, "I've done all I could to welcome Sally into the family."

"Yes"—Sally took a quick look up to meet the eyes that had scared her in the portrait of Julian's grandfather—"the family present and past"—an implied criticism.

"Well"—Julian felt the faintly defensive pride of race in him—"dull but respectable, darling."

Sally felt a shock of absolute relief, and as it took her she reacted like lightning, striking with all her force: "Dull?" she questioned. "What about that vicious old heel."

"Great-grandpapa, vicious. Only, oh so pompously, hopelessly good. They called him the Bishop."

"He didn't build a house in a tree."

"No, no, that was darling Aunt Agatha—just her fun. He only built a church on an island."

"Well——" Sally looked Angel up from the feet and down again, slowly. "Aren't you the works. Aren't you the whole damn works."

Angel spoke through her most brilliant smile. "I must be gentle with you, I must be patient. I daren't ask you to understand. How could you understand? You and I, I should say, are eternal strangers."

"You and I," Sally amended, "are two very tough common women; that's why we understand each other so perfectly."

"I'm a mother——"

"You're a classical let down to motherhood. You're a predatory, conceited, vain old doll, and a most inexpert liar."

"Inexpert?" strangely, that was the barb that really stuck in Angel's bleeding flank—"Inexpert—oh, that's really the last—that's the end. Let me tell you two things, Mrs. Wood. An excellent train leaves the local station at midnight, and there's always room for one more on the mail-boat."

"Thanks." Sally lit a cigarette. "I'd hate to deprive you of that vacant place—because you've certainly bought it."

Angel pulled out her last stop. "Julian," she said in a faint, and frightened whisper.

Julian looked most uncomfortable and poured himself out a drink he didn't want.

"Slaney," she whispered on, "you love and believe in me, darling, don't you."

"No, I don't," Slaney spoke in a new voice, "because, do you know, I'm a hardened cynic—that's what you've done to me, that's me, old and cynical."

"Oh, Slaney," Chris implored gently, "don't grow up on me any more."

Rather pleased, she picked up the cue he gave her; "Yes, I've changed from a child into a woman. I'm going to drink Scotch Whisky and inhale my smoke—don't touch me— give me a cigarette—give me time to think and know my own mind."

Chris limped across and leaned over her with his cigarettes. "You know," he said, "you ought to be state-controlled."

Slaney looked up. "Would it be nice?" she asked in her own silly voice.

"You've turned on your own mother, Slaney." Slaney only looked at Chris. "You're breaking my heart." Slaney only looked at Chris. "Nobody left." The flatness of the moment was really sad. "Tiddley my little one—I'll give you another chance."

Tiddley said steadily: "And will you give me another piano?"

"Oh, my God!" Angel flung to her feet, a tree in a storm was not more sensational, not arms but grieved torn branches. "This is getting beyond me. Don't be morbid, dear. You've always got your mouth-organ."

Tiddley said with deadly reasonableness: "But I can't make the top notes on my mouth-organ."

"Really! Selfish to the last!" Hot with anger Angel tore everything up by the roots: "If it comes to that, dear, you can't make them on the piano, either."

"Angel—you—oh, I'm through. Oh, oh dear; oh, God, oh, please——" Tiddley's head went down into the lap of the white dress, its skirt rose ungracefully up her planted feet and short legs—her despair was awkward, not pretty, after the previous scene even a little exhausting.

Angel, looking down at her, made a little gesture of despairing boredom to all. It was enough. They rose as one bird to flock and kneel around Tiddley, kissing and comforting, offering their love and handkerchiefs, their drinks and cigarettes. She had been martyred—the lucky thing.

"Oh, what a shame," they said . . . "Be tough . . . It's not true . . . Play to us, Tiddley, always . . . Tiddley, we love you . . ."

Suddenly Birdie was there again, with her blue cooking apron tied over her white coat, giving her hips and a behind and somehow recalling that flannel apron of bath-time that good nannies sport every night of your young life.

" Come with Birdie, my lambs," she said. " It's late—your bottles are in, and your beds turned down, and I've made Ovaltine for all."

" God bless all nannies," Sally put out her cigarette and picked up her bag, " and make Sally a good girl."

" Come with me, darling." Julian put his arm round Tiddley. " You shall have the Peter Rabbit mug with all the baby bunnies on it."

They were gone. Angel was alone in the warm vindictive room. She was without a clue back or forwards to any happiness. She was with her poor wicked self alone. Her silly scheming heart was a hat blown in the dust, ridiculous, skipping and bowling into nowhere at all, a lovely long trip to nowhere. If someone caught it, and gave it back to her it was ruined, it was not her pretty hat any more. She didn't feel guilty towards the young in any way, rather grieved and insulted by them. She sought for a way back to where she had been only this morning with her children, with Tiddley and with Birdie—but she did not seek it through any confessional cleansing. She could not see where there could be any beneficial change in her behaviour. She had acted entirely and absolutely for the best and for their benefit—they had misunderstood her intentions, and failed her bitterly.

When she thought of Sally—of the little body and gross humanity, her savage tongue and fearlessness—her heart hammered, she felt sick and hot, pregnant with her dislike of this animal by whom her child had been taken. Towards Birdie and Tiddley she felt most strongly. A wondering revulsion at the betrayal of her trust and love. She thought of all the years through which she had kept the spark of life and romance alive in them—who but she had nursed them through the sad unacknowledged crises of lonely women? She had been their innocent outlet for all wordless, nameless loving.

Angel, who mercifully required no real loving, for whom
Oliver's exotic friendship had been more than sufficient, could
understand, could provide and direct all the shadow play of
romance in the adolescent and the middle-ageing. Now, with
actual loving in her house, she was in a torment of mistrustful
jealousy, despairing at their escape from her, catching at lives
as uselessly as though she caught at straws on a flood of water.

She sat still as a mouse in her unhappiness, looking at the
places where Sally and Chris had been sitting, with dislike
active even for the dinted cushions, shadows of their presences.
As the emptied room calmed, assuming the self rooms wear
alone, she sat cold amongst all the pretty fancies she had
invented. The pieces of furniture and the silk stuffs and the
lamps which had been like persons to her, retreated to a
distance, their beauty or their comfort shrunk and chill. The
slight summer evening fire fell to nothing in the grate and
the scents of Tiddley's flowers became disgustingly rich, as
though they gargled out their throats upon the air—only
white roses smelt a little fresh and wooden, more of their
stems than of themselves, a delicate thread of sanity and
restraint.

She was waiting, she in all her business, was waiting here
alone because she was unwanted, because to-night she must
not go and kiss and tuck in bedclothes and ask if bottles were
hot and whether the bedside book amused, all the happy
kindness of her life was outed like a candle. She was once
more in that ice-bound, limitless place which she had known
when she was first a widow, the terrible country where she
had bravely refused to dwell or have her being. She had fled
its desperate and natural melancholy, and denied its hellish
emotion from the first, although all her little pretences of
content, her strict bright disciplines of self had been like pouring sand through empty hands. She had looked at those two

loved children, thinking: pretty, yes—how pretty they are, and feeling no warmth or glow. "Those darling children must be such a comfort to you," they said to her, and she smiled and nodded, and held her hands to a painted fire.

But time and work, and the fact that she was a cold woman and an able and managing woman too, had brought her peace, and she loved her children fully again. She built her whole life again on their lives. Her own importance to them was her being. And to-day, in one day, in less than a day, she could see herself left once more with the sand running through her hands, and before her eyes an aching horizon to nowhere. She put her forehead down in the cold cage of her fingers and bent her ageing, pretty head and tucked her long youthful legs up under her like an agonising schoolgirl. There was no prayer in her moulded heart, only fear, that terrible deathly fear for self. But I shall go mad, she thought wildly, I shall go mad alone, I can't be alone.

Only then, through the tumult of defeat it came back to her—Oliver's strange proposal to her to-day. Words she had taken as gay tribute to her power and self, were they now translated into strength and comfort, and a reason to be? —together they would loose their pleasant power over this place of Julian's where together they had worked—might it not be solace and at the same time rather of the breath of life, to rescue some other wilderness and set a house and lands in order? Only on her death should a child inherit, and it must be a good, obedient, sensible lamb, a very changed lamb from the sullen outlawed flock she had known to-night. How relieved Angel felt to have remembered this shaft of light in her darkness. It primped her up, got her on her feet again, set her shaking cushions and twitching furniture to rights with some of her old spirit of order and possession.

The whole idea now seemed to her rather charming and

suitable. She clothed it and accepted it, gathering new power in its consideration. The idea was far from any true contact with the real Oliver—the Oliver who scolded and disapproved and stuck pins in all life's gayest balloons—that reality was submerged and swallowed in this mythical affectionate cavalier who was to walk beside her, comforting and carrying suitcases for the rest of life.

When Oliver opened the door and stood within the room, rather smartly dressed and oddly enough, carrying a suitcase in either hand, she hardly felt surprised, or questioned his appearance other than as a comforter and friend. She swooped, gracious and giving: " Oliver, dear, you've come back for your answer—the answer is—Yes—I'm very happy and," she waited till the right word arrived to her, " proud, that you want me." Then she forgot her grand pose and sat down. " They've all run out on me, darling, and I'd love to marry you, truly."

He put down the suitcases and came forward: " Angel, you don't mean this? Not genuinely? "

" Oh, I do, I do," she promised him. " Absolutely. Oh, Oliver, the children have turned on me—can you believe it? "

" Unhappily, yes."

" I can't understand. Why, I'd rob a bank, I'd stop a train, I'd believe I'd even lie for them."

" And they've found you out? "

" Yes, wasn't it disgraceful of them? "

" Disgraceful," he said blankly. God, why couldn't she see the nimbus round his head? Question his blue suit, his hat, his suitcases at this hour of night—give him an opening of some sort?

" You'll help me round this cruel corner? " she said, hands out towards him, chin high and pretty.

"Listen," he said, "I have to tell you something. I've got to——" He went towards her rather desperately.

"Must it be to-night, my dear?" Angel always prided herself on her ability to bypass what she thought of as an awkward male moment, without unduly wounding the advancer. "I'm tired, rather tired—you know I'm not ready for happiness."

"Wait—Angel, you've got to."

A rapid enough stream of talk carries all sense out on its drift; still talking, she was at the window . . . "I need to be by myself. They've rather done for me you know, but I'll be all right—I'll say good-bye to my garden I think—I hope I'll be sensible about it . . . No, don't come with me, dear——" And then the last neat instruction: "Bolt the window after me, I'll come in by the side door. I'm sure those boys have forgotten the rat poison. Good night—*à demain*! and don't forget the lights, dear, will you . . ."

She was gone. She turned once to see him still standing, a fold of the curtain in his hand. "Quite emotional, poor lamb, I hope he doesn't forget to bolt the window . . ." Her vigilance knew no exhaustion.

* 33 *

OLIVER DROPPED the curtain. He looked very touching, Sally thought, nervous as a kitten in his lovely blue suit, none of the confidence of the wicked eloper about him—nothing to help her to be unkind. He said gently: "The stars are terrific to-night—you'd think Vienna was reborn."

"You know Vienna's full of Russians." She must break this mood, this charm of words.

" All right, then they're for us alone—Aldebaran and all the rest of them." He took her by the elbow. " Come on, we've got to make this train."

She stood quite still within his arm, as far removed from love as a tree inside a paling.

" All dressed up for the wedding journey." Her hands were folded on her arms, one in each sleeve—only her eyes touched him. " I can't come along," she whispered. " Darling, I can't come along."

" Think again—think straight."

" Oliver, I'm staying. Believe me, it's no good—the kid needs me too much—you don't know all that went on here to-night, how he fought her for me. Can I walk out on that? Can I ? "

" You're a symbol, darling, that's all. Julian's got a whole life you can't share—his engines, his boats, his broken clocks. Sally, you overestimate your importance."

" Maybe, what do we know ? We just take these Julians, these kid cynics for granted—suits us."

" Suits them—they're tough kids. Don't dramatise."

" They left school to bomb Berlin—what have they had out of life ? Teddy bears, conic sections, and operationals—I tell you he was on the edge when I got to know him out there, he'd skipped death once or twice too often."

" That's over now. You've done all you can for him."

" I'm sticking around—he's pretty proud to bring a smart girl home. Do you want me to tramp on that ? "

" You're his vanity—you're my life."

" As you are mine." It was the most quietly spoken oath. Hearing it he knew that he had failed. He heard her saying, " We're the grown-ups in this nursery tale, Oliver, and Angel's the most dangerous adult of us three."

" Surely you're wrong. Surely I am—kiss me——"

" No."

" Once."

" Once."

Nothing on earth is more horrifying than to be the disturber of lovers. Nothing can compare with the embarrassment of this disaster. Even Angel, sailing into the matter in a very fury of righteousness, felt somewhere a brief and dreadful stab in the heart at her own enormity and her own loneliness. But the overwhelming size of the situation, its choice particular horror, filled her like the wrath of God and gave her the strength of a mob of witch burners. Sally, her son's bride, and Oliver, her own friend and affianced, met for the first time to-day and to-night, kissing in this desperate yet somehow grievous embrace. Sally's arms might have been those of a lover in stone and Oliver bent his head searching her face with eyes that might never again, in love, behold it.

On a great whistling breath, her dress flaring in the wind of her approach, Angel spoke: " You must forgive my most unpardonable interruption——"

They drew apart, almost negligently, as gracefully as they had kissed. Sally did not even put a hand to her hair.

" You're welcome! " Sally said in her little sing-song voice. " Believe it or not, that was just good-bye, *auf wiedersehen*."

" Good-bye—what kind of fool do you think I am. What kind of mother do you think I am? How am I to tell my son that I found you seducing Oliver, three hours after your first meeting? "

Oliver said gently, " Steady, Angel. Don't leave me out of it altogether. It takes two bad people to make one good seduction. Anyhow—shall we all have a cigarette and calm ourselves? Seduction's the wrong word—Sally and I were lovers years ago. She's the girl who left me to die by myself in Austria when you, my dear, rescued me, and gave me back my health. Sweet business, isn't it? I mean, pretty."

Her eyes always on practical detail, Angel pointed to the two suitcases. "And you imagine I believe it's good-bye, to-night? What are those two awful suitcases doing here, smelling of intrigue?"

"Two heart breaking anti-climaxes, that's all—and here's another," he kissed Sally with extreme gentleness, "*Auf wiedersehen*, my darling."

"Oh, *auf wiedersehen*." Angel was still using her avenging voice. "Now I see it all. So she carted you at Innsbruck and left you with a withered gentian in your hat band, one lung and a broken heart for me to piece together?"

"That's right—you've tumbled—now, you've got the whole set up. What do you want to do about it?"

"What does she want to do about it?" Sally moved forward, a dangerous slant to her head. "Here's where I tell her what to do about it. She's double-crossed every soul in this house to-night, now she's going to get hers."

"You dare to dictate to me?"

They faced each other—two street cats could not have been nearer to earth, tooth and claw, fur or feather.

"I'm in a good position to dictate," Sally said, "because it rather looks as though I had my hooks in both your men —doesn't it? Not one, but both. Oliver and Julian. Julian and Oliver. Oliver, I should find it bitterly hard to release, you know how it is. On the other hand Julian's need of me is so desperate—I can't decide. Can you help me to decide?"

Angel could only think: "I've thrown men over, I've held out on them, I've never lost a man, not yet—I never can." Aloud she said: "To-day Oliver asked me to marry him and I gave him my word. It may come as a surprise to you, Mrs. Wood, that there is such a thing as faith in this world."

"From that I gather that you pick Oliver and I take care

of Julian. Listen, it's not enough. You keep your hands off Julian and off Slaney and off Chris—I'm interested in their happiness, too. You leave them undisturbed by lies and influences, let them work out their own poor little fates and lives, and then I promise you, I give you my cold word, I'm through with Oliver."

" Oddly enough," Angel said, " I believe you."

Oliver felt the moment to be one of truth between the two women—he who was so deeply concerned had the balance and readiness of mind to withhold himself from the contest. Not now his time. Not to-night, with all this inebriated emotion, this power-lust and sacrificial lust thickening the air.

" Remember," Sally said, " any funny stuff and I swop to Oliver at the altar rails."

" Under these interesting circumstances, dear Angel, do you feel as keenly as you did about our marriage? " Oliver permitted himself the inquiry.

" You can trust me, Oliver," Angel said with a grave and childlike simplicity, a kind of faith that went over and under any cheap sarcasm and left her the winner.

" And how will you keep your bargain." Sally was letting nothing slip—she was steel bright, her words were steel.

" In a big way," Angel flung it out, suddenly alight with new purpose and power. " Yes—what about a triple wedding in the island church? "

" A triple wedding, three weeks from now—not three months or three years? "

" All right, three weeks——" the great new plan ran through her like a fire in dry grass. " Bishops in starched sleeves—champagne in magnums."

" You'll have some fun? " Oliver said it indulgently.

" Yes, I'll have some fun." She threw up her beautiful

head and looked round upon the room that had been all her doing and her life and her own. " I'll exit to music."

" We've passed our words then, have we? " Sally said.

" Yes." They shook hands like two prefects in a girls' school.

" It all seems very tidy," Oliver sighed, " but what has been arranged for Birdie and Tiddley? "

" They're outside this treaty," Angel said. " Aren't the children enough for one night's work? "

" Poor loves—I've made an error there all right," Sally sighed, " or maybe "—she thought it out stiffly and very tired—" you have."

" Who knows? " Angel did not even shrug her shoulders. There was a stillness of enmity about her.

* 34 *

THE COLOUR of the sand went through the water and into the air, the weed melted and sucked at the rocks, the water was down to the bottom of the iron ladder that led up to the harbour jetty from the sea. The dirty smell of the sea was as definite as the taste of a fresh oyster. It was past eight o'clock but the sky was so big and light, night seemed a day away still. Little boats bobbed about gently in the low tide, they seemed to be suspended in air by the wet ropes that tied them to the iron rings driven into the cement of the quay side.

Standing on the sea wall, among the salty swags of fishing nets hung to dry, Tiddley's piano looked like the corpse of a ravished governess; the pale slipper-like pedals, the modest prettiness, the air of upheaval in a meek and useful life were all in evidence as it waited, almost complacent in its unsuitability, the publicity attendant on this fate worse than death.

Angel looked at the piano with a cold, unrepentant eye. It was not the only incongruous object on the boat quay this evening, for she was erecting with the help of Finn a terrifying wedding arch in which oars, glass balls from fishing nets, and a wealth of blue delphiniums were used with awful dexterity and lack of humour. She looked young and strong and relentless in her blue flannel coat and skirt and flat white buckskin shoes. In contrast, Finn, running up and down the wet steps to the boat below, looked wild as a spiney sea-creature caught in a net. There was a wicked air about him that seemed to inflame the occasion with a feel of bad fairies, ill-wishing and merciless joking.

"Finn," Angel called from her perch on a step-ladder, "more delphiniums."

"Only three left, madam." He stood under the arch of flowers, gazing up at her with eyes golden as a goat's in the light that filled water and air with gold. "The leg of the font in the island church whipped a lot on us. Will I run up to the house for another few?"

"No, no, I'll manage." She bound wet moss and flowers together and stretched her tireless arms.

"By gum and pardon me"—Finn stood in slavish admiration—"but that looks great for the three bridals in the morning."

"Perfect, isn't it?" Angel surveyed her work without any annoying spirit of self-criticism. "The Island Church looked lovely, too—thank you for all your help, Finn."

"I done nothing, indeed."

"I'd never have managed the lilies on the altar without you."

" Ah," he said with a true poet's fancy, " when the morning sun hits in on that cold stone spot, they'll be gorgeous."

" Yes, yes," she flamed out in agreement, " I see it—Miss Slaney in white from head to foot, veil down—myself in simple, graceful mist-blue."

" And Mrs. Wood?" he prompted, longing to complete the picture.

" I think I heard something about a purple brocade coat and skirt and orchids. I feel certain there will be a spray of orchids."

Finn sighed: " Will the morning ever come, when we'll see ye three brides?"

Angel seized on the moment of enthusiasm to improve her instructions for that morning. She leaned on the wall and took a little notebook out of her pocket.

He was looking out to sea, away from all domestic ties: " Is that Colonel Christopher's boat I see?" he asked the air.

" Nonsense——" Angel was turning the leaves of her spruce little book. " I gave him a very strong hint to keep away to-night. Now, Finn, about the morning. You must keep to my time-table. What do you do at twelve o'clock?" she pinned him pencil point to page.

Finn answered in his grand manner: " Take his Grace the Bishop, and the three bridegrooms off to Church Island in *Julietta*." He paused, listening to a throb over the water and the outdoor thought gave back his poacher's voice: " Begod I think Colonel Christopher's on his engine now."

Angel ignored the matter. " And remember——?"

" To give his Grace a double brandy before we start."

" He's a shocking sailor," Angel said, slightly condemnatory.

" My cellar's here, glasses and all—would you ever guess?" Finn opened the lid of Tiddley's piano. " And a bottle for the bridegrooms." He peered in like a squirrel.

" Be sure you take everything out before the schoolmaster starts the ' Voice that Breathed o'er Eden '—that's when we disembark after the ceremony. And be down here to help him load the piano into the turf boat when we are all gone on our honeymoons. How well everything fits in. I don't let grass grow under my feet. And that reminds me, did Miss Tiddley run the Atco over the tennis court ? "

" I doubt it, madam." Finn was leaning over the sea wall, his present interest centred entirely on the boat approaching anchorage. " Easy, sir, easy does it," he called, and prepared to catch the rope Chris threw up with a slapping impatience.

" How tiresome and difficult," Angel said to nobody. " Now will you attend, Finn—twelve-thirty—brides to the island."

But Chris, rather lion-like in the sandy, tawny light, was with them. " Hallo, dear, what a surprise." Angel was cool.

" I've got to see Slaney at once," he said. " You do understand it's rather important. Where is she ? "

" In the house having her hair set; and forgive me, dear, but don't you think you'd better leave her alone—you know what girls are."

Chris did not answer. Head low, hands in pockets, he went gently away in his rubber-soled shoes. He was not rude. He seemed just a little desperate.

Finn looked after him and back again at Angel: " But Miss Slaney's prawning on the far rocks, madam," he offered.

" I know nothing about that." Angel reverted to the note-book. " Now then, brides to the island."

" And, oh, won't it be a fright if it rains, madam." There was a gloomy relish about this suggestion. " By George, it can peg rain on Church Island, too."

" Oh—Finn—don't. Anyhow, Birdie can bring three big umbrellas in the boat—I'll put them on her list." She wrote it down. "Three big umbrellas. Bridegrooms carry them anyway."

"Put the umbrellas on my list, madam"—Finn shook his head—"if to-night's coup comes off, we can put no dependence on Miss Birdie to-morrow."

"For her own sake, poor old thing," Angel murmured, amending the entry in the notebook, in her tiny, precise writing.

"Her luck have went—there's black trouble crossing her every time she'll box the cards." Again the wicked glint of relish. "The smiles and the wiles and the salmon soufflés can't beat the cards."

Angel thought of the last three weeks and the course things had taken; the little trousseau-buying trips to Dublin, when Birdie and Walter had been left behind; long days to know each other better as together they worked out improvements on the garments bought for the brides, and together designed, both in fact and fancy, models that filled them with satisfaction, mumbling to each other through mouthfuls of pins; they were busy together; they worked together; they understood an identical importance. Angel had not under-estimated the danger, but had been over-ruled by the absolute usefulness of the combination. She always felt that when the moment became too ripe, she could, if necessary, destroy.

Birdie, looking oddly indestructible in happiness and a charming new hat, came gaily down and stood smiling up at the wedding arch. She wore a pale pretty coat almost ahead of the mode and the hat was as sympathetic to her face as water round a bend of land.

"Well, Birdie, how smart you look," Angel said with rather insulting indulgence. "Your hat," she finished faintly. It was all so contrived that anyone should feel overdressed and slightly absurd, but Birdie knew she was all right.

"Isn't it lovely?" She moulded it a shade more closely to her head. "Walter made it."

"Sweet, dear." Angel's garden scissors snapped on a stalk, "You don't think, just a trifle ageing?"

"He wanted me to have a halo," Birdie went on. "No, I said, Walter, I'm not the halo type."

"Right first guess, miss," Finn agreed.

She was not distressed. "Ah, go on with you and your nonsense, Finn." She had to tell them. "I can't be cross to-night, Walter and I are just off to make our final arrangements with Father Scanlan."

"Well, well," Angel received the news indulgently, as one who has a matter in hand and can afford forbearance. "I suppose you know your own business best, my dear. And are all the brides' suitcases packed?"

"Including my own——" The iridescence of the word bride was a wonderful rapture for Birdie to share. "To the last whiff of tissue paper and my dream nightdress in blue satin on the top."

"That'll paralyse him," Finn spoke to the air.

"Hush, Finn." Angel spoke more to enlarge on the absurdity than to reprove. "Now, Birdie," she became practical as one does with a child at bed-time, "Did you make your special lobster sandwiches? We'll need them to-night, after all this hard work."

"My lobsters are all mayonnaised for the wedding breakfast."

"Ah "—Angel got by that one quickly—" Finn, pop down and get a couple more from the box."

"Very good, madam." He looked out to the store box wavering on its moorings outside the jetty and ducked under the wedding arch and down the steps to the boats, singing, "My mother she said I could marry—marry—marry."

" Oh, that boy." Birdie took it in good part. " Madam, you'll excuse the sandwiches I know, but Walter and I are due at Father Scanlan's this minute."

" Really ! " Angel was busy sticking sprigs of greenery into her arch. " And where is Walter ? "

" Mrs. Wood wants to know that, too." Birdie shared a joke. " She's ringing bells through the house for him and her wedding hat unmade in his work-box."

" Funny."

" He's meeting me here at eight o'clock," Birdie spoke with confidence.

Angel glanced at her watch. " Only twenty minutes past now."

" Is it as late as that ? " Birdie spoke with sudden sharp anxiety, and then as Finn came gaily up the steps, a dark blue lobster flapping and clapping in either hand, she recovered herself to ask with gallant insouciance, " You couldn't tell me, could you Finn, where is Walter ? "

Finn put the lobsters down to writhe and bubble on the cement. " Slipped it off, did he ? Oh crimes ! "

" And there's words from a butler's lips." Birdie was still gay.

" You're not worried, are you, Birdie ? " Angel asked solicitously.

" Not a bit—it's all safe in the cards and the tea leaves. I'm confident."

Finn looked out to sea. " Don't you forget you have the biggest trouble card in the pack tucked up in the marriage bed—and on a Friday, too."

" Oh, that's out now—'twas the wedding mayonnaise that wouldn't thicken for me."

" You wouldn't cut the pack just once more," Angel proposed, as though she saw all trouble resolved.

"And the marriage cards tumbling over one another at three o'clock to-day." But there was a faint break in Birdie's impertinent confidence—Finn saw it.

"The ace of spades across them and a big change on the moon to-night."

"Is there? A change on the moon—well, maybe I'll just give the pack a run through while I'm waiting." They had shaken her.

"Boil the lobsters, too." Angel took advantage of old habit.

"There's a saucy dog." Finn handed over the lobsters.

"Now, what's next on the list——" Angel reverted to the notebook. "Tell Slaney about almost everything gently— well I may as well get it over in the open air as long as I don't slip up on the seaweed." She went down the steps off across the black gleaming sand and oily rocks as light on her feet as Finn himself.

"Finn!" Birdie appealed suddenly to the enemy. "Do you know something I don't know?"

"Will I tell you?" Finn leaned towards her.

"Do—and I'll not forget it to you. Where is he, boy?"

Finn's face became quite inhuman: "He's gone to pluck a nesting swan to make a feather quilt for two—sixpence now if you find him—I'll chance a shilling to the sight of my eyes, but you never will."

It was then that Chris came quietly back: "Birdie, where's Slaney?" It was the child who had lost the other child.

"Getting her death over there in the cold water," the nannie spoke; and then the anxious girl: "You didn't see Walter anywhere?"

"No——" Chris was not interested. "Is he lost?"

"We have reason to believe that he's done a small disappearing act, sir." Finn spoke in his butler's voice again.

"It's a lie," Birdie cried out, "it's a pack of lies—there's trickery and roguery and the cards will show it up, for they never lie to me." She was gone, flinging away up to the house, the bride and the nannie consumed in the witch. It was like Mrs. Tiggy-Winkle running up the hill, all the humanity and cosiness lost in the wild evening. Chris felt the faintly nightmare quality of the hour. He needed a pipe-stem to clench. "Finn," he said, "I've got to find Miss Slaney."

"It's not ten minutes since I seen her," Finn offered casually. "Now which way was it she went? She was off out to sea in her own little dinghy. They're all in low spirits to-night. It's the weddings, I suppose. Look at Master Julian, now—you'd think it was carrying his coffin he was."

Chris saw Julian and Tiddley approaching wearily under a burden of lobster pots. He advanced on them, charged with his quest. "Have you seen Slaney?"

"She's getting her hair set, I suppose." Tiddley offered the suggestion. She did not mind.

"She is not having her hair set," Chris said angrily.

"All right, Colonel—don't be so savage about it." Julian sat down. "I wish you'd kept away. I hate bridegrooms. They remind me about myself. I only want a bit of peace down here to mend my pots."

"I must find her." Chris was idiotically frantic.

"I should try somewhere else." Tiddley was winding up a length of string. Julian took it away from her nervously. "I've got my own troubles."

"I think I have her," Finn gazed out to sea. "Now. No, over—now do you see? Out by the head——"

"No, I don't," Chris said miserably.

"Ah, well, it mightn't be her at all, only my fancy." Finn took it easily. "I'd take a whisk around the bay with you, and see did I see her, only I'm cot for time."

"Come on, Finn, five shillings if you spot her." Chris was suddenly determined.

Finn yielded, and together he and Chris went down to the boat, leaving Julian and Tiddley alone. Although they were working on the pots there was the air about them of head-in-hands.

"Were we unsympathetic?" Tiddley said dully.

"We don't want our last evening mucked up." He raised his head and flinched. "Oo, isn't that wedding arch frightening? Lucky, lucky Tiddley—three times a brides-maid——"

"That's me all right, dear." She was determinedly brisk. "Well," she put out a hand for the string, "let's keep our minds on our lobster pots."

"All mended up and a very nice job too," Julian patted his like a dog. "It's taken us a week to do, but they're worth the trouble."

"You know Angel wanted to put them on the garden bonfire, but I hid them in my little tool-house." She paused. "Locked up."

"Sensible Tiddles—everybody knows new pots don't fish well. Got another bit of string on you? Good girl. You always keep what I need. Oh——" for a moment his mind left the work in hand. "Look at your poor piano. I know, play me your old piece while I finish this pot."

Tiddley moved across the quay suggestible and obedient to the last. But when she reached her absurd piano something hit her into sudden anger. The more trivial insult that edges a grosser injury.

"My stool going too"—she was shrill—"and the wrong height—they couldn't even leave it my own height."

She sat on its withered velvet circle and like a faithless friend it let her down with a curly bumping run—an absurdity.

" She did that to me on purpose." Tiddley blamed one person, wickedly.

" Never mind," Julian laughed, " you're the sweetest stooge I know. Go on, ' 'Twas on the Isle of Capri.' "

Tiddley shut the lid on the keys, sour white teeth in the evening. " Can't, can't. It's like when our pet monkey died."

" I remember—we couldn't look at him."

" That's it——" She drew back from the **pia**no. " And fancy—out all night like this, when I treasured it so—an oil stove in winter—yes, and damp days in summer too, sometimes."

" Never mind, sweetie." Julian was a bit too big for the moment. " I'll buy you a baby grand for Christmas—I would now, only I'm over and over and overdrawn."

" But by Christmas," Tiddley said, her eyes bravely on the horizon, " I'll be gone for a lady gardener."

" Come off that nonsense." Julian put the pots in a neat row. " Don't spoil my last evening—you know I couldn't live here without you."

" You won't need me and you'll have Sally. Aren't you thrilled ? " She had to ask. It was the last moment before the execution.

" Tiddley," Julian spoke deliberately, " I'm not. If you know what I mean, not thrilled. Not exactly."

" Julian——" The whole sea and air trembled for her. " Why ? "

" Oh, you know, I expect. It's all Mummy's beautiful plans for triple weddings. Everything going our way in such a big way—I just feel rushed into it. It's not my responsibility any more. It's only an awful, awful wedding."

" I don't see how you can blame Angel, she's been terrific, making it all so easy. You wanted to get married, you brought Sally home specially."

" Of course I did." He was nearly angry.

" She loves you too "—Tiddley spoke low—" so what's the matter? "

" I don't know, I don't know." He sat down despondently. " I wanted wings till I got the bloody things. Tiddles," he came across and leaned over her in a breathless moment of confidence, " keep it to yourself but it's like this—I'm afraid I'll never be able to teach her to suck out a blocked petrol pipe."

" Perhaps you will——" Tiddley choked back the tears. " After you're married."

" Oo, I do funk being briefed to-morrow." Now Julian wanted someone else to dread to-morrow, too. " And what will you do, little Tiddley, when we're all gone, and the ground is covered in rice and dirty bits of paper, and you smell the tide out like now, smell—and far too many lilies and champagne dregs and opened telegrams? "

" I'll be too busy to think," she said with ghastly brightness.

He had to hurt her: " And your piano gone, too."

" Julian, please stop teasing."

" All right," he said. " Listen, you won't be alone, among the dirty glasses, to-morrow evening Sally and I will come back to you. We'll have bacon and eggs for dinner and set the lobster pots—how's that? "

" Julian! " The horror of these constrained hours with lovers nearly killed her. " Don't do it—promise—I, I couldn't bear it if you came back to-morrow, I couldn't."

So he had her in tears again—an old sense of power delighted him quickly when he saw her tears. " Darling, stop crying. You know: ' Stoppit Miss Tiddley now do? ' " He pulled her hands away from her face: " Look, you're making mud in your little grubby paws. Idiot, what is it? Tell me."

233

" No, I can't. It's nothing—let me go." She was as stubborn and dumb as a child's pony.

" Say—Julian come back to me to-morrow——" Suddenly he caught her closer. " Say it."

" You don't know how you're hurting," she whispered.

" I love hurting you and teasing you, and I hate hurting you and teasing you. I'll kiss you better."

" No, Julian."

" Let me."

He kissed her. There were the sea and tears fresh in her mouth and no other scent or taste than if he kissed a child. Even for this contrasting excitement he was in Sally's debt. " I know now why I wanted to hurt you," he said.

" Things don't change." She was oddly calmer; with this first knowledge of love a sort of woman's kindness moved in her.

" No," he said, " I owe Sally far too much to change anything."

They sat down on the sea wall, talking quietly, looking at each other, but steadily. No touching of hands.

" You see," Tiddley said, " I must go."

She heard him say, and it was as if heaven opened to pour down light to her: " Darling, it's always been you, but why couldn't I know."

" The war and Sally grew you up so quick."

" For you—and not for you ever—try and help me, Tiddles —I'm flying blind."

All the wild mature practical instinct quickened brilliantly in Tiddley to save him pain. " Julian, do you want to give me a good-bye present?" she asked quite briskly.

" When I look at you I'm giving you the whole of Cartier's to choose from," a breath of the old nonsense was between them, " Don't you see the bills in my eyes?"

" That's better, darling "—she was on her feet—" but I don't want anything from Cartier's—I only want my little piano." Business-like she went on: " The schoolmaster wants ready money and a fiver profit—I asked him."

" That's twenty-three pounds," Julian said doubtfully.

" You'd get that for *Julietta's* new engine, but I suppose you'd have to fix up the old one and put it back in her." She threw the idea away. " You couldn't do it—not in one evening."

" Couldn't I, now? You think I couldn't do that for you, do you." He turned her chin to him with one finger. " Well, you're wrong, I'll work at it all night if necessary." He drew a big breath of resolve and dropping down from the wall, beside her, went across to where *Julietta's* old engine lay.

He took off the shrouding tarpaulin and peered and thumbed and muttered.

Tiddley sat still watching him. She was huddled like a little animal, a small elemental creature that crouched its body over a treasure. Now she had given him reason enough to forget her during their few dangerous hours together, she would thankfully have died that they might kiss again—the terror and nausea that follow on sacrifice went over her spirit and body in deadly waves.

" Ah, there you are—looking for you *partout petite*." It was Angel walking back strongly across the rocks; Slaney, in a swim-suit and blue jersey with blown hair and pale face, followed, her prawning net and bucket slightly absurd like toys at a funeral.

" Well——" Angel mounted the steps to the sea wall, " what are you doing, darling? "

" Oh—just playing," Julian grinned, and jerked at a bit of *Julietta's* mechanism. " Got any sandpaper on you, Tiddley—good girl."

" Playing? Really! " Angel showed beautiful patience.
" Now, Tiddley, have you washed the dogs and put the
bouquets in water? "

" *Pas encore*," Tiddley spoke with mechanical politeness.

" You can let my bride flowers die." Slaney rather de-
claimed the line. She sat down crossly when it passed by
unnoticed.

" And where's the spanner? " Julian was intent.

" Under my bed," Tiddley turned to the house. " Shall I
get it? "

" Do."

" *Un moment*," Angel fluted, " *et avez-vous*," she made
gestures of mowing grass, "*oh mowed le* tennis court."

" *Non, je n'ai pas*." Tiddley stood squarely.

" *Et pourquoi?* " Angel was still gently grieved.

" *Parce-que je ne veux pas. C'est pourquoi*——" Tiddley
paused. " And from this moment take notice I'm speaking
English."

She walked away towards the house in search of Julian's
spanner, leaving Angel with an open mouth full of French.
She shut her mouth on the French, shook back her pretty hair
and faced her children with startled eyes. " Changed, quite
changed."

" We've all changed," Slaney insisted.

" And not for the better, either. But what can have come
over Tiddley? "

Julian looked from the piano to Angel, caught her eyes and
brought them back to the piano with his own. " You don't
suppose," he spoke quietly, " that's got anything to do with
it, do you? "

" Oh, it's not that at all. Don't be so silly. Everyone's
in love, except her, that's what makes her so boring and
unnecessary."

Julian flamed at the cruel implication. "Mummy, how dare you talk like that about her? It's my own Tiddley."

"Your own maid of all work. Now, please hurry, Slaney. Why do you think I got that expensive little hairdresser all the way from Dublin—she's done nothing for the last hour—and look, I ask you look, at your nails?"

Slaney bent her knuckles inwards to look: "But don't you understand, it doesn't matter?"

"Don't let her put anything brighter than coral on them." Angel swirled past, a feather on a flood. "What about a face mask? Then get your feet right up and read that little booklet on wedded love I've just given you."

"You can take back your little booklet." Slaney was out for drama.

"Now, darling," Angel fussed. "It puts everything so nicely and I do insist on your reading it."

"Well, I won't. I don't want it—I've got my own ideas."

"Now Slaney," Angel spoke with some sincerity, "and when you should be preparing heart and soul to be a beautiful bride, where are you?"

"Up to her waist in sea water, prawning," Julian threw in without raising his eyes from his work.

"I *like* standing in sea water," Slaney insisted with awful calm. "It draws the blood from my brain."

"Oh, dear, why is the blood in your brain?" Angel inquired, in the tone one employs towards a nervy child. ("Not another sore throat, darling?")

"Because I'm doing something I've never done in my life before—I'm thinking."

"There'll be lots of time for thinking after to-morrow," Julian said resignedly.

"Brides shouldn't do too much thinking, anyway." Angel

237

popped it in in a dreadful sane matter-of-fact little voice.

" But I'm not a bride in a cellophane parcel "—Slaney had their attention at last—" and I'm not going to be—not to-morrow. Not with Chris."

" You don't want to marry Chris? " Angel spoke almost stupidly. " Julian—you heard her? "

" She doesn't mean it."

" I do. I do mean it. I've written. 'All's over,' I said."

" But my dearest "—Angel's voice came from some holy calm—" when I gave in, when I planned everything, when it's all to-morrow."

" That's it. I'm planned silly, darling. I don't want a wedding planned by you and a husband planned by you and a honeymoon planned by you—I tell you, it's not marriage—it's pollination."

" My darling baby, use words your own size, please," Angel implored.

" I'll choose my own words and my own men."

" But of course——" The triumphant moments reeled from Angel in a benignant catalogue. " You have utter freedom—even now at the eleventh hour, with the Bishop coming and the hairdresser here and the trousseau bought and the island bell ringing and the champagne corks popping and the press photographers clicking——"

The children cried out together, Slaney for all she threw away from her, Julian with a giddy sense of horror.

" Stop it," they shouted. " Stop it, Angel, stop it."

Slaney said, with tears: " It sounds so lovely."

Julian said, battering grimly away at *Julietta*: " It sounds so awful. Please try to remember I've got to go through with it."

" You've got to go through with it "—she took him up, incredulous—" Julian, before it's too late, tell me, tell me darling—I'd give up anything for you—I'd remould your happiness."

There was a pause while the incoming tide sucked and swirled at the rocks and the pier foot and the little boats moved and grunted in the silence. Then Julian said: " Hands off my happiness, if you don't mind."

" Julian, should I tell you? Perhaps I shouldn't? I will. Slaney, I suppose you are old enough to hear it, too, darling, you think you know all about Sally, don't you? "

" I know everything that matters." This was from a cool distance and an angered Julian.

" Full detail of her month in the Tyrol with Oliver? "

" With old Oliver? " It was Slaney who answered. " How terribly pre-war and old-time's sakes. I never heard such a silly scandal."

" How far away and long ago," Julian said dully. " What difference do you think that can make. Why should I mind after all these years? "

" Well, I would, I think, after all I'd mind——" Slaney was rather pleased at her own inclusion in this grown-up chat. " I'm going to take all my marriages most seriously. Nothing 1930 about me."

" You go back to your paddling," Angel coaxed. " Mummy'll fix your bother like she's fixed everything, always."

" I've fixed it my own self." Slaney picked up her bucket and net suggestible as ever. " But let me break my heart my own way, that's all I ask—let the damn thing break." She went back to the rocks and pools with some sort of infant grandeur in spite of her bathing drawers.

" Julian, darling, I don't want to force anything," Angel picked gently on, " but tell me, can you face to-morrow, can you go on? "

" Of course I'm going on," he persisted. " What you've told me is all over—dead and finished before the war."

So she had him. She had him recaptured. " She didn't tell you they were on the point of eloping the first night of your home-coming ? "

" Mummy——" He sat down. " Mummy—have you got this right ? You're saying Sally's in love with Oliver ? Still in love with Oliver ? "

" Yes, yes ! Mad about him." Everything went in her torrential insistence in this which she knew to be true—her own vanity that had clung to Oliver; her own hatred of that grave woman who had dared to come from nowhere to shatter the entire structure of Angel's living. With both children back to her of their own wills, Angel could afford to break all bargains and let promises whistle down the wind—her sense of power and love was big as a sail and carried her grandly out in this new sea.

" Yes," she repeated, " mad about him. But I made her give him up for your sake, darling."

He ignored this—he looked gloriously happy. " And Oliver's in love with her ? Are you sure, Angel ? Certain ? Or have we all gone mad ? He was going to marry you, wasn't he ? "

" Well—" Angel spoke as from a fat dog-eared novel of 1909—" all the best in Oliver belongs to me, naturally. But I did try to save the beast in him from Sally."

" You mean Sally's keen on the beast in him ? I can escape without hurting her ? "

" Escape," the light blessed word. " Escape—but of course you escape. I can't interfere in a young life, it's not in me somehow—or I'd have told you before."

" And you've only told me just in time—only just—oh, Mummy, you are a sausage, actually." He kissed and shook her, wildly and joyfully. Her eyes and heart were full of tears and laughter and she trembled, her pretty straight shoulders clicked and trembled in relief and pride and a crazy sense of success. She felt like the poker player who wins £100 on a broken straight, rather weak and terribly delighted. She sat down when he had gone, rushing like her little remembered child back to the house, bucket and spade forgotten. She pulled the tarpaulin back over *Julietta's* dismembering. She joined her hands and stood looking out to sea and to the first star, and was still standing so when Oliver came down from the house, stepping into the night like an evening cat. He stopped, appalled at the sight of the wedding arch. " Oh," he shivered, " oh, what a terrifying nuptial erection."

Hurt and immediately on the defensive, she answered, " No need to crab what you couldn't do yourself. It took me hours to get that up."

" I believe you." He still looked at it malevolently.

" And all for nothing." Relief and triumph blended in Angel's voice again. " Oliver my dearest, I've got to tell you something—something that's going to hurt—hurt a lot."

Oliver sat down, glaring out to sea in a moody constipated way. " Go on—I'm past caring."

" It's the children—don't think I cheated "—she felt quite humble in the truth of what she was saying—" I haven't. But they've come back to me themselves. Both of them—they don't want to marry. It's only—they need me still."

He didn't look up: " Undue influence and wedding hysteria, that's all."

" Not influence, Oliver, I promise you. I was simply pushing them into marriage."

" Exactly."

" You know it's true—they need me—they belong to me."

"Forgive me—but where have I heard this one before?"

"But don't you understand—I'm giving everything up for them—even your happiness. Oliver, will you set me free? Free for them now that they want me?" Before his answer, as a wave turns, her mood was changed and broken: "Do I hear that tiresome Chris's engine?"

"One thing at a time." There was a pulse going in Oliver's neck like a bird's heart in your hands, but his words were spoken without triviality, he dare not accept such a joy, and entirely doubted Angel's word. "Do you mean, you don't want to marry me?"

"Frankly, no dear." Angel came charmingly back to normal. "It's off, and I'd be so grateful if you could remove Mrs. Wood just as soon as you can."

So that was all—the thing was still unchanged—yesterday here again. "I'd love to help you," his voice was cold and dull, "but I'm afraid you underestimate Mrs. Wood, if you think she'll walk out on Julian now. That's going to be a real headache. He's her crusade, you see, her Holy War—like you were mine."

"Was I?" She breathed it out. "How beautiful—but 'Crusade,' that's a new word for baby-stealing."

"That will do from you my bird-wit," but he spoke patiently. "Hadn't you better call up the Bishop before the telephone shuts down? He's sure to be interested in to-morrow's change of programme."

"Yes, yes, ten million things to undo." Ability, organisation, life itself flowed from her, she turned towards the house, embracing the occasion. It was then that Chris and Finn came bouncing up the steps from the boats like a couple of frustrated pirates. And Sally, wearing a faint lilac brocade nonsense for breakfast on a French balcony, sleeved to the backs of her hands, skirted to her sandals, yet somehow shameless with the air of bed-time, came down from the house and across the stones as strongly natural in her romantic dress as Finn and Chris in their patched trousers and wet plimsolls.

Angel she ignored, even Oliver. "Finn," she demanded, "what have you done with Walter? My wedding hat's in six bits in his work-box this moment. Won't it look swell in the morning?"

Finn looked to Angel for direction. "Has Julian told you nothing, dear?" she asked.

"I haven't seen Julian. Come on, Finn, where's Walter?"

"Maybe I shouldn't say it," Finn hesitated, "but I think himself and Miss Birdie has hopped it off to the priest for a marriage licence."

"That situation——" Sally paused for the surest word— "doesn't exist."

"The entire situation," Oliver said, "is out of hand."

Angel, swinging in easily on the flood tide, full of power as strong as the closing hour, spoke. "The situation, as it happens, has evaporated. And now, if I may have a word with my butler—hop on your cycle, Finn, and call off the organist, while I cancel the Lord Bishop."

Chris caught Angel by the arm. "It may sound extremely silly to you——" there was a grey look beneath his sunburn— "but if you don't tell me where Slaney is this moment I'll twist your arm."

"Chris," even then she mastered the difficulty. She put her hand over his and looked up like a trusting little girl— "you wouldn't."

"Tell me."

"As a matter of fact, she's in bed, dear. So don't you think——" But he was gone.

"And I'm sorry for you if you're lying again." Sally expressed all their views of the matter.

Angel ignored her and continued to instruct Finn. "And don't forget—counter-order the twelve packets of paper rose-leaves. It's too late to send back the confetti."

Finn turned his eyes sadly from the wedding arch. "Oh, madam, madam, what's happened our bridals?" He followed the brisk tide of her retreat.

"Let me tell you——" Sally faced Oliver, she was strung above the state of tolerance on a nervous tension, unsafe in its extremity. "This is about the craziest wedding evening I've had yet. All alone, darling, up there in the old château you know, ever since dinner, I was getting stinking with the hairdresser, so friendly I thought I'd show her my new hat, just to pass the time away—no hat, no Walter, nobody."

"No Julian?"

"Julian——" She reached suddenly the true heart of the matter. "Julian—tying rotten mackerel in filthy lobster-pots with his childhood's pal; and what's more, in confidence, dear, he plans to return here to-morrow evening, row me out in a small boat till I'm sick to my stomach, while he and Tiddley fix their lobster-pots. Now, can you beat that one for a long wedding evening?"

"Darling, you should keep back just a few surprises for these long wedding evenings."

"Oh, all my tears are shed and I haven't any more surprises." She was exasperated, she was looking out at the creeping sea with eyes staring against tears.

"Sally, I've got a surprise for you."

"Oh, fine." She was cold.

"Angel has thrown me over." He paused. "What? No reaction?"

"Well, you're due for a little break, honey—that's swell—my congratulations."

"And why, because she's slipped the silver cord back on

244

those two children. Slaney has gone back on Chris and Julian won't have you."

"For heaven's sakes, am I jilted too? Oh, she's pulled a fast one on us somewhere."

"Don't think me rude, but you do understand that it's Julian who's doing the jilting."

She answered flatly, without excitement: "Well, listen, I'm holding out on him, see? I'm not giving that poor kid up till mother takes that Indian sign off him forever. Anyhow, leave Julian out of it. Look at that——" They both saw Slaney coming wearily back across the rocks. "Doesn't that poor child convince you something's got to be done?"

"Don't start telling me she's on your hands, too. You wouldn't let Chris and nature take their course, would you? Look, here he is again. It's like the lover in the French farce."

"He didn't find her in bed, that's the only difference." Sally turned to meet Chris. "Take it easy—there she is, coming home with her bucket and spade."

"Keeping everything on ice for the future," Oliver said, sourly—he felt sour.

Sally said; "Listen, dear—if I were you——"

"You'll forgive me, but I'm not looking for advice." Chris spoke rudely, desperately. His eyes were on Slaney's slow approach, head down, weighed with her bucket, careful over the rocks. "I know exactly what I'm going to do, but I'm not talking about it. There's been too much talking."

"Hardly from you." Oliver spoke with desolate unkindness.

"All right, I know I'm not one of the clever ones." He looked inconceivably handsome and sure as he claimed his stupidity.

Slaney, looking up from her bucket of sea water and prawns, saw him above her on the pier against sea and nets and sky,

immoderately the larger of the group of three. She set down
her bucket and took a deep breath as she stood with the
incoming tide washing faintly over her cold feet and her
thick dark jersey swallowing all prettiness as a shell houses its
tortoise. They were both silent as he came down the pier
steps to her.

Oliver and Sally watched their meeting intently. The young
had stepped into a place in life they had known once, when
belief is absolute and you sign on love for ever. They looked
backwards into the entranced state, that youth unknown till
its hour is done with. They listened to Slaney's unsteady
attack.

"Hallo, what are you doing here? Didn't you get my
letter?"

"That's why I'm here." Chris took the bucket away from
her and put it carefully on the lowest step of the sea wall.

"Didn't you understand it, then, my poor old boy?"

"Take that back, I'm not your poor old boy, and don't
think you're leaving me either."

"I shall marry to please myself, not to amuse my mother.
It's all turned into her—it's not you and me any more. Do
you know whether you love me or not? Do you now?
Truly now?"

"I love you a hell of a lot too much for my comfort—I
won't say more than that."

"You'll get over it."

"Yes," he said, "I'll get over it. We'll get over it together."

"Chris," she stood away from him, "my mind's made up,
I'm not being married in that Island Church to-morrow."

"Neither am I." He caught her shoulder. "But you're
coming with me now—midnight express and a London
registrar as quick as God'll let us—Come on, into my boat
now——" He swung her off her feet. She was appalled. She

was enchanted. From nowhere, suddenly she was afraid, a child at its own party—he knew it. He put her on her feet in the sand and water and took her hand and stooped low to kiss her.

" It's all right," she whispered.

" All the same, I don't trust you." He picked her up again, and walked out towards his dinghy.

" Never trust me, never trust me for a minute, Chris. Promise——"

They did not hear Chris's answer. He rowed strongly out to sea.

" My dear——" Oliver and Sally leaned on the sea wall, watching the boat, the lovers, the evening sea and sky—" it could be like that, you know. Come with me."

" Don't talk to me, Oliver. Please—don't you think it hurts at all to see that little boat just off to Eldorado? "

" Yes—on such a night. Sally, my only love, it's now or never for all our lives."

" I know that's true."

" Oh, my dear, please think carefully."

" Thinking hurts."

" Look then."

" I only see you."

" Listen to me—you love me."

" Yes, I love you."

" We'll never love again."

" Never."

" So what do you do? Mess up both our lives for a kid who walks out when Angel crooks her finger."

" Walks out, says who? I've saved that kid from hell, yes hell, and I'll save him from Angel, too. She's a destroyer."

" And you."

" I'm human love." Sally said the words with humble truth. Their awful strength at last seized on Oliver's mind.

So it had been all along. The stupidity and force of human loving had taken her from him, twice, back to an old man who missed her; now to a nervous boy whose confidence she had set like a star in heaven, a candle she would never out.

"You win," he said lightly. "It's the Pilgrim Mother in you I suppose. The undefeatable American Mother."

They lit cigarettes—two separate darts of flame from two separate lighters—the stone they leaned on grew colder beneath their arms, the incoming waves penetrated the harbour chill and gentle, and flowed out across weeds and sand in inevitable symmetry.

Oliver put out his cigarette. "Now the darkness gathers," he quoted unforgivably. And, as he meant, all the desolation, all the sense of danger and loss and lonely watching in that hymn for little children pressed so unbearably on Sally's heart that her head went down and tears as full-bodied as Slaney's splashed and steamed on the salt-cold stones. Again his arms were round her, his cheek against her hair again.

"And you see Julian—you see for yourself how it is, always *auf wiedersehen*."

Angel plunging down the steps from the house drove Julian and Tiddley before her. Between them they carried a box of tools like a baby's coffin—they would not be hurried. Julian put down his end of the box and came slowly over to take Sally's tear-stained face between his hands. Tiddley opened the tool-box and put her head in it. Oliver moved across to Angel—a tiger ready to spring at a tiger.

"Sally, is it true?" Julian asked. "Don't you want me any more?" His slight dramatisation was put forth in absolute fairness. She was not to know his mind until he had the truth of hers.

Cool and steady, as if her tears were part of pleasure, she answered him: "Well, don't you have the damndest notions.

Ah, sweets, of course I want you. What about Thursday evening in Paris?"

"Evening in Paris?" Angel cut in. "You flatter yourself. He'll settle with you for a calm afternoon in *Julietta*."

"My dear," Oliver relieved the ugliness, "just subdue those natural impulses for a moment, and shut your trap."

Angel was off and away. "My child's martyrdom goes through me and through me——"

"And comes out the other side." Sally turned from her to Julian: "Well, Julian, passing me up, I understand."

"Yes, he's through with battle-axes——"

"Be quiet," Oliver said, "or I'll throw you in the sea."

"Passing me up, Julian? I'm yours. Really. Stop or go, honey, which is it?"

Both Angel and Sally leaned savagely expectant towards him—their anxieties devoured the air. Each was strung to a point of inattention to outside things so fine that they heard no wave break, while Julian childishly delayed his answer. At last it came: "Sally, will you let me go?"

Angel did not wait. Bursting free from Oliver, she flew over to his side.

"Oh, Julian, our life begins again. I knew you couldn't break with me, darling—you're still six years old and mine, aren't you? Come on—own up, aren't you?" It was a disgraceful display.

Sally said with a dry shudder: "I saved you once from drowning, kid, have sense. Stop in the boat."

"It's because of you, Sally." Julian left them both and took a tool away from Tiddley. "That's not the way, stupid." He went on with her job on *Julietta*, seeming to draw calmness from the actual using of his hands. "It's only because of you I've got the sense to choose—and it's Tiddley I want."

Angel and Sally, for once in all time, shared an exact sensation and staggered momentarily together, under its impact.

"Tiddley!" Angel found the most cruel word. "It's ludicrous."

"But it's me he wants." The ever-ready tears sprang to Tiddley's eyes. "He does, really, and my piano he says, too." She put the flat of her palm on its lid, claiming it faithfully.

"Pardon me, babe"—Sally's voice lifted the matter a little from its tragic depths—"but do you take on the piano?"

"I do," Julian's response was serious, and made to Tiddley more than to any outsider.

"Then it's love—it's the great big stuff that lasts for ever." She turned to Oliver, tears as big as Tiddley's tears pouring down her face. "Darling, am I humiliated?"

"You've got to remember," Oliver said with an indecent amount of restraint, "that all the best crusades ended in disasters." He took her handkerchief out of her bag and gave it to her. "Glorious disasters." He lit two cigarettes and gave her one, then he sat down by himself on the sea wall because the evening was reeling in ecstasy round him.

With gathering menace, Angel turned on Tiddley. If Tiddley had been the twelve-year-old she looked at the moment, a good shaking would have settled the matter—to-night it would have done less harm than the tumbling angry words. "Disaster is right, and traitor is the word for it. Yes, liar and thief and planning little half-wit."

Julian met the attack with brilliant ease. "Don't stop," he murmured, unscrewing an auful tube and considering it closely, "the more you crab her, darling, the more she's only mine. It's better than six broken watches or a blocked jet any day."

" And another thing—she's got the piano—you know what that means—' The Isle of Capri ' for the rest of all time. Julian, Julian, think——"

" Yes, thank God I'm unmusical, and in every other way Tiddley's my ideal of womanhood. Here, darling "—he handed Tiddley the end of *Julietta's* vital—" suck this, while I blow."

" You—you changelings." Even Angel accepted their absolute unity. She turned from them, the terror of defeat chilling her sadly—what should help her now? " Where's Slaney? " she asked in such a tiny voice that Oliver could have wept for her.

" Half way to heaven," he said gently, " if that makes it any better, dear."

" What d'you mean? "

" She started a few minutes ago," Sally had the asp in her voice, " with the Colonel."

" Chris—gone with Chris? I don't believe it—it's a bad dream—it's a plot——" Angel put her hand up to her mouth and turned her round about from the faithless ones, looking up to where her house leaned out above the evening sea; her house, so full of wedding clothes and tiers of sugared cakes and bottles of wine and ribbons and flowers, made ready by her own love and unsparing work, and for the first time her house seemed to sicken on her hands, bulging with all this gross expense and useless grace. Her mind turned from the thought of its disposal. But then there was something more to be done about it all—there was her principle and her salvation and the core of her sanity, that something which always had to be done. She pulled in a deep, brave breath of sea air, and lightly on its buoyancy, went from them.

But down the steps from garden to sea, Birdie came

violently and met her face to face, so that she fell back, almost
for protection, to the group on the sea wall—she actually
feared the strange winged look of Birdie—the tremendous and
swift descent was somehow more purposeful and avenging
because she wore a hooded duffle coat Julian had brought
home from the wars, sandshoes instead of high clicking heels,
and behind her, Finn subjected and mumbling, carried a
lighted stable lantern.

Tremendous, Birdie spoke: "How many flashes in S O S?"

"Good gracious, don't ask me," Angel tried to bring the
matter down to normal—but even Finn was no more with her,
something had changed his faith, she could tell it.

"Madam," he spoke in the air. She was the alien. "We're
played up—the blazing truth is on the cards, and you can't cod
God."

"Three times I cut the pack, and each time it was fire over
water and hands across the sea, so look now, were the cards
lying to us?" Birdie shot out an arm enormously muffled
in the strange coat, and following her pointing hand they saw
a Robinson Crusoe fire, as small as the fire in an opal, capering
and leaping minutely on the shore of Church Island. "I'll
row it out now to the island for that's where my boy's
marooned. I'll not deny the cards and let my own chance
slip to-night. Love will steer me out and this light will guide
me back." She took the stable lantern from Finn and set it
down on a stone, like a night-light in its saucer, and turned
determinedly to the boats.

But they all blocked her way, surrounding this changed,
impassioned creature, checking and impeding her in her
undertaking. She struck out through the crowd as if she was
swimming and they caught her coat and her arms and pleaded
with her. "The tide's running too strong." "It's dangerous,
really." "Birdie, you can't." "I utterly forbid it." "Steady

ducky, let me come too." It was Oliver, but she shook him off, she was free even of her friends.

"Leave off my hand, I'll follow my luck——"

"*Prenez-garde. Elle s'enrage a folie.*"

Birdie was ready even for the domestic French: "That's easy"—she plunged free from them all—"the old cracks barking," and she was poised, indefeatable, on the top step, ready to descend to the boats and open sea, when strangely, romantically, with a suggestion of the sea giving up its dead, Walter, naked but for a jock strap and hair net, his brown body gleaming with sea water, phosphorus and lantern shine, staggered exhausted up the steps and fell into her arms. With a calm from heaven, Birdie turned to Angel; "Madam," she asked, "do you know the French for love?"

Walter was shivering and babbling: "Sea fog, and night falling, my hair full of bats, really dear, and the church full of rats—oh, I'd rather drown. Finn, you've let down our friendship. Birdie, keep me, keep me safe."

Awed, Finn asked: "Did you swim it back from Church Island?"

"An arm of the sea back to his Birdie." Birdie took off her duffle coat and wrapped him in it, as a nannie muffles her own in care and safety. "Look, lamb, look, child, keep warm."

Up the wet steps in the dusk, Chris and Slaney came, hand in hand, inviolably remote. "We picked Walter up in the bay," they said.

"You two back so soon?" Angel turned on them, for once uncertain what line to take.

"We had to," Slaney answered, "Walter was nearly drowning."

"Only nearly," Angel flashed round to Finn. "And who left that box of matches with him?"

" Oh, pardon and excuse me, but what's a box of matches against the stars ? " Finn was still appalled and paralysed by the train of events, natural and supernatural.

Chris said : " Tide's turning. Come on, Slaney. We're off to make the midnight express—Dublin to-night—London to-morrow."

" Good-bye, Mummy "—she said it with polite gentleness.

" You're not going like this—you can't." Angel stood back against the sea wall, crucified in their desertion, immensely, treacherously sad, and Slaney stepped towards her to comfort, to be lost again. Oliver, not Chris, came between them, like a sword. " Listen," he said, " we're going, we've got to leave you, Angel, everyone of us—now or never. Come on, Birdie, Walter, Sally my love, into the boat with you. Julian—Julian———"

" Half a minute," Julian was making a frenzied assault on a nut—" I've got to free this gasket."

Inspired, eyes great with love, Tiddley said, " Bring it for the honeymoon."

" Clothes," Sally protested while she bunched those lilac skirts in her hands and got ready to run down to the boat. " Make-up ? " She was panting with laughter, they were all less or more than sane—the whole adventure was so necessary and so silly. Oliver was right. It was the moment out of all their lives—the moment when fate was ripe to a change, the moment before the star falls or the wave turns. . . .

But Angel barred their way to the boat. She stood in front of the steps. " Wait—wait till to-morrow. You can't go like this, it's madness—I need you so—think of me."

At Tiddley's piano, Finn provided a brilliant diversion—the bottle of champagne was whipped out and the glasses. " Madam," he said, his fingers on the wine, " this'll hold them."

Champagne, it was the perfect sparkling weapon with which to gain a minute at this latest minute. "Oh, open it, Finn, quick we'll drink it to all our lives together."

Mesmerised by it, they stood, while she put glasses in their hands and filled them, laughing and crying: "Remember, remember, don't go."

"We must," Oliver put an arm round her shoulders gently, as one takes the living from the beloved dead, "we're only going because we must." He touched his glass with his lips and gave it to her. "But first—our love to you, Angel—and listen; you've picked us up—you've let us right down—you've loved us and played hell with us—you've been our danger and our fortress—our boiled eggs for tea and our most God-awful despair. But, precious, promise not to change. Stay just like you are. Be there, ready to fulfil your fate and perfect future. Children, before we go, let's drink to her—the Fairy Grandmother."

It was theatrical and lushly sentimental and exactly what was needed. It was to-morrow in her hands—to-morrow, bunched in daisies and bassinettes and ribbons—her to-morrows, her importance, and her insurance against the years—she saw it for the first time and cried now in this delicious relief from loneliness, this absurd lightening of her darkness.

"Oh, Oliver"—she kissed him with real affection—"what a wonderful thought—grandchildren—real babies again. Oh, how slow I've been not to see it."

"Yes, darling——" Slaney was round her neck—"I dedicate my eldest to you. And good-bye, good-bye for now."

"Good-bye—my eldest too—you were quite perfect till I was twelve." Julian kissed her.

"I liked you best at two—and I'll be seeing you again! *Au revoir*, my Julian."

" And don't we make a swell team? " Sally took Oliver by the arm. Angel produced only a glittering smile: " Oh— no, I won't say it—a smart crack now may cost me a god-child."

" Be good, Sally." Oliver was between them. " Don't say it either, whatever it is. Bundle in, honey, time's short."

" Yes, yes——" Angel was magnificent—" what are you all waiting for? You'll miss the train. Bundle in, hurry up! Oh, wonderful, wonderful, grandchildren. I'd like dozens and dozens, cuddley ones, curly ones, pretty ones, plain ones. Good-bye, little Tiddley—Birdie, Walter, do your utmost— Julian, stop sucking and blowing—you'll be too late. *Allons! Dépêches-toi! Au revoir! A bientôt!* "

She pushed them down the steps with her laughter, her tears, her farewell words. She looked more beautiful and more hopeful and more kind than any one of them could remember to have known her as she stood there on the quay, the ghostly nets and dark stones behind her and the sea and the night sky for company—only Finn was left to her. And as the oars took that heavy-laden boat out to sea, the children could see them clinking glasses and drinking healths and laughing still. Oddly, they felt not so much relief at their escape, as a feeling that perhaps after all they were out of the fun—they would have to come back to her.

FOR THE BEST IN PAPERBACKS, LOOK FOR THE

In every corner of the world, on every subject under the sun, Penguin represents quality and variety—the very best in publishing today.

For complete information about books available from Penguin—including Pelicans, Puffins, Peregrines, and Penguin Classics—and how to order them, write to us at the appropriate address below. Please note that for copyright reasons the selection of books varies from country to country.

In the United Kingdom: For a complete list of books available from Penguin in the U.K., please write to *Dept E.P., Penguin Books Ltd, Harmondsworth, Middlesex, UB7 0DA.*

In the United States: For a complete list of books available from Penguin in the U.S., please write to *Dept BA, Penguin,* Box 120, Bergenfield, New Jersey 07621-0120.

In Canada: For a complete list of books available from Penguin in Canada, please write to *Penguin Books Ltd, 2801 John Street, Markham, Ontario L3R 1B4.*

In Australia: For a complete list of books available from Penguin in Australia, please write to the *Marketing Department, Penguin Books Ltd, P.O. Box 257, Ringwood, Victoria 3134.*

In New Zealand: For a complete list of books available from Penguin in New Zealand, please write to the *Marketing Department, Penguin Books (NZ) Ltd, Private Bag, Takapuna, Auckland 9.*

In India: For a complete list of books available from Penguin, please write to *Penguin Overseas Ltd, 706 Eros Apartments, 56 Nehru Place, New Delhi, 110019.*

In Holland: For a complete list of books available from Penguin in Holland, please write to *Penguin Books Nederland B.V., Postbus 195, NL-1380AD Weesp, Netherlands.*

In Germany: For a complete list of books available from Penguin, please write to *Penguin Books Ltd, Friedrichstrasse 10-12, D-6000 Frankfurt Main I, Federal Republic of Germany.*

In Spain: For a complete list of books available from Penguin in Spain, please write to *Longman, Penguin España, Calle San Nicolas 15, E-28013 Madrid, Spain.*

In Japan: For a complete list of books available from Penguin in Japan, please write to *Longman Penguin Japan Co Ltd, Yamaguchi Building, 2-12-9 Kanda Jimbocho, Chiyoda-Ku, Tokyo 101, Japan.*

FOR THE BEST IN PAPERBACKS, LOOK FOR THE

☐ MILLENIUM HALL
Sarah Scott

First published in 1762, *Millenium Hall* was one of the first novels to show that marriage need not be the only ambition for a woman. In it, six women come to the mansion and establish a utopian community based on female friendship and support. *224 pages*   *ISBN: 0-14-016135-X*   **$6.95**

☐ THE RECTOR AND THE DOCTOR'S FAMILY
Mrs. Oliphant

These two short novels will delight all who love Austen, Eliot, and Trollope's *Barsetshire Chronicles*. The setting is Carlingford, a small town not far from London in the mid-1800s. The cast ranges from tradesmen to aristocracy to clergy . . .   *212 pages*   *ISBN: 0-14-016151-1*   **$6.95**

☐ HESTER
Mrs. Oliphant

Catherine Vernon is seen as a none-too-benevolent despot by her dependent relatives living in the "Vernonry" near her home. Then fourteen-year-old Hester arrives, and as Hester grows up, Catherine finds she has met her match. *528 pages*   *ISBN: 0-14-016102-3*   **$7.95**

☐ FAMILY HISTORY
Vita Sackville-West

Since her husband's death in World War I, Evelyn Jarrold has behaved impeccably. Then she meets Miles Vane-Merrick, a rising Labor politician who is fifteen years her junior, and embarks on a love affair that will change her life forever. *336 pages*   *ISBN: 0-14-016156-2*   **$6.95**

FOR THE BEST IN PAPERBACKS, LOOK FOR THE

☐ **A GAME OF HIDE AND SEEK**
Elizabeth Taylor

In her youth, Harriet falls in love with Vesey and his elusive, teasing ways. But when he goes to Oxford, Harriet never hears from him again. She marries the respectable, steady Charles, and is happy for years, until Vesey enters her life again . . .   *274 pages   ISBN: 0-14-016137-6*   **$6.95**

☐ **TAKING CHANCES**
M.J. Farrell (Molly Keane)

First published in 1929, *Taking Chances* perfectly captures the leisured Anglo-Irish lifestyle of that era, but most of all it explores allegiances and love, as orphaned Roguey, Maeve, and Jer search for love and happiness.
                                     288 pages   ISBN: 0-14-016173-2   **$6.95**

☐ **NO SIGNPOSTS IN THE SEA**
Vita Sackville-West

Edmund Carr is an eminent journalist who learns he has only a short time to live. So he leaves his job and buys a ticket for a cruise—for Edmund knows that Laura, a women he secretly admires, will be on board.
                                     160 pages   ISBN: 0-14-016107-4   **$6.95**

☐ **MY NEXT BRIDE**
Kay Boyle

Young American Victoria John comes to Paris in 1933. In her Neuilly lodging-house she meets artists and eccentrics, and finds herself drawn into an artistic community with alcoholism and emotional chaos close behind.
                                     336 pages   ISBN: 0-14-016147-3   **$6.95**

FOR THE BEST IN PAPERBACKS, LOOK FOR THE

☐ **A STRICKEN FIELD**
Martha Gellhorn

Mary Douglas, a detached American journalist, arrives in Prague in October 1938 and finds the city transformed by fear. Through her friend Rita, a German refugee, Mary becomes irrevocably involved with the plight of the hunted victims of Nazi rule. *320 pages   ISBN: 0-14-016140-6*   **$6.95**

☐ **THE RISING TIDE**
M.J. Farrell (Molly Keane)

An absorbing tale of three generations of an Irish family in the first decades of the twentieth century, *The Rising Tide* centers around Garonlea, the huge gothic house which holds each family member in its grasp.
336 pages   ISBN: 0-14-016100-7   **$7.95**

☐ **DEVOTED LADIES**
M.J. Farrell (Molly Keane)

It is 1933. Jessica and Jane are devoted friends—or are they? Jessica is possessive, has a vicious way with words and a violent nature. Jane is rich and silly and drinks too much. And when Jane goes off to Ireland with George Playfair, the battle begins. *320 pages   ISBN: 0-14-016101-5*   **$6.95**